JAKE ATLAS

AND THE HUNT FOR THE
FEATHERED GOD

JAKE ATLAS

AND THE **HUNT** FOR THE
FEATHERED GOD

ROB LLOYD JONES

**WALKER
BOOKS**

First published in Great Britain 2018 by Walker Books Ltd
87 Vauxhall Walk, London SE11 5HJ

2 4 6 8 10 9 7 5 3 1

Text © 2018 Rob Lloyd Jones
Cover illustration © 2018 Petur Antonsson

This book has been typeset in ITC Veljovic

Printed and bound by CPI Group (UK) Ltd, Croydon CR0 4YY

British Library Cataloguing in Publication Data:
a catalogue record for this book is available from the British Library

ISBN 978-1-4063-7771-2

www.walker.co.uk

MIX
Paper from
responsible sources
FSC® C020471
www.fsc.org

For Jago,
the coolest stormtrooper
in the galaxy

1

I took a deep breath, held it, and stepped into the dark.

"Night vision."

My smart-goggles switched to a gritty green view of arched granite walls, as suddenly I could see. I was in a secret tunnel, deep beneath a five-thousand-year-old temple. Or a pyramid. Or an ancient shrine or something. OK, I didn't really know where I was. I'd not paid attention in the mission briefing because I'd been bursting for a wee. But we were somewhere *really* cool.

I felt three quick taps on my shoulder: the signal to stop. My twin sister, Pan, had spotted something. Digital information flickered across the lenses of her smart-goggles, reflecting off her cheeks, so her face looked even paler than usual.

"Sami?" she said.

A voice spoke, crisp and clear in our ears – the technology of the smart-goggles transmitted sound waves from their frames directly into... Actually I missed that briefing too, but it was high-tech stuff. The voice we heard was that of its inventor, Dr Sami Fazri, computer genius and supplier of gadgets to the world's top treasure hunters.

That's us – treasure hunters. Cool, huh?

"What going on in there?" Sami replied.

"There are some inscriptions here on the wall," Pan said. She crouched and traced a gloved finger over the carvings, a series of slashes and lines low down on the stone that looked to me as if a toddler had attacked the wall with a knife.

"I think it's the ancient Akkadian script," she continued. "I'll take a photo. Can you send it to Mum for a translation?"

Pan leaned closer to the writing and blinked three times. Her smart-goggles recognized the instruction and flashed, taking a high-res photo of the inscription.

"Got it," Sami confirmed. "But your mother isn't happy."

"You've known Mum for longer than us, Sami," I said. "Have you *ever* seen her happy?"

"I can hear you, Jake," another voice snapped in my ear. "But I am *not* supposed to be helping you."

"Mum, can you read the script or not?" Pan replied.

"Why can't you?" Mum asked.

"Because I can't read Akkadian!"

That wasn't entirely true. In the few months that our parents had been training us to become treasure hunters, Pan had studied several ancient languages. I was pretty sure I'd heard her talking about Akkadian, an ancient language from the Middle East. My sister was a genius – a proper one, with a photographic memory and terrifying mood swings – but she can't yet have mastered Akkadian. There was no way she'd ask Mum for help unless she absolutely had to.

Mum sighed deliberately heavily, intending for us to hear.

"First off, the inscription is Sumerian, not Akkadian," she said. "You failed to notice the lack of prefixes on the triconsonantal root words."

I spotted Pan's fists clench at her sides and knew she was struggling to contain her frustration. I gave her shoulder two taps, a signal that had come to mean something like, *Don't scream a load of swear words at Mum.*

"Jane," Sami said. "Pan's not an expert in ancient languages like you."

"Nevertheless," Mum replied, "the inscription is Sumerian and *not* Akkadian. So what does that tell you?"

"That you two spend too much time in libraries?" I suggested.

"No, Jake!" Pan said.

She was getting into this now. My sister didn't

often show that she was excited. Her favourite mood was grumpy, sulking under her dyed-black fringe and behind gothic make-up that made her look like a cross between Dracula and someone dressing like Dracula but going way over the top. When she got talking about clever stuff, though, she couldn't hide her excitement. Her eyes widened and sparkled, and her jaw clenched as she failed to fight a grin.

"That means the inscription was carved *before* twenty-five hundred years ago, when people still used the Sumerian script," she explained.

"Good, Pandora," Mum said. "Keep thinking."

"So the king whose tomb we're looking for," I asked, "did he die before twenty-five hundred years ago?"

"King Ashurnasipal," Pan said. "And he did."

"So this passage *does* lead to his tomb. Result!"

Pan and I went in for a high five.

"Stop fooling around," Mum snapped. "Perhaps you are close, but I can tell you from experience that this is when you should be at your most alert."

"Really?" Pan muttered. "You never mentioned *all your experience* before."

A third voice spoke in our ears. "Less of the sarcasm, young lady."

"Dad?" I asked. "You're listening too?"

His voice was distorted by crackling so loud it caused Pan and me to wince.

"Sami?" I called. "I think the comms network is breaking up."

"No," Sami said. "That's your dad. He's eating crisps."

"You call *that* concentrating?" Pan asked.

"Pandora is right," Mum agreed. "Stop eating crisps, John."

"It's my lunch," Dad replied.

"It is not lunch," Mum said. "A sandwich is lunch. Crisps are a snack."

"So what's a crisp sandwich?" I asked.

"Guys?" Sami said. "The mission?"

Sami was right; Pan had done her bit, and now I needed to do mine. I breathed in deeply and held the breath again, in a sort of meditation technique Dad had taught me to help focus my mind. Pan was a genius, but I had a skill of my own, if you can call it a skill: an odd knack for thinking fast and making plans in tricky situations. They were instincts and impulses that had got me into a lot of trouble in the past, but I was learning to control them.

"Sami," I said, "can you give us a thermal report for a radius of fifty metres, and an ultrasonic scan of this entire tunnel? Send a 4D plan of the tomb to my smart-goggles, as well as coordinates for the extraction drone pick-up, and suggestions for a back-up exit if the drone fails. Pan and I will take proof of find from the king's burial chamber and return with a full archaeology team once the discovery is verified."

"All right," Sami replied, "but you may have trouble. The thermal scan shows three heat signatures in your proximity. Two are you. The third is not. Whatever it is, it's approaching with speed."

This didn't sound good.

"How much speed?" Pan asked.

"Sami," I said. "Can you use high-sensor thermography to tell its blood temperature?"

I heard him tapping at a screen. "Blood temperature suggests it's not human," he replied. "The creature is ectothermic. An insect. But the thermal reading is way too big for an insect."

"Bring up a list of native insects in ... in wherever we are."

"It's too big for an insect, Jake."

"Can you check anyway, Sami?" Pan asked.

"Good, Pandora."

It was Mum again. I felt a pang of jealousy and hated myself for it; it was childish to think about this right then, but Mum never complimented *me*.

"OK," Sami said. "I'll send a list of insects to—"

"It's a scorpion," I said.

"It could be," Sami agreed. "But it would have to be some sort of—"

"Giant mutant scorpion," Pan said.

"Yes. How do you know that?"

"Because it's right in front of us."

Pan and I edged closer until our sides were touching. Panic rose from my stomach, but I swallowed it back down and kept my eyes on the creature scuttling closer. It was as long as a crocodile, with chunky claws raised and snapping. Its tail was curled back over its body, as if it were attempting one of Mum's yoga moves, and the stinger at its tip was as long as a dagger.

I reached to my waist, feeling the gadgets holstered around my utility belt: climbing clips, a micro-laser for cutting stone, a grappling gun, a compressed oxygen breathing tube, a flare gun and a clasp to release the inbuilt bungee cord. Where was a giant-mutant-scorpion-killing device when you needed one?

The creature scuttled closer, its claws tapping the stone ground.

"Jake," Pan hissed. "Get us out of this!"

I turned away from the creature and my sister, and scanned the tunnel walls. My breathing slowed as my instincts kicked in again. My eyes moved faster around the tunnel walls. I remembered my parents' training: *there is always another way out if you clear your mind of fear, and think.* And then it happened. It was as if someone had hacked into my brain and taken control, making it work in ways that it usually wouldn't.

"The inscription," I breathed.

"What about it?" Pan asked.

"The stone it's carved on is different from the rest of the wall."

"I... But why?"

I crouched lower, studying the block carved with the ancient script. There was a thin gap around its edges, as if it could be taken out or pushed in. But the gap wasn't *that* thin. In fact it was pretty obvious, almost like we were *meant* to spot it…

"It's a trap," I realized.

"Isn't the *giant mutant scorpion* the trap?" Pan yelled.

"Look at the ground where we're standing," I replied. "It's a trapdoor, rigged to collapse if we press that stone."

"What's down there?"

"How do I know?"

"So how does that help us against the *giant mutant scorpion*?"

Pan was yelling now, her panic mounting as the creature's tail curled up tighter, like a spring. It was about to strike.

"I'm going to laser it," Pan said.

"No!" I said. "Let it come closer."

"Do you know how scorpions kill their prey, Jake? They paralyze them and eat them alive. *Alive.*"

"Just trust me, Pan. Use your grappling gun. Fire it at the ceiling the moment the scorpion steps onto the trapdoor. I'll push the stone and grab hold of your legs. The trap will open, the scorpion will fall, and we'll stay hanging."

"Are you sure?"

"Yes. No. I think so."

The scorpion tapped even closer.

My palm trembled as it pressed against the stone

block. My heart was like a machine gun in my chest. "Get ready..."

The scorpion stopped. Its claws clacked together – and vanished. Then the whole creature disappeared, and a loud whirring noise filled the tunnel. Around us the walls began to flicker. The scorpion reappeared for a second, upside down on the tunnel roof, and then it was gone again.

Pan yanked her smart-goggles from her face. "Hey!" she yelled. "The simulator's broken again."

Stark yellow lights came on. More of the "tomb" vanished – the tunnel walls, the stone floor and trapdoor. Instead I saw slatted wooden walls, hay bales and the rusty remains of a tractor in the corner of a barn.

I couldn't help a small groan – for a moment I had forgotten that we weren't really in a lost tomb or anything like that; we were actually in the Yorkshire Dales, up in the north of England, at the country estate of an old family friend. We were hiding out here while being trained as treasure hunters. Only, the training part wasn't going so well...

Sami balanced on top of a stepladder, checking a hologram projector fixed to a barn wall, one of the high-tech bits of kit that had created the simulation of the tunnel in the barn. His face was as wrinkled as a raisin, and his bald head glistened with sweat despite the chilly autumn winds that rattled the barn. His *jellabiya* – a traditional Arabic dress – clung to his back.

He muttered and cursed in Arabic. Sami was one of the world's leading experts in future technology. He didn't like it when his gadgets went wrong.

"Stay in position," he called. "It's just a glitch."

"Leave it, Sam."

Mum rose from a hay bale.

She closed her laptop and pulled off the smart-goggles she'd been using to talk to us in the simulation. She rubbed her eyes, seemingly exhausted by the sheer weight of disappointment.

"They've already failed," she added.

"Failed?" I said. "We were about to kill the scorpion."

"You were about to kill *yourself*," Mum insisted. "And your sister too. Sami, what was beneath the trapdoor?"

"Boiling oil," Sami replied.

"Boiling oil?" Pan protested. "In a five thousand-year-old tomb? How was it still boiling? And the Akkadians never discovered oil."

Mum's jaw clenched. "*Sumerians*. The point is that you were not certain. If that was a real situation—"

"How realistic is a giant mutant scorpion?" Pan complained.

"You faced a giant mutant snake in Egypt," Sami said.

Another breeze rustled through the barn, but that wasn't why I shivered. A few months ago we thought Mum and Dad were just boring old ancient history professors. Pan and I had travelled with them to Egypt, but they'd vanished. Our search led to a meeting with Sami and another treasure hunter named Kit Thorn, in whose home we were now hiding out. We'd found a secret tunnel in a pyramid, and a lost tomb of an Egyptian god. *That* was where the mutant snake attacked us. But we'd discovered something even more shocking: that Mum and Dad were really super-high-tech tomb robbers.

Actually, that's not quite true. They were tomb robbers *once,* rescuing relics for museums before other hunters could sell them on the black market. Now they were coming out of retirement, and training me and Pan to work with them. Only, it wasn't going so well...

"Fixed it!" Sami announced.

All at once the simulator came back on. Hologram projections beamed from a dozen cameras, recreating the 3D image of the tunnel. One moment we were in the barn, the next we were back in the tomb, and the trapdoor opened.

The simulation shifted up, as if we had fallen into a pit. The scorpion splash-landed beside us in an image of dark, bubbling liquid: boiling oil. The creature writhed and screeched and sank deeper.

I looked to Pan, who shrugged.

"No *way* this oil would still be boiling," she muttered.

2

Mutant scorpions, giant man-eating bats, pits with spikes, pits with *poisoned* spikes, swinging blades, closing walls that squash you like a bug if you can't find the secret release mechanism...

Each new horror appeared in front of my eyes in pin-sharp detail so realistic that I instinctively reached to my utility belt to defend myself, even though I knew each scene was just another simulation. I'd seen them all several times now.

I pulled off my smart-goggles and set them on the workbench. I knew how much effort Sami put into creating these tomb-training simulations, and they really were amazing. But the truth was I was getting a bit bored of them.

"They're great, Sami," I said.

Sami cursed in Arabic. "You've done them all before, haven't you?"

"A few times, yeah."

Sami cursed again, louder. His bald head gleamed in the light from a dozen holograms – scenes from the simulations he'd created for our training. The projections beamed from a glass table screen, a sort of 3D computer we called a "holosphere". Sami swiped several of the files away with his fingers, and tapped frantically on the screen, causing new holograms to whoosh up – scenes of mountains, deserts, jungles, caves...

"Your mother wants a new simulation for your training *tomorrow*," he grumbled. "How about one in Antarctica? I could build a lost tomb at the South Pole, with crazy polar bears and mutant penguins."

"Aren't polar bears in the north?"

"They're *crazy* polar bears, Jake!"

"Crazy lost?"

"OK, how about one hidden beneath a volcano? Or *inside* a volcano! Not even your parents have found a tomb inside a volcano."

"Wait. But they have found one *beneath* a volcano?"

"I need ideas, Jake!"

"I'm not allowed to help you, Sami! It's cheating. I'll know the solutions to the traps."

"Since when did you care about cheating?"

I didn't, and usually I'd have loved to get involved, but that afternoon my heart just wasn't in it. I hung out with Sami in his workshop most days after training, mucking about with the tech he built for us to use on missions. It was fun watching him work. He was older than my parents, with dodgy eyesight and small, wrinkled hands, but he had the energy of a teenager when it came to his gadgets. He'd set up his workshop in one of the many rooms of Kit's mansion, and the place was cluttered with cool things: flare guns, smoke bombs, compressed oxygen breathing tubes, laser cutters, gloves with in-built metal detectors...

"Your knee is twitching, Jake."

"Eh?"

Sami flicked a few of the holograms aside to see me better. "Your knee. It shakes like that when you're frustrated. What's wrong?"

I smiled. I'd only known Sami for a few months, since our adventure in Egypt, but he already understood me better than most people.

"The simulations are great, Sami, but shouldn't we be doing this for real now? And all this equipment... We should be out there using it."

"That's up to your parents, I'm afraid."

"They don't trust us yet, do they? Even after everything we did in Egypt."

A few months ago, in Egypt, my sister and I had tracked down a sinister organization we called the People of the Snake, who had kidnapped our parents. They'd tried to force Mum and Dad to locate a lost tomb, but Pan and I found it first. We'd saved our parents and blown up the People of the Snake's secret base.

Sami and Kit Thorn had helped us a lot back then. Kit ended up in hospital, and was still there, but he'd let us use his home to train as treasure hunters. We were on the run from the police so we couldn't go to school, but I was studying way harder than when I *was* at school. Our parents had taught us about archaeology, ancient civilizations and loads of other stuff. None of it was easy for me – I wasn't a genius like my sister – but after three months I could just about tell the Olmecs from the Toltecs, or hieroglyphs from hieratic.

There had been physical training too. Mum and Dad were experts in several martial arts, but they refused to teach those, insisting we'd never need to fight. Instead, Dad made us run laps around the grounds of Kit's mansion. It was a properly big stately home, and it was autumn in Yorkshire so basically raining all the time. You should have heard Pan moan!

"Jake does the action stuff!" she always yelled. "I read the books."

That was rubbish – Pan was as tough as anyone I knew – but no matter how much Dad tried to encourage her with chants of "You can do it!" she just flicked her fringe down over her eyes and hollered back, "No, I can't!", except with more swearing. But, really, I think Pan loved it all as much as I did. We were training to be treasure hunters!

But Sami was right; I had been getting more and

more frustrated. I stared around his workshop, and all the cool gadgets we still hadn't been able to use. Would we ever?

Again Sami seemed to be reading my mind. "It will happen, Jake. Besides, you don't even know what to hunt for."

"We do know, though, Sami."

We had one clue: a mysterious emerald tablet that Pan and I found in Egypt, one of several hidden in tombs in different countries. Together, the tablets revealed some sort of secret history of the world that the People of the Snake were trying to hide. We'd planned to travel the world hunting for the tablets, protecting the history they were trying to erase. Only, we needed a clue to the next tablet, and so far Mum and Dad hadn't found anything useful on the one we had. So we were stuck here.

Eager to take my mind off it, I picked up an object from the workbench – a tiny device, no bigger than a fly, with mini rotors on top.

"Is this the world's smallest helicopter?" I asked.

Sami flicked away the last of the holosphere files, but his eyes were brighter than ever. He loved talking about his work. "*That* is a nano drone," he said.

"A drone?"

"A very *small* drone. It can fly through cracks to explore tombs you can't access."

"There ain't no tomb I can't access, Sami."

He knew I was joking, and grinned. He took the

device super-gently, as if it was a delicate living thing, and held it in his palm. "It's entirely soundless, with a built-in microcamera, echolocation scanner and geothermal sensor. It's—"

"It's off!"

As Sami was speaking I'd put my smart-goggles back on, and the device had instantly connected. Its tiny rotors spun but made no noise as it rose from Sami's hand. It really did sound helpful for treasure hunts, but right then I had other plans for it.

"How does it work?" I asked.

"Just tell it where to go."

"Turn ninety degrees and fly forward ten metres," I instructed.

I saw the drone's video feed in my goggles as it flew silently from the workshop and into a corridor decorated with antiquities Kit had nicked from tombs: Ming vases on stands, jade dragons, Egyptian *shabtis* in display cases.

"Fly forward thirty metres."

I guided the drone to an oak door at the end of the corridor. It was open a fraction. Blue and green lights flickered from beyond.

"Thermal camera," I said.

My view changed to a geothermal pattern of the drone's surroundings – dull grey broken by a bright orange blob: a human heat signature. Someone was in that room.

Good.

"Jake?" Sami sounded nervous. "What are you up to?"

I sensed he was considering snatching my goggles, so I turned away slightly. "Training, Sami. We're meant to learn how to use this, aren't we?"

I guided the soundless machine into the room – and saw my mum. She sat at another holosphere, studying files projected from its table screen. With her hand, she swiped through holograms of ancient texts, pinched one to enlarge it, ran a finger along a line of ancient writing, and then discarded it with a frustrated flick of her hand.

I guided the drone closer as Mum lifted an object from beside the screen – a relic about the size of a laptop computer but made of shiny green stone.

"The emerald tablet," I breathed.

"What?" Sami asked.

"Nothing..."

Just to see the tablet quickened my pulse. This was the closest I'd been to the thing since I'd found it in Egypt. Mum kept it in the study, and had banned me and Pan from going in. I think she feared I might do something crazy, like steal it and put it on eBay to flush out the People of the Snake. It hurt that she didn't trust me, but I can't sound too outraged because I actually had considered doing that.

The video was so sharp that it felt like I was right there in the study, and I spoke in a whisper.

"Zoom."

The drone's camera showed me a close-up of the tablet, gleaming in the light from Mum's holo-sphere. I'd forgotten how beautiful it was, carved on both sides with the same symbol – a snake in a circle, eating its own tail. There was ancient script inside the circle, which my parents hadn't been able to decipher. They didn't even know what language it was.

Mum had stayed up late and woken early, studying the tablet. She'd read dozens of books, examined hundreds of images from archaeology sites, searching for anything to understand the treasure better. So far she'd not learned anything about the location of the next tomb. The bags around her eyes had grown into black bin liners.

Guilt nagged at the back of my head. I shouldn't have been spying, but why did Mum have to keep everything so secret?

"Why can't she trust us to help?" I muttered.

"She?" Sami asked. "Jake, are you spying on someone?"

"I... No. Yes. Kind of."

"What? Which?"

"Yes."

"Oh, God. Please tell me it's not your mother."

"OK. It's not my mother."

"But ... is it your mother?"

"It is, yes."

"Jake! Get the drone out of there before she sees!"

I took off the goggles, looked at my friend and cringed.

Sami sighed. "It's too late, isn't it?"

Right then a shrill scream rang from along the corridor.

"JAKE!"

3

All families fight, right? Before my sister and I learned about our parents' past, all we *did* was fight. Then, for a little while, we actually seemed to get on. We'd been so excited about treasure hunting together; thrilled, even. But recently the fighting was back.

The fights usually followed the same pattern. Pan and I sided with each other, even if we didn't actually agree on whatever we were fighting about, while Dad tried to keep the peace, and Mum wouldn't let him. Sami hid in his workshop until the dust settled, but I knew he listened in.

That evening, after I was caught spying with the drone, the yelling lasted over an hour. You don't want to hear it all, but this snippet should set the scene. Imagine it to a soundtrack of doors slamming, Mum sighing, and Dad muttering for us all to calm down after every other sentence.

"I will not calm down, John! This is serious! Jake, you are grounded."

"I'm grounded? That's crazy, we never leave this stupid house."

"I don't know what's come over you. You never behaved this badly when you were at school."

"That's not true, Mum."

"Stay out of this, Pandora."

"But don't you remember the Ant Farm Incident?"

"Of course I remember that! But spying on me is even worse."

"Worse than tipping red ants over schoolgirls?"

"Hey, I was helping you out, Pan. Those girls were bullying you."

"Still, Jake ... those ants were stingers."

"How is this helping us right now, Pandora?"

"Just pointing out that Jake has done *way* worse things. He blew up a tomb in Ancient Egypt."

"I said sorry about that!"

"Please do not ever mention that again, Pandora!"

"Listen, everyone just calm down."

"Stop saying that, John! How can Jake expect us to trust him if—"

"Trust me? You hide the emerald tablet from us. You won't even let us look at it. *We* found it. Pan, I don't remember Mum and Dad being in that tomb, do you?"

"Nope. It was just before we *saved their lives*. In fact, the tablet is technically ours."

"Yes! Finders keepers! The first rule of treasure hunting."

"That is most certainly *not* the first rule of treasure hunting. Honestly, it's as if we have taught you nothing, Jake."

"OK, this is interesting. Jake, Pandora? What would you say *are* the main rules of treasure hunting?"

"John, this is not a lesson! Jake was spying on me!"

"Because you don't trust us!"

"Because you don't *think*. Spying on me with a drone? It wasn't even a sensible plan. I can think of at least half a dozen better ways to have invaded my privacy. Can you?"

"I thought you said this wasn't a lesson."

"You didn't *think*, Jake. It was just a silly drone."

"Actually, it was a carbon-filament nanodrone with a built-in high-definition—"

"Stop listening in, Sami. This is a family dispute!"

"Sami *is* family, Mum. You go ahead and listen, Sami!"

"I'm staying out of this!"

"Everyone just calm down. I'll make some dinner, and we can all just get along like normal."

I don't know what world Dad lived in where "getting along" for us was normal. The only time we ever had was when we were treasure hunting in Egypt. Then, the Atlas family had *worked*. *That's* what we needed to be doing.

None of us spoke for a while after that. Dad

29

cooked something with chickpeas that I knew none of us would eat, either – even Pan, who is a vegetarian. It was another part of our training: to introduce us to foods from around the world so we didn't moan when we went on adventures. Only, Dad was *such* a bad cook. He burned every single chickpea, so my meal looked like a pile of rabbit poo.

Mum didn't even look at the food. She just sat staring out a window and stroking the Egyptian amulet she wore around her neck – a symbol of the mother goddess Isis that she'd swiped from one of the first tombs she and Dad discovered, way before Pan and I were born. I wondered if she was thinking how much easier life had been back then...

Some of the things she'd said seriously worried me. More and more, Mum had been mentioning school, as if this was all just a holiday. In training, she'd taught us to always have a back-up plan, to know two exits for every entrance. I suspected she and Dad had a way out of *this* too, a plan to clear our names so we could go back to our old lives. That scared me far more than anything.

Before this our lives were *rubbish*. Mum and Dad were pretending to be happy as boring college professors. I was always getting into trouble, kicked out of schools for stealing and fighting. Pan had been miserable too. Bullied for being so clever, she'd turned into a Goth, dying her hair black and wearing dark clothes. We were constantly at each other's throats.

But our adventure in Egypt changed everything. Pan became proud of her big brain, and I'd stopped feeling bad about myself, too. I wasn't a troublemaker anymore. I was a *treasure hunter*.

Only, was it ever going to really happen?

We *had* to make this work.

Dad tapped his fork against the side of the table. I could tell he was trying to think of something to say to break the silence. He looked at me and Pan through the thick lenses of his glasses, which made his eyes seem freakily big.

"So what went wrong in the simulator today?" he asked.

"We were attacked by a giant scorpion," Pan replied, rifling through chickpeas with her fork for any that might be edible. "That's a bit dumb, isn't it, Dad?"

"Well, your mother and I were once attacked by a monitor lizard in Malaysia."

I pushed my plate away, always keen to hear more about their adventures. "How did you get away?"

"I jumped on its back. Except dozens of baby lizards ran out from behind a rock."

Pan edged closer too. "What then?"

"One of them bit my hand. That's why I can't use this little finger, see?"

"You told us you broke that in a rugby match."

"Well, that's sort of true."

"It's not true at all, is it, Dad?"

31

"No, not at all."

I grinned, adding it to the list of stories they'd told us to cover for their treasure-hunting past. I loved picturing them travelling the world and getting into danger, but the stories stung, too. I was desperate to have tales of my own.

"Do you want to hear something *really* strange?" Dad said.

Pan and I leaned even closer. We *definitely* wanted to hear. Dad had a look that I'd only seen since we'd come back from Egypt – his eyes wider than ever, and twinkling like he'd just heard the best bit of gossip. He and Mum had hidden their past for years. Now, at last, he could talk about the good old days, and he loved it.

"This one time in China," he began, "we saw a rabid panda bear bite another treasure hunter right on his—"

"John?"

Mum tucked her amulet back under her shirt. She sighed, stretching her back where it ached from leaning over the holosphere screen.

"I think they've heard enough," she said.

She looked at her plate of food as if she'd only just noticed it was there. "What is this, anyway?"

"Gheimeh," Dad replied. "It's Persian. We ate it in Iran when we were hunting for the temple of—"

"I remember," Mum interrupted. "But it wasn't black, was it?"

She flicked one of the burned chickpeas off the plate, a perfect shot that hit Dad on the chest. Dad *humph*ed and flicked it back. I noticed Pan smile at the exchange, even though she looked away to hide it.

The atmosphere seemed to be perking up, so I decided to ask what had been on my mind since I spied on Mum in her study.

"Did you discover anything today?" I asked. "On the emerald tablet?"

Mum sighed again, so heavily this time that the chickpeas rustled on her plate. "No, Jake," she said.

"Where do you think the tablets will lead? If you had to guess."

"Never guess," Dad replied. "*That's* the first rule of treasure hunting."

"Yesterday you said the first rule was 'never go into the study without my permission'," Pan said.

"But if you *had* to guess," I asked. "About the tablets?"

Dad nudged his glasses up his nose. "Remind me what she said."

She. He meant the woman who had tried to kill us in Egypt. She was one of the People of the Snake, maybe their leader, although we weren't sure. She wore their symbol on a brooch, so we'd called her the Snake Lady. We'd discovered her real name was Marjorie, but that just sounded silly.

"The Snake Lady said there were several emerald tablets around the world," I replied, thinking back to our encounter in her headquarters in the Egyptian desert.

"They're all in lost tombs," Pan added. "The people buried with them were from a civilization that was older even than Ancient Egypt, but was somehow wiped out. The People of the Snake are trying to find the tablets and destroy the tombs, to hide a secret about who those people were and what happened to them."

"And how much of that do you believe?" Mum asked.

"Pretty much all of it," I replied.

"Just like that? Because someone told you?"

"We have the emerald tablet," Pan said. "That's evidence."

"That's evidence of *something*," Dad agreed. "But we don't know what."

"Whatever it is, the Snake Lady is trying to hide it. We have to stop her, right?"

Mum looked at Dad, but neither of them answered. Mum smiled painfully, as if the effort had used up her last scrap of energy.

"I'll cook us something else," she said. "It's been a while since we had spaghetti. How about that?"

I glanced at Pan and noticed her watching Mum with the same concern. Pan loves spaghetti. So do I. But right then we wanted burned chickpeas.

Mum collected our plates and scraped the leftovers into the waste disposal unit. Blades whirred, grinding up the chickpeas. She stared down into the sink, watching the food vanish in a mush, and then she said something else. It was hard to be certain with all the noise from the blades, but I was pretty sure I heard her right.

"Perhaps it's time we let this go."

4

That night I lay awake watching raindrops race each other down the windowpane. I kept imagining one of them was the Snake Lady going after an emerald tablet and the other was my family trying to get there first. The Snake Lady won every time.

Mum's words rang around my head.

Perhaps it's time we let this go.

I'd dreaded this moment for months, but expected it too. Our parents were chickening out. The longer they studied the emerald tablet, the crazier they thought this whole thing was. At times Mum seemed to trust Pan, but she'd never been convinced that I was up to the job of being a treasure hunter.

If we just had a clue to the next tablet, things would be different. Mum and Dad wouldn't be able to *stop* themselves from going after it. I had a back-up plan to make that happen, a last resort. If it didn't work, Mum and Dad would probably never trust me again. But they never really had anyway, so I had to try.

I slid from bed and strapped on the utility belt loaded with Sami's tomb-hunting gadgets. Wearing it felt like putting on a favourite T-shirt, and gave me confidence I shouldn't have had for such a crazy plan.

I crept barefoot along the hallway, stopping, listening. Kit's house was several hundred years old; it reminded me of stately homes that my parents used to take us to at weekends, with a grand, sweeping staircase that looked great but was totally rubbish for sneaking. Getting to the bottom was like a tomb-training exercise: seeking out the route with the fewest creaks to wake my parents.

I waited again at the bottom of the stairs, but all I heard were thundering snores from down the hall. Sami was fast asleep in his workshop.

I kept going to Mum's study and slid a gadget from my utility belt, a device the size and shape of a lipstick tube. As I held it to the lock, a laser beamed into the keyhole, where it scanned the grooves for lock pins. A thin pick slid from the gadget and opened up like a claw inside the lock. I heard a *clunk* and a thunk, as the skeleton key picked the lock. Grinning, I stepped inside and closed the door.

Just enough moonlight fell through the leaded window to see the holosphere table screen, piles of Mum's books and a mess of papers fanned out across the floor. I slid my smart-goggles from their slot in my belt, and put them on.

"Ultrasonic," I whispered.

The goggles switched view to an echolocation soundscape – a graph pattern of squiggly lines made by sound waves bouncing from empty spaces. Sami had invented it to help us to see things in tombs that our eyes couldn't, like secret passages or cracks behind rock walls. Right then I needed it to find something else.

I turned, breathing slowly... There!

"Torch," I said.

A super-lumen beam, as bright as daylight, shone from the frame of my goggles. I rushed around the holosphere screen and removed a painting from the wall. Behind it was a safe. It didn't take long to open with the skeleton key, and then I rose to tiptoes and shone the torch inside.

"Looking for this?" a voice asked.

I whirled around, yelping in fright.

Pan stood behind me. She had the emerald tablet in her hand! "Get that light out of my face," she snapped.

I yanked my goggles off.

Pan wasn't wearing her utility belt, so didn't have a skeleton key – but she'd got in here somehow, and locked the door behind her. Did she have the *actual* key? I stared, confused.

"What are you doing here?" I asked.

She sat at the holosphere and tapped a code into the screen. Half a dozen holograms rose into the air, archaeological reports and ancient documents that I was sure Mum had already checked. Pan was *double-checking*.

"Mum said I could look at this stuff," she explained, "to see if I spot anything she missed."

"Wait. She *lets* you come in here?"

"Sometimes, so I know where she hides the key. She'd be furious if she knew I was here this late, though."

I nodded like I understood. I *did* understand; it was sensible of Mum to let Pan look at the tablet. Pan was smart enough to find a clue, which was what we wanted, after all. But it stung to hear that Mum had trusted her to look at it. She'd barely allowed me to touch the thing since I stole it from the Snake Lady in Egypt.

"So what was your big plan?" Pan asked.

"Plan?"

"You just broke in here."

"Oh. I was going to steal the tablet and send it to the British Museum. It would be on the news, and the Snake Lady would see. She'd try to get it back, and we'd be waiting with a—"

"That is a dumb plan, Jake."

It wasn't my best, but I was desperate. "You heard what Mum said at dinner?" I asked.

Pan nodded, her eyes still glued to the hologram

files. "That's why I've got to find a clue *tonight*."

I glanced around the piles of reports and plans, wondering if it was worth having a look, but I didn't even know what I'd look *for*. Instead I stepped up to a corkboard, which displayed the few clues we actually had on the Snake Lady. Sami had searched for her face in the background of photos on social media sites. He'd had over fifty hits, but we were only sure that three were the Snake Lady. In each photo she wore a crimson wig to hide her snow-white hair, but she couldn't disguise her sharp cheekbones or arrogant smile. She looked smugly satisfied, as if she'd just watched a noisy dog get run over in a street.

"Horrible witch," I whispered.

I remembered how she had left me and Pan to die on an island in Egypt. Then, after we'd escaped, she'd actually asked us to work for her. I couldn't help wondering what might have happened had we agreed. We'd know everything about her organization, and be out there hunting for emerald tablets. We'd be treasure-hunting, not hanging around this mansion doing nothing.

"She goes to cool places," I muttered.

"Eh?"

"The Snake Lady. These photos were taken all over the world."

Pan flicked away several hologram files to see me better. Her face in the projected light was deathly pale, but her eyes were wide and shiny.

40

"Where *are* they taken?" she asked.

"I don't know, but look at the car number plates, and the shops' signs."

Pan rushed to join me at the corkboard. "Jake, that's it! We've been so busy trying to decipher the tablet, we never properly studied the clues we *had*."

Pan loved these moments, deliberately drawing out a discovery to wind me up. I wasn't going to beg, so I turned away to watch the rain patter against the window.

"Reckon it'll brighten up tomorrow?" I asked.

"What?"

"Wonder what's for breakfast..."

"Jake! We've just made a big discovery!"

I whirled back. "Well, why don't you just tell me?"

"I was about to!"

"No, you weren't. *You never just tell me!*"

"Just wait here."

And then she ran off!

I waited for a minute in the dark, unsure if she was even going to return. I was about to put the tablet back in the safe when she rushed back, dragging a sleepy-looking Sami by the arm. Sami wore boxers and a T-shirt, and as he staggered into the room he waved a closed umbrella wildly around in the dark. I knew that the umbrella wasn't just an umbrella: it was another of Sami's gadgets, a stun gun in disguise.

I stood back from its aim. "Don't shoot!" I cried.

41

Sami lowered the weapon and stared at me, confused. "Where's the burglar?"

"I lied about that to get you to come," Pan replied coolly.

"Are you crazy? This stun gun is loaded with *concentrated midazolam*. It would have knocked Jake out for twelve hours!"

Pandora waved away his concern as she rushed back to the corkboard. She was so excited about whatever she'd discovered that her words came out in gasps.

"Sami, we need your help."

Sami set the stun gun on a side table and rubbed his eyes to clear away the last of his sleep. "I'll get your—"

"No. You can't tell our parents. We won't leave this room, Sami. And if we find a clue, I promise we'll tell Mum and Dad."

Sami sighed and muttered something in Arabic, but he wasn't as torn as he was acting. In Egypt he'd talked Mum and Dad into letting us become treasure hunters, and he knew how close they were now to giving up.

"What do you need?" he asked, finally.

Pan tapped the images on the corkboard. "These photos of the Snake Lady. Where are they from?"

"Social media accounts," Sami replied.

"But which accounts?"

"I don't know. I found them using a biometric

interception programme. It extracts facial recognition matches from the web. The Snake Lady is only in the background of these photos. Whose actual accounts they are isn't relevant."

"It's totally relevant," Pan insisted. "Not *whose* accounts, but where they took the photos. Can we find out?"

"Well, yes, but only by hacking into those accounts. That's illegal."

"So you can do it?" I asked.

Sami stared at me. "Did you hear the part about it being illegal?"

"I thought you were on our side, Sami," Pan said. "Not Mum and Dad's."

"Pan, there are no sides. You're a family."

"Tell that to them. You know they're going to give up, don't you? What will happen to us then? I'll return to that gross school for the gifted."

"School for *geniuses*," Sami said.

"For freaks, Sami. I hated it. And what about Jake? He'll go back to being a troublemaker and a thief. He'll probably end up in jail, Sami, for life, without the possibility of parole. If you visit him, you'll look into his broken eyes and know that all of his misery, as well as that of his victims, was caused by *you* right now, not helping us in our hour of need."

I tried not to laugh. From the way the wrinkles curled up even tighter around Sami's mouth, I suspected he was fighting a smile too. Sami had become part of our family over the past few months, and Pan had him wrapped around her little finger.

"Sami," Pan pleaded. "Can you do it or not?"

Sami did another groan-sigh-Arabic-mutter combo, but I knew he'd help us: not just because we needed to find a clue, but also because of how we hoped to find it. He couldn't resist the challenge. We were testing his skills.

He typed on the holosphere screen, and dozens of files projected into the air. Most were home pages from social media sites, but one was different. It looked like a creature from an old computer game, a Space Invader, and it was flashing. Sami gazed at that file in wonder, like a pilgrim visiting holy relics in a church.

"This is an extremely aggressive parasite," he explained. "A program that hacks social media accounts."

"Which social media accounts?" I asked.

"All of them."

Light from the holograms gleamed off Sami's bald head. His hand trembled as he touched the Space Invader with two fingers and slid it into one of the flashing files.

It was as if someone had pulled the plug from the holosphere; everything just vanished. We stood for a moment in the dark, breathing hard. I was about to ask if it had gone wrong, when a million files suddenly shot up from the screen. I know people say "a million" and don't mean it, but it was *at least* that many. Each was a dot of light, so it looked like we were staring at a galaxy of stars.

"What are they?" I gasped.

"Every social media account on the internet," Sami explained. "Two and a half billion of them."

The files began to move, shooting sideways and vanishing, replaced by thousands more and thousands more, gathering speed until they were a white blur.

For a moment we stood in silence, mesmerized by the stream of rushing light. I noticed Sami glance at me, and then at Pan. He was one of the world's leading experts in future technology, with qualifications from top universities, but when it came to speaking his mind Sami was ... well, not so clever.

"You know," he said finally, "I mean, listen, guys... I was just thinking, really, that maybe, well – and don't take this the wrong way or anything because I think you've got real promise as treasure hunters – maybe your parents might be right about—"

"They're not," Pan said.

"Right," Sami said.

A single file shot from the stream. It floated by Sami's face as if it were in orbit around his head. Two more files followed it, and hovered beside the first. The light stream vanished, leaving just those three little glow-fly files.

"Those are the accounts that caught the Snake Lady in their photos?" Pan asked.

Sami nodded. He expanded the files with finger swipes. Two Instagram pages, one Facebook. "You sure you want to open these? It's a gross invasion of privacy."

Pan and me spoke at the same time.

"Definitely."

They were pretty normal social media accounts – filled with photos of meals and holidays, mostly. After several minutes of searching, we found the snaps with the Snake Lady in the background. All three were selfies of the account owner, tagged with a location and date.

"Where were they taken?" Pan asked.

"This one was in New York," Sami said. "This one in Vienna, and this third photograph was taken in Shanghai."

"So why was the Snake Lady in those places?" I asked.

"*Exactly*," Pan replied. "Sami, can you cross reference the dates, see if any similar events took place in those three cities?"

I was still amazed by the speed with which Sami worked the holosphere. He was a bit older than my parents – so *properly* old – and often moaned about his bad back and aching knees. But when it came to tech stuff, Sami had the energy of a child. His fingers worked like a concert pianist's across the table screen, and web pages whooshed up into the air.

"There were several similar events in each of

those cities," he said. "Music festivals, movie premieres, auctions—"

"Wait," Pan said. "What auctions?"

Sami enlarged the websites of three auction houses. "This is interesting," he muttered. "They were sales of antiquities."

I edged closer. "So the Snake Lady was buying ancient stuff at sales? Do the auctions have lists of what they sold?"

"Yes, auction catalogues," Sami replied.

"Cross reference the catalogues from those three auctions," Pan said.

Sami was on it already. More taps on his screen, more projections, and this time he couldn't fight the grin that creased up his whole face. He'd discovered something.

"Have you guys heard of the Aztecs?" he said.

"The burrito restaurant in High Wycombe?" I asked.

He looked at me. "No, not the burrito restaurant in High Wycombe."

"He means the ancient Mexican civilization," Pan said.

"That's right," Sami agreed. "Each of the auctions the Snake Lady attended was selling an Aztec codex."

Pan answered my question before I could ask. "A codex is an Aztec document with writing and pictures."

"I knew that," I lied.

47

Sami scrolled through the web pages. "The auction houses sold three of four codices recently found in Mexico. They all date from the Spanish Conquest."

"The time when Spanish soldiers invaded Mexico and conquered the Aztecs," Pan whispered to me.

"I knew that *too*," I mumbled. "Sami, you said there were *four* of these documents. So is the fourth on sale too?"

"I'll check."

"If it is, *that's* where we'll find the Snake Lady," Pan said. "And I bet those Aztec codices are a clue to the next emerald tablet."

Sami flicked several files away, like he was swatting flies, until he was staring at a single web page. He suddenly looked confused, as if he'd hit a surprisingly tricky question in an otherwise easy quiz.

"I don't know whether this is good news or bad news," he muttered.

"What is it?" Pan asked.

"The auction where the fourth codex is being sold is here in England, in London."

He looked at us through the hologram, and I really couldn't tell whether he was smiling or grimacing about what he'd discovered.

"The sale is tomorrow," he said.

5

"What in blue blazes is going on?"

I grabbed Pan and Pan grabbed Sami and Sami grabbed me, and we all yelped.

Mum stood in the doorway. She was in a "blue blazes" mood – the phrase she saved for her very angriest moments. Her sleep mask was pulled up over her head, but her eyes were wide awake and full of fury. Dad stood behind her in his dressing gown, looking a little less sharp.

"I asked you a question," Mum snapped.

"It's not as bad as it looks," Pan replied. "We were—"

"Don't answer back," Mum barked.

"But, Mum, we—"

"Sam," Mum continued, "I am astonished that you are involved in this. I thought you were on our side."

"Sami is on *our* side," Pan insisted. "Aren't you, Sami?"

Sweat glistened on Sami's head. Right then he looked like he'd rather not be on *anybody's* side.

"No one has to take sides," he said. "Jake and Pan have found—"

"Enough, Sam," Mum said.

Dad stepped past Mum and into the study. He placed the emerald tablet back in the safe and rubbed his eyes beneath his glasses.

"We can talk about this in the morning," he said.

"But, Dad—"

"I said, in the morning."

Dad locked the safe. He saw Sami's umbrella stun gun on the side-table and sighed, as if it somehow confirmed his worst fears about Pan and me.

"Look," he said, "your mother and I understand your enthusiasm. But we have studied that tablet for weeks. There is simply no way that we can locate the Snake Lady, or—"

"She'll be at an auction in London tomorrow," Pan blurted.

Dad stared at her, his glasses slipping down his nose. He nudged them back up and glanced at Sami, who nodded to confirm our discovery. Then he looked at Mum, and they had one of their silent conversations – a whole argument in nods, headshakes, widening and narrowing eyes.

Mum must have won, because she spoke next.

"Jake. Pandora. Your father and I are ... delighted by your interest in our old lives." She said *delighted* like she meant *disgusted*. "But we were hasty in suggesting it could continue. Isn't that right, John?"

Dad sounded less sure, but it was obviously something they had talked about – giving up the hunt for the emerald tablets, and going back to our old lives. "I... Yes. Perhaps we got carried away."

"What?" Pan said. "But we can't go back to how it was before."

"We were all safe before," Mum replied.

"We hated each other before," Pan said. "You and Dad were bored stiff teaching at that college. So instead of treasure hunting, you want to be miserable for the rest of your lives?"

"I would never be miserable," Mum said, "if I knew you were safe."

"But we can't go back anyway," I said. "We're wanted criminals."

"I am confident that we can convince the authorities there was a misunderstanding," Mum replied.

"Misunderstanding?" Pan said. "Jake blew up a tomb! He did actually do that, remember?"

Mum winced, as if the memory caused her physical pain. "Yes, I remember. All too well."

What did *that* mean? Did she fear it would happen again? Was Mum trying to protect *us* by keeping us away from danger? Or did she just not trust *me*? Did she fear I might do something that crazy again?

My arms began to tremble. Something was boiling up inside me. A volcano. "But we have a clue,"

I protested. "We have to follow it."

"We're not saying we can't," Dad replied. "From libraries, after school or at weekends."

"Libraries?" I scoffed. "We should be out there kicking butt!"

"Watch your language, please," Mum warned.

"You watch *yours*."

I was out of breath and out of ideas. I could tell that Mum and Dad had made up their minds, but how could we just act as if the past few months had never even happened? Treasure hunting was all I wanted to do, the only thing I was good at. Before this, I was no good – a thief, a troublemaker. I was scared of that person, the old Jake Atlas. Treasure hunting had given me a focus, a way to use those skills for something good. We'd trained, worked hard, but it wasn't good enough for Mum and Dad. Or at least, *I* wasn't good enough.

"It's me, isn't it?" I said.

"Jake?" Mum asked.

"Pan is a genius," I replied. "You know she's good enough for this. But you don't think I am. You've never trusted me at all."

"You need more time, Jake, to learn composure. Today, with that scorpion—"

"I had a plan!" I insisted. "It would have worked."

Mum and Pan broke into another argument, as my sister defended me, insisting we'd never *actually* encounter a giant scorpion. I didn't listen. The volcano inside me was about to erupt.

"Mum, I'm sorry," I said.

"For what, Jake?"

I grabbed the stun gun and shot her.

It wasn't something I'd planned. I mean, who *plans* to shoot their mum? I barely even knew what I'd done until it had happened, and then I was even more shocked than Mum.

I staggered back, staring, as a stun dart fired from the tip of the umbrella and dug into Mum's arm. Mum had flipped at me for far smaller crimes, but now she remained weirdly calm. I think she saw the panic in my eyes, and understood how desperate I felt.

"Jake, put that weapon down," she said, still so calmly. "It's a stun gun, loaded with *xylazine*. You know that your father and I built up immunity to that drug decades ago."

I did know that. But there was something Mum didn't know.

"Mum," I gasped. "It's not *xylazine*."

Her eyes widened. I think she was about to say something else but her legs gave way and she collapsed, unconscious, to the carpet.

Dad edged closer, arms out and palms raised. "Jake," he breathed, "give me that weapon. Don't do anything silly."

Don't do anything silly? I'd just shot my mum with a stun gun! And now I had to shoot Dad too. There was no chance now that he'd let us go after the Snake Lady at that auction. Not while he was conscious, anyway.

The stun gun trembled in my grip. I had to be careful; Dad looked big and clumsy, but I'd seen how good he was at fighting, and how fast.

"Jake," Sami warned, "Put the gun down."

"It's not a gun!" I insisted. "It's just a stun gun!"

"Do not shoot me, Jake," Dad added.

"I'm not going to shoot you, Dad. Stop saying *shoot*. It's just a stun gun."

"Jake..." Pan hissed.

She wasn't convinced about this plan either, and I couldn't blame her. There was no going back now, though.

"It's just for twelve hours, Dad," I said. "You look tired, so it's a nice long sleep. We'll find the clue. Then we can still do this as a proper family."

"Proper family?" Dad said. "Jake, you're aiming a gun at your father."

"A stun gun, Dad. And I'm really, really sorry."

I think I screamed as I fired again, but my memory is a bit of a blur. The dart hit Dad in the chest. He stumbled back and then forward, slurring his words as the drug rushed through his bloodstream. "Jake..." he rasped. "Don't... Too dangerous..."

The umbrella fell from my hands and I edged further back, shaking almost as hard as Dad, as he swayed from side to side like a drunk staggering from a pub. Finally, he slumped to the floor beside Mum.

Sami rushed to them, cursing in Arabic. He took their pulses and lifted their eyelids to examine their pupils. They were both fast asleep; nothing worse.

"They're unconscious," he gasped. He whirled around, yelling so loud he sprayed me with spit. "You just shot your parents!"

"I didn't have a choice!"

"Yes, you did! The choice was shoot your parents or don't shoot your parents! And you shot your parents!"

"He's got a point, Jake," Pan said. She leaned over Mum and Dad, grimacing. "They're going to be *so* mad when they wake up."

I closed my eyes and groaned, wishing I'd thought about this more. Maybe Mum was right; I was too reckless for this job. Look at what I'd just done! Right then I only knew one thing for sure: we had to make this worth it.

6

The moment I walked into the auction house, I felt an urge to do something crazy, to charge at one of the display cabinets and knock it to the floor. I used to get the same feeling at the museums where Mum and Dad gave lectures. They were hot and stuffy and so *serious*, and everyone was looking down at me. I just wanted to cause some trouble – *any* trouble.

I breathed in deeply, held the breath and let it out slowly. The last thing we wanted to do was draw attention to ourselves. We needed to focus – was the Snake Lady here right now?

Everyone was too caught up in their own worlds to notice us anyway. Around the entrance hall, posh-looking men and women peered into glass cases displaying the various antiquities that were up for sale: garishly painted pots, gold jewellery, fragments of stone sculptures. A banner at the side of the hall announced the auction: TREASURES OF PRE-COLUMBIAN ART. It showed a golden sun disc with a face carved in its centre, and a jade snake that was coiled and grinning.

"What does Pre-Columbian mean?" I asked.

"It means before Christopher Columbus discovered the Americas," Pan explained. "In the year 1492. After that the Spanish conquered a lot of Central and South America."

"So where do the Aztecs fit in? That's what the Snake Lady is after, right? Something from the Aztecs."

"Their civilization was in Mexico. They were conquered by the Spanish too, and basically wiped out."

"Ouch."

As I followed Pan through the crowds I realized how much Mum and Dad would have hated this place. There were some amazing antiquities on display, but this was no museum: everything here was for sale. Rich people buying up history to hoard it in private collections stood against everything Mum and Dad became treasure hunters for.

A man in a blazer and cravat glanced at us over the top of his spectacles and sneered, as if we were something he'd just discovered on the sole of his fiercely polished shoe. I sneered back and muttered a few things I shouldn't admit to muttering, and the guy hurried off towards a security guard at the entrance.

Pan dragged me deeper into the crowd. "Don't cause trouble. We have to blend in."

"Blend in?"

I glanced down at my dirty jeans and yogurt-stained T-shirt, and wished we'd planned this better. Getting here this morning had been a scramble. It had taken ages to drag Mum and Dad to their bedroom and tuck them in for their stun-drugged sleep. After that we'd had to convince Sami to drive us to London in his van. The journey had taken several hours from Kit's mansion in Yorkshire. In the end we'd arrived minutes before the auction, with no plan for what to do next.

Now that we *were* here, my guts twisted up with nerves. We'd spent three months looking for the Snake Lady; I'd become obsessed with finding her. But now that we might actually be close, part of me didn't *want* to find her. The truth is, I'd forgotten how much she scared me. I remembered how close she'd come to killing us in Egypt.

No, we *had* to find her. After what I'd done to Mum and Dad our only hope of ever being treasure hunters was to find a clue to the next emerald tablet, and one they couldn't ignore.

Pan pulled me towards the next room. "The auction is about to start."

The auction chamber was packed. About a hundred people sat in rows around the large sky-lit hall, shifting in their seats to get a better look at a stage where an auctioneer – the snooty-looking guy in charge of the sale – stood at a wooden podium.

"Do you see her?" Pan hissed.

We stood at the back, scanning the crowds for the Snake Lady, but people kept getting up and moving around to greet someone or talk on their phones. We knew the Snake Lady would be here in disguise, if she was there at all.

The auctioneer banged a little wooden hammer against his podium, and everyone settled down. He glared at them as if he was guarding school children at detention rather than about to make a fortune flogging ancient relics.

"Right, let's get on with this, ladies and gentlemen. The first item for sale today is this rather fabulous clay drinking vessel painted with an image of an Inca god."

The crowd sat up to get a better look as a stagehand raised the antiquity for everyone to see. Most of the buyers had what looked like a table tennis bat with a number on the paddle, which they raised to bid on an item.

"I shall begin the bidding at five thousand pounds. Will anyone bid five thousand pounds? Yes, you, sir, good. Do I have ten thousand?"

After that, the auctioneer talked at machine-gun speed, raising the price by ten grand each time someone waggled a paddle, and then banging the hammer against his podium to signal that the highest bid had won. You wouldn't believe the amount of money stuff went for. That clay cup went for seventy grand! A cup!

Pan was fascinated by it all. She kept gripping my arm as the stagehands brought in new items.

"Jake, I recognize that from Mum and Dad's books. It's Olmec. And that's Mayan! Those were the civilizations that came before the Aztecs in Mexico."

My eyes remained on the crowd, but all I could see were the backs of people's heads.

The auctioneer cleared his throat. "Now we come to the final item in the sale; this rare Aztec codex from the time of the Spanish Conquest. This magnificent document is one of four, the other three having already been sold at auctions earlier this year."

Pan's grip tightened on my arm. "That's it, Jake! The Aztec codex."

This was the item we thought the Snake Lady was here to buy. It didn't look like it could be worth much – a scrap of brownish paper painted with colourful figures. It looked like an old, dirty comic book.

The auctioneer banged his hammer. "I shall begin the bidding at five thousand—"

"One million pounds."

A gasp swept across the room.

The auctioneer stared. "I... Did you say *a million*?"

He tapped his hammer on its stand, weakly this time. He looked dazed. "I... Any further bids? No. Sold for, um, one million pounds."

The room erupted in claps and whispers. Everyone in the crowd shot up from their seats to get a look at the buyer. Pan cursed as we moved around the scrum of posh people, trying to get a look. They'd blocked our view, but I didn't need to see to know who had bought the codex.

"It's her," I said. "It's the Snake Lady."

"Can you see her?" Pan asked.

"I just know, Pan. Who else would pay a million for something when the bidding is only at five grand?"

Pan understood. The People of the Snake seemed to have unlimited funds. They needed the codex, so they made sure they got it. Price wasn't an issue. But even so, we had to see the Snake Lady if we hoped to follow her. Glancing around the room, I spotted security cameras mounted in high corners. I pressed my comms bud deeper into my ear.

"Sami?"

He'd insisted on staying close in his van, and on us wearing ear buds so he could remain in contact.

"I'm here," he replied.

"Can you hack into the CCTV system to see who's in the middle of that crowd?"

"I can," Sami muttered. "Except that's—"

"Illegal, I know, Sami. But it's important. Can you do it?"

"Hold on," Sami said. "All right, I'm watching the feed now, but I can't see the buyer. Whoever it is, the person must be short."

"It's *her*," I said.

"We don't know that, Jake," Sami warned. "Don't do anything stupid."

I was desperate to do something stupid – to scream about a bomb, or smash one of the relics – to get the crowd to clear. But I forced myself to stay cool, to think.

"Jake," Pan warned, "we've got trouble."

A security guard was heading for us, tipped off – I guessed – by the posh guy I'd scowled at earlier. The guard spoke into his radio, and one of his colleagues approached from the other direction. We were going to get thrown out. We'd lose the Snake Lady.

Think! Think, Jake!

"Sami?" I said. "Can you bring up the blueprints for this building? And yes, I know it's illegal."

"All right," he replied. "I've got them."

"What room has the Snake Lady gone into?"

"We don't know that it is her, Jake."

"What room, Sami?"

"A side annex off the auction hall."

"Jake," Pan hissed. "The guards are coming."

"Is there another way out from that annex, Sami?" I asked.

"Yes, there's an exit onto St George Street."

"That's where she'll come out," I said. "People buy stuff worth a fortune here. The auction house must help them leave securely through a different exit to everyone else. Sami, meet us with the van at the main Bond Street entrance in thirty seconds. And I need you to do one more thing."

"I'm listening."

"Set off the fire alarms."

"What?"

"We're about to get caught. We need a distraction. It's either the fire alarms or I'll smash an ancient relic."

I'd barely finished that sentence when alarms began to shriek around the auction hall, a noise so piercing it caused people to cover their ears. The security guards immediately turned away from us and began to guide the crowds surging for the main exit. Pan and I moved among them, back through the entrance hall. I shoved one guy out of the way and shoulder-barged past a couple of others, ignoring their protests. One of the guards spotted us and reached to grab Pan, but she stamped a heel into his foot and he tumbled back, more out of shock than pain.

I pulled Pan with me out onto Bond Street, where Sami's van was waiting. Its side door opened and we piled in.

"Get to St George's Street!" I cried.

But the road was blocked with traffic as people rushing from the auction house hailed taxis or scrambled into private cars. I leaned from the passenger seat, trying to look through the crowds and the rain that had begun to batter the windscreen. We needed to see the car the Snake Lady got into, to follow her...

"Drive on the pavement," I demanded.

"Jake, this is central London," Sami shot back. "I'm not driving on the pavement."

"Please, Sami!"

"Jake, no!"

Think, Jake, think!

"Can you hack into the street CCTV at the St George Street exit?"

Sami tapped the van's dashboard, and part of the windscreen turned into a high-definition computer screen. After a few seconds the screen changed to show a black-and-white blizzard. Static.

"This is strange," he muttered. "The camera for that street isn't working."

It wasn't strange. It made perfect sense – the Snake Lady's organization had disabled the camera so she wouldn't be seen. I cursed, and punched the seat. I was so tightly wound that I almost hit Pan too. She touched my shoulder.

"Jake," she said, "breathe."

She could see that I was freaking out. I had to remember my training, to think past my panic and make a plan. I closed my eyes and breathed in. My mind cleared, changing from a muddy puddle to a crystal clear pool. In an instant I knew what to do.

I scrambled to the back of the van, flipped open the armrest of the seat and pressed a button hidden beneath. A side panel of the van slid open, revealing various mounted gadgets that Sami kept ready for missions. I pulled a sleek silver rifle from the rack.

"Is this the tracker gun?" I asked.

"That's a stun gun," Sami replied.

I grabbed another device. "This?"

"That's an actual gun."

"Which one is the tracker gun, Sami?"

"The one that looks like a tracker gun!"

"I don't know what a tracker gun looks like!"

"Why not? You had a lesson!"

"I didn't listen in that lesson!"

"Why are you yelling at me about this?"

I didn't know – my blood was up. The Snake Lady was getting away.

"Here," Pan said, taking one of the weapons. "It's this one."

The tracker gun didn't look like a gun at all. It was disguised as a fancy gold pen, but with a tiny silver arrowhead poking from its tip. I remembered now: the tip was the GPS tracker. As it fired it spread open and used magnets to cling onto any metal surface it hit.

Pan tried to hand it to me, but I shoved it back into her hands.

"You have to do this," I said. "Get to St George's Street, see which car the Snake Lady gets into and fire the tracker at it. Then we can follow her."

"What? Why me? Jake, *you* do the action stuff."

"Stop saying that, Pan, that's crazy. You're the best shot by far."

We'd all seen her sharpshooting in Egypt, when

she took down the Snake Lady's mercenaries with a stun gun. Pan knew I was right, but she still looked horrified. I didn't blame her; this wasn't a training simulator. It was a real mission.

"Jake, I ... I don't think I can."

"Pan, you've got this," I said. "Just aim and fire."

"Aim and fire," Pan repeated, in a voice as shaky as her hands. She looked back at us as she opened the van door. "At least there won't be any giant scorpions."

"You hope," I replied.

She ran into the crowds and the rain.

I slid the door shut and we waited, listening to the rain on the van roof, praying Pan pulled it off.

"Your parents should be waking up around now," Sami said. "I'm in so much trouble."

We were all in so much trouble. If this didn't work, treasure-hunting was over, and the Snake Lady had won. I'd do my best to shield Sami from my parents' anger. I'd tell them that I'd forced him to help, but even so, I'd be amazed if they ever spoke to him again. He didn't deserve that – he'd looked out for us since Egypt, helped us every step of the way. He wasn't just our friend: he'd become part of our family.

"I'm sorry, Sami," I replied. "We shouldn't have got you into this."

Sami smiled. "Your parents got me into this over thirty years ago, when they first became treasure hunters. I joined them very willingly, and I'm here by my own choice now, too."

For a second I forgot about Pan and our mission and I seized the opportunity to learn more about Sami's past adventures with my mum and dad.

"Did you go on every mission with them?" I asked.

"Not all, but many. I was always in the comms van, keeping watch."

"You had their backs."

"Not that they needed me. Your parents knew what they were doing. They didn't take risks."

I looked away, trying not to show how much that comment upset me. "You mean like I do?"

"Your parents wanted to rescue artefacts for museums, but other hunters were paid well to find those treasures first, often very dangerous people. Your mother and father knew that, but they believed in what they were doing. They planned everything very carefully. They didn't just charge into tombs, even though at times that meant they might fail, and the relics would be lost."

"I can be like that too, Sami."

"Maybe, Jake. That is what your parents wish. But I wonder if that is for the best."

"What do you mean?"

Sami hesitated, choosing his words carefully. "Your sister is a genius. Her value to the team is clear. Your parents know your value too, but it scares them, Jake, especially your mother. In truth, it terrifies her."

"I don't understand, Sami. What value? What scares them?"

Sami was about to answer, when a thump on the side of the van caused us to jump. I slid the door open, and there was Pan. She was soaked, but smiling. She held up the tracker gun.

"Bull's-eye," she said.

"You saw her?" I asked. "You actually saw the Snake Lady?"

She clambered in, wiping rain from her face with her coat sleeve. "Not exactly," she replied. "I saw someone leave through that other exit. The security guards helped the person into a car, and I got it with the tracker. But I didn't see who it was for sure."

That was enough for me. It *had* to be her. The Snake Lady thought she was so clever, but we were on to her.

I pulled the door shut and barked to Sami, "Let's go!"

7

It was getting dark by the time we hit the motorway. The rain was coming down so hard we could barely see ten metres ahead, even with the windscreen wipers going at full speed. Other cars were smudges of red and orange light. The rain was so loud on the van roof that we had to wear our smart-goggles and speak to each other through their microphones.

"Are you sure we're still following her?" Pan asked, rubbing mist from the window to see outside.

Sami tried to explain how the tracker worked, using words like "triangulate" and "global positioning satellites" which made more sense to Pan than me. The result was a flashing light on a street map, pro-jected onto part of the van windshield – the light we were following. We hoped it was the Snake Lady, but couldn't be sure.

"We're heading into Sussex," Sami said.

I checked my watch. If Sami's drug worked as he said, Mum and Dad had already been awake for a few hours. I noticed Pan grimace slightly as she gazed out of the window, and wondered if she was thinking about it too.

We followed the tracking signal for another hour as it led us deeper into the countryside along pitch-black country lanes. Lightning flashes revealed rolling hills, a creepy old windmill, horses staring from the rain.

"Why is she coming all the way out here?" Pan asked. "Do you think it's a trap?"

"Switch to night vision," I said.

The headlights cut out, and we saw the road ahead through the green filter of night vision.

"The car we're following has stopped," Sami said. "Half a mile up ahead."

"Keep going. Slowly."

The van rattled as we crawled along a pot-holed lane, past thatched cottages and a village primary school. We stopped.

"The signal is coming from outside that house," Sami said.

Pan and I shifted into the front of the van to see through the night-vision screen. My heart was pounding harder than the rain on the roof, but what I saw left me confused. From what we knew, the People of the Snake were a powerful organization, able to influence governments, destroy monuments, do whatever

70

they liked. Their headquarters inside the mountain in Egypt had been ultra high-tech.

But this was just a cottage. The car we'd followed was parked outside a white cottage with perfectly symmetrical windows and neatly trimmed hedges, like a child's drawing of a house. There was a farm shed nearby, and a village pub with hanging baskets and steamed-up windows. The place wasn't scary. It was ... pretty.

"Sami," I said, "can you scan the house with thermal imaging?"

"Already have," he replied. "Nothing unusual. I see heat signals from one person and a small animal."

"A mutant animal?" I asked.

"A dog, I think."

"Try an infrared scan."

"Done that too," Sami said. "And ultrasonic. There's nothing unusual about that house, Jake. Either someone is blocking the signals, or it's just ... someone's home."

"We need to see more," I insisted.

"No, we do not," Sami replied. "We don't even know who we followed here."

"It's the Snake Lady, Sami. It's Marjorie. She's just spent a million pounds on a document that could have cost a tenth of that, then driven to the middle of mud-soaked nowhere. She's not just watching TV. That's not *her*."

"Jake, you barely know this woman," Pan said.

"I know enough."

"You're obsessed with her."

Maybe Pan was right. I *had* thought about her a lot over the past few months. In fact, I hadn't thought about much else. She'd tried to kill us, but I didn't entirely hate her. In a weird way, Pan and I had her to thank for something, although we never would. It was her organization that had forced my parents to come out of retirement as treasure hunters. That was the only reason Pan and I had found out about Mum and Dad's past, and had a chance to make it our future.

"We can't go back to how things were, Pan. Do you remember how bad that was? You and I didn't talk. We didn't even *know* Mum and Dad, not the *real* them. But in Egypt, the Atlas family *worked*."

"We can still work, Jake."

"No, Pan, they'll never let me do this unless I prove that I can. Then they'll trust me."

"Trust you? You shot them, Jake!"

"It was a *stun gun*!"

We sat in silence for a moment, listening to the rain on the roof.

"Jake," Pan said finally, "we've done well. We've found something. Maybe this is their headquarters, or maybe it's—"

I don't know what else it might have been, because right then I threw open the van door and ran for the house. I guess Mum was right; I am reckless. And that was about to get me in more trouble than I'd ever known.

8

"Jake! Wait for me, you idiot."

I glanced back and grinned as I saw Pan rushing after me from Sami's van. I was very happy to take a few insults from my sister in exchange for her coming with me. I really hadn't fancied sneaking around the Snake Lady's house alone; the place may have looked like a sweet country cottage, but my heart had begun to beat as if I was running towards a torture chamber.

The closer we got to the place, the more it made sense. In Egypt the Snake Lady had acted so sweet and kind while also plotting to kill us. This house seemed just right for her – sweet on the outside, but with something much darker going on within, I was convinced

"Stay low," Pan hissed.

We hid behind the hedge that fronted the house

and slid on our smart-goggles. The rain had eased a little, and my night vision could just pick out Sami's van down the lane.

He spoke to us through the goggles' microphone. "You're right outside the house," he said.

"We know, Sami," Pan replied.

"Come on," I whispered.

Pan hissed a protest, but I was already off – darting from behind the hedge and across the cottage's small front garden. I tried to remember my training, and look for traps or alarms, but it was hard to concentrate. I wasn't just scared of the Snake Lady or being caught, but also of failing. It would confirm Mum and Dad's suspicions that we weren't ready to be treasure hunters. Or at least that I wasn't.

"Jake, get down!"

We sank to the grass beneath a sash window. Firelight flickered from inside the house. I heard classical music: an opera singer wailing. One of those annoying, yappy-type dogs began to bark.

"Sami," I whispered. "Can you tell us where she is in the house?"

I expected him to grumble, but instead there was silence.

The yapping grew louder, competing with the opera singer. The volume caused the window to tremble in its wooden frame.

We scrambled through a gate, to a glass-panelled door at the back of the house. A muddy pair of wellies sat beside a dog bowl, and a doormat with the message HOME SWEET HOME. It was all fake, I was certain. The doormat may as well have said SECRET EVIL HEADQUARTERS.

Pan examined the door frame with her goggles. "Don't see anything odd. No wires, lasers or heat sensors around the grooves. It's just ... a door."

"Then we should open it."

I slid the skeleton key from my belt and used it on the lock. There was a soft *clunk*, and the door opened.

"Good old Sami," I breathed.

I grasped the handle, but Pan grabbed my arm.

"You said we'd only look."

"We *are* looking," I replied.

It was a dumb thing to say, but I couldn't stop myself now – I had to see more. The door opened without any sound. The dog had gone silent too, although the opera singer was still screeching – an annoying sound like an alarm going off.

"Looks like we're in a kitchen," I whispered.

"Really?" Pan shot back. "Was it the sink or the fridge that gave it away? Jake, this is *just someone's home*. Let's go."

It wasn't. I had that feeling in my belly, that instinct I had learned to trust. There were eggs in a helter-skelter holder. A basket for the dog. A reminder note on the fridge to pay the milkman. It was all so boring, so normal.

It wasn't right at all.

I crept across terracotta tiles, through a doorway and into a dining room with wood-panelled walls and a wood-beamed ceiling. Moonlight cast a shadow across a long oak table that had just one chair. A vase at its centre looked expensive, like an antique. The opera music was coming from the next room.

"Jake," Pan hissed. "We need to go *now*."

I can't explain the next few seconds. Had I agreed, maybe everything would have been different. But something in me refused. A cosy cottage, cheesy doormats, opera... This was all so wrong.

I think Pan said something else. She might have even tried to grab my arm and pull me back, but I didn't hear, and barely even noticed. I just stood, staring at the entrance to the next room, listening to the music, and realizing something for the first time.

She knew we were here.

I don't know how I was so certain, I just was. The Snake Lady had known we were following her, and she knew we were here, right now, in her home.

She was in the next room.

She was waiting.

9

The moment I saw her I froze. I don't just mean I stood still; it was as if my insides had literally turned to ice, the blood frozen solid in my veins.

The Snake Lady was facing the fire, so all we could see was her white hair and the black woollen cape she wore, but I knew she was smiling. That smug grin had haunted my dreams: cheekbones popping out. Ruby lips curled into a sneer.

She spoke in that candyfloss voice, sweet but sickly.

"Darlings!" she said. "Welcome!"

That's right, you witch, we found you.

That was what I *wish* I had said. Instead, I slid my smart-goggles off and stared. It was as if she had me under a spell, an ice queen's magic. I'd thought about this moment for so long, being face to face again with the Snake Lady. I'd practised it in my head, and even in the mirror. But now I was here I didn't know what to say or how to act.

She turned. Firelight glinted off her perfect white teeth. I stepped back an inch, more out of shock than fear. I'd pictured her so often, but in none of those daydreams had she been so pretty. Her cheekbones and painted lips, her pale skin and snow-white hair catching the firelight... She looked more like a film star than a villain. Only her eyes reassured me that she was as horrible as we remembered. They were so dark – almost no whites at all – but also shiny and bright. We called her the Snake Lady but her eyes looked more like those of a shark.

She stepped closer. Her dog – a little brown thing that looked like a bigger dog's poo – scuttled by her feet, wagging its tail frantically.

"Darlings," she said. "I would not move if I were you."

"Yeah?" Pan shot back. "Why not?"

"Because you have broken into my house. You are currently surrounded by an electromagnetic force field. An invisible cage, if you like. It is a horrible device, and I hate to use it, but I am a poor frightened woman who lives alone. I was forced to defend myself."

"You're lying," Pan spat.

"Am I?"

I wasn't so sure. I couldn't see any gadgets in the wall panels that might generate the force field, but that didn't mean they weren't there. We'd seen the crazy technology the People of the Snake used at their headquarters in Egypt.

She slid leather gloves from her hands, folded them neatly and set them down on a side table. "Now," she said, "who *are* you?"

I dared a step forward, so the firelight caught my face. "I'm afraid it's us again, Marjorie," I said.

Her black eyes stared. "No, seriously. Who are you?"

"I..."

Words caught at the back of my throat. *She didn't recognize us?*

"We're ... Jake and Pandora Atlas," Pan said.

"Do we know each other?" she asked.

Was she serious? She had tried to kill us! We'd blown up her headquarters, stolen an emerald tablet that she'd spent a fortune trying to find.

"We... You know, in Egypt..." I stammered.

At last her eyes lit up. "Oh! Oh, yes of course! But whatever are you doing here in my— Wait, have you been thinking about me ever since *then*? You *have*, haven't you? You've been trying to find me. Am I your *nemesis*? Oh, how utterly delightful."

Anger boiled inside me unlike any I'd felt since, well, the last time I saw this woman. She had a way of making me feel like I was the last to be picked for a school sports team. She knew exactly who we were. She was just messing with our heads.

"You tried to recruit us!" I yelled.

Her smile vanished, and her marble eyes gleamed. "And you refused," she replied. "But I shall give you another chance."

"Chance?"

"To work for me."

I laughed, but her face was totally serious.

"We don't need to work for you," Pan replied. "We've deciphered the emerald tablet. Mum and Dad are going after the next one right now. They've probably already got it."

"Really? Then why are you here spying on me?"

She *definitely* knew who we were, and that we'd run out of clues.

She picked up a document from the side table and slid it from a protective plastic slip. It was the Aztec codex she'd bought at the auction. Up close, it looked even feebler than it had in the auction room – a tiny slip of paper, with those cartoonish Aztec gods.

The Snake Lady held it close to the fire, considering it in the flickering light.

"This just cost me a million pounds," she said.

She threw it on the fire.

"Hey!" Pan cried. "That belongs in a museum!"

The codex was already ash. Pan swore at her, but I wasn't surprised. In Egypt this woman and her mercenaries had destroyed tombs and priceless treasures. They were trying to hide a secret about a forgotten ancient civilization. No, not forgotten – *erased*. It made sense that she'd burn the codex.

"That was a clue, wasn't it?" I said. "To the next emerald tablet."

The Snake Lady brushed her hands. "Of course. We cannot allow anyone else to acquire that tablet, so we must erase the clues."

"But you don't have it yet either," I realized. "Or else you wouldn't need to destroy those clues."

"Such a perceptive little boy."

She poked the fire, watching the sparks crackle up the chimney. A million pounds going up in flames, and she just smiled. The money meant nothing to her organization. They would, and could, pay any price to protect their secrets.

"What tomb are you trying to hide this time?" I demanded.

"Have you heard of Quetzalcoatl?" the Snake Lady asked.

"Quetzalcoatl," Pan said. "The Aztec god, shown as a snake with feathers."

"The Aztecs had many gods," the Snake Lady replied, "but Quetzalcoatl was special. He was inherited from older civilizations in Central America. The Toltecs, the Maya, the Olmecs... They all worshipped him. They gave him different names, but depicted him the same way, as a feathered serpent. To each of them he was the bringer of civilization."

"Like Osiris in Egypt," Pan said.

The Snake Lady clapped her hands – a limp sound, like raw steaks being slapped together. "You noticed!

Such a clever girl. You see, the Aztecs did not really inherit Quetzalcoatl. They *stole* him. His worship and, we believe, his body."

"His body? But he's a god."

"Oh, darling Pandora. You were being so clever. In Egypt, did you not insist that Osiris was 'just a god', right up to the moment you discovered his coffin?"

"So you're looking for the coffin of this god, Quetzalcoatl. You think the emerald tablet is inside it, like it was in the coffin of Osiris in Egypt."

"I do not think that. I know that. Tell me, Pandora, for Jake's benefit. Who was Hernán Cortés?"

"Hernán Cortés was a Spanish soldier. He led the army that conquered the Aztecs."

"Conquered?" the Snake Lady replied. "*Massacred* would be a better word. Cortés and his troops slaughtered the Aztecs. They destroyed their temples and burned their cities."

"They sound like your kind of people," I muttered.

"You know so little about *my people*, Jake Atlas. What we are doing is more important than you could ever imagine. Hernán Cortés and his soldiers were thieves and pirates."

"What's he got to do with anything, though?" Pan demanded.

"An awful lot, Pandora. Those Aztecs that survived the massacre fled, gathering whatever they could take, including Quetzalcoatl's coffin and its emerald tablet. That was why we bought and destroyed those codices. They told of the flight of those last Aztecs, with the coffin of their feathered god."

"So you know where they hid it?"

"Yes and no. The documents mention particular mountains in the jungles of Honduras, in Central America."

"We know where Honduras is," Pan spat.

"*You* do, Pandora. Jake, however, has no idea, so please forgive me for filling in these little details."

I swore at her, although I wasn't bothered. I wanted to know more about the tomb. "What other clues did the codex give you?"

She watched me for a moment, her eyes narrowing to dark slits, and then stepped closer. "There were indeed other clues," she said. "The Aztecs did not want the knowledge of the tomb to be lost among their people. The codex is the first of three markers, which together lead to the tomb of Quetzalcoatl. It states that the next marker will be discovered at a location called the Place of the Jaguar."

"The Place of the Jaguar?" Pan repeated. "What does that mean?"

"Precisely," the Snake Lady replied. "We employed two of the world's best hunters to find out."

"Let me guess. They failed."

"No. They vanished."

"Vanished?"

"Do you wish me to explain that word, Jake?"

"No! Just ... how could they vanish?"

"The last we heard from them, they believed they were close to locating the first marker. Then, nothing. But that is only half of the mystery. This team – we called them Alpha Squad – carried a tracker beacon, so we could follow their progress. When they vanished, so did the signal. For almost a month, it was as if both hunters simply disappeared. Then, last week, the tracking signal was reactivated."

"Reactivated?"

"Darling Jake, are you a parrot? Yes, reactivated. Yet we have heard nothing from Alpha Squad at all. It is very curious. Only one thought gives me comfort. Alpha Squad were among the best in the business, but not *the* best. There is another team that I believe might fare better in the quest."

"Who?" I asked.

"She means our parents, Jake."

This time my laugh was real. "You think Mum and Dad will work for *you*? No chance. Even if you have us prisoner."

"Oh, no! I am not keeping you prisoner. You proved yourself most capable in Egypt, and I need my best team possible. That means the Atlas family. The *whole* Atlas family."

"But..." I was confused. "If you let us go, why would we work for you?"

"Ah ha! My big reveal!"

The Snake Lady picked up a tablet computer from the side table and tapped the screen. Behind her, one of the wooden wall panels slid to the side, revealing an array of weapons.

"Not that one," she muttered.

Another tap on the tablet, and another wall panel opened. I glimpsed a control centre with black-clad figures and holospheres, maps and photographs pinned to boards.

"Not that one either," she said, and the panel slid shut.

It was as if she was pressing buttons inside me, doubling my rage with each tap. She was winding us up, like a bully flicking your ear. Anger boiled from my belly and suddenly I charged. I don't know exactly what happened, only that sparks sprayed, and an electric shock thrust me back to the floor. It felt as if I'd ... well, as if I'd run into an electric force field. Spit ran down my chin, and a blizzard of white spots filled my vision.

"We'll never work for you," I groaned as Pan helped me up.

The Snake Lady looked up. Her jaw muscles clenched and her cheekbones stood out sharper than ever.

"Oh, Jake," she said. "Of course you will."

She tapped the screen again, this time without looking. A third wall panel slid away, revealing another chamber. It looked like a hospital room, except that it was lit by soft red lights. Machines monitored a patient lying in a bed, attended by two black-suited mercenaries – ex-military thugs the People of the Snake hired to help them keep their secrets.

"Jake!" Pan gasped.

I shook my head, clearing the spots in my vision, blurrily aware that something was suddenly very wrong. Was that...? No, it *couldn't* be. With a shaky hand, I slid my smart-goggles back on and pressed their frame to my ear to talk into the microphone.

"Sami?" I said. "Sami, can you hear me?"

No reply.

He wasn't there.

He was in the bed.

The Snake Lady stepped into the chamber and stood beside the bed. She laid a palm gently on Sami's chest, watching it rise and fall with his short, shallow breaths. Then, suddenly Sami shot up. His eyes bulged so wide that they bled, and he began to writhe in agony, as if he was covered in stinging insects. His hands twisted, and his scream was so pained that even the black suits stepped back in shock. Recovering, they pinned him to the bed and injected him with something that stopped the seizure. Sami slumped back, unconscious.

"What have you done to him?" Pan screamed.

"It's complicated," the Snake Lady replied. "A poison. I cannot tell you which – only that it acted swiftly. These machines will keep him alive for another fortnight, or until he is given the antidote."

"Give it to him!" I yelled. "Now!"

This time the Snake Lady didn't fight her smile. In the chamber's red light her teeth looked like they were covered in blood.

"That is not how this works," she said. "You *are* going to Honduras. You *are* going to find the Tomb of Quetzalcoatl. You *are* going to retrieve its emerald tablet, and you *are* going to deliver it to me. *Then* I will give you the antidote."

Her smile spread wider. "Any more funny jokes, Jake? Any more clever lines, or silly threats? No, I thought not. Now, a driver will take you back to your parents. He will give you a bag containing fake passports, visa documents, tickets for your flight and credit cards. You will also find details of our contact in Honduras, who will supply you with any equipment you require for the expedition. If you return too late, Sami will die. If you return empty-handed, Sami will die."

Tears blurred my eyes. "What if we don't return at all?"

"Ah. I wish I could say that Sami would survive. It would not be as if you had not tried. But these days it is too easy to fake your own death." She waggled a finger. "No cheating! Also, if you do die and I let Sami live, he will come after me for revenge, and that gets *so* tiresome. So let us just say that if you die, then Sami dies too. That way it is nice and neat. Are we clear, darlings?"

"If he dies I will kill you," Pan seethed.

The Snake Lady clutched her chest as if she'd been stabbed in the heart. "Darling Pandora! After everything I have done for you?"

"Done for us?"

"I *made* you. My organization, and the work we are doing, is the reason your parents came out of retirement. It is the reason you are being trained to aid them, even though that training is going rather poorly, do you not think?"

She came even closer, her eyes glinting when she saw the looks of surprise on our faces.

"Oh! Did you really think you were *hiding*?" she said. "Did you not think that we have followed your every move since you caused us so much bother in Egypt? We bugged Dr Thorn's house, listened to your conversations. You have been so desperate to find me. I felt honoured to be at the heart of so many family squabbles. Jake, Pandora, I feel such affection towards you. It is almost..."

She touched her heart again, this time a gentle stroke.

"*Motherly*. However, I have a job to do. You see me as a villain, but you have no idea the danger you cause by opposing us. If I must be villainous to carry out our work, then so be it."

Behind her, the door to Sami's hospital chamber swished shut and the panel to the control room opened. The Snake Lady's dog followed her as she walked through the entrance.

"No more training," she said. "This is now real. Bring me the emerald tablet or your friend dies."

The door closed, and she was gone.

10

We were driven back to Yorkshire by one of the Snake Lady's mercenaries, who didn't say a word the whole journey. Pan and I didn't talk much either. We had no idea what to say. Things couldn't have gone worse. We'd got what we were after – a clue to the next emerald tablet – but now we were working for the Snake Lady. If we failed, Sami was dead.

Mum and Dad were waiting for us at the kitchen table when we got back. They went berserk, of course, and even berserker when we told them what had happened. Dad shouted, doors were slammed, and Mum went into her silent mode. She sat staring out of a window and stroking the Egyptian amulet she wore around her neck, a sure sign that she had reached boiling point.

The next day we were on a plane to Honduras. We were off on another treasure hunt, only now I wished to God we weren't. I kept picturing Sami in that bed, eyes bulging and hands twisted... He'd warned us so many times to be careful, not to take risks, but I'd never listened. I had done that to him. Sami, my friend.

No one blamed me, but everyone knew it was my fault. I had shot my parents, chased the Snake Lady, and broken into her house. Mum was right: I was reckless, and I might have got one of our best friends killed.

No. We could still save him.

We *would* save him.

None of us spoke on the flight. Mum slept and Pan swotted up on the Aztecs. I watched an *Indiana Jones* movie to take my mind off Sami. Dad watched a bit too, but didn't seem impressed.

"No one is going to find the Ark of the Covenant in *Egypt*," he mumbled.

He seemed to have calmed down, so I tried a bit of chit-chat.

"Have you been to Honduras before?" I asked.

Dad glanced at me. I could tell he was considering changing the subject, but there was no point in keeping secrets now.

"No," he said. "Never there. It was too unsafe."

"Unsafe?"

"Honduras has the world's highest murder rate. It's as close to lawless as any place gets. The area we will be exploring, in the east of the country, is called the Mosquito Coast. It's one of the wildest, least known parts of the planet."

"That's where the Snake Lady's team was searching for the tomb of Quetzalcoatl?"

"Yes, somewhere in there."

"But people don't just vanish, not in real life."

Dad thought about that for a second. He leaned closer and got that excited look on his face again.

"Jungles aren't like anywhere else you'll ever go, Jake," he said. "People *do* just vanish, and often. You're never less than five metres from something that could kill you. Savage animals. Poisonous insects. And the Mosquito Coast is the most dangerous of *all* jungles. Smugglers and bandits use it as a passage from North to South America. There are professional kidnappers, illegal loggers and the constant threats of dehydration, exhaustion, disease. If you do die it's unlikely you'll ever be found. Jungles are warm and wet, so corpses decompose at incredible speed, aided by various creatures that will eat your flesh. In some ways you're better off dead. If you get seriously injured in a place like that there's little help. Gangrene can set into a wound, and your body starts to rot from the inside. You become easy prey to animals. There is little you can do but watch in horror as they stalk closer, waiting for the moment to—"

"John?"

Dad looked up. Mum glared at him from across the aisle. "I think Jake has heard enough, don't you?"

"Right," Dad said. "I'm going to have a nap."

There was no way *I* could sleep after *that*. By

the time we reached Honduras I'd watched all the Indiana Jones films and not slept a wink.

We landed in a city named San Pedro Sula. I'd love to tell you about it, but I only saw the airport. I do know it was hot. Not dry hot, like the desert, but steamy hot, like a bathroom after a shower. Even in the middle of the night, the short walk from the plane to the airport left my T-shirt clinging to my back. The air smelled of damp laundry.

It was only as we waited to pass through security that I remembered we were wanted criminals. Dad obviously hadn't forgotten: he double-, triple- and quadruple-checked the fake passports given to us by the Snake Lady. "Remember," he whispered, "we are the Brown family. Not the Atlas family. We are *not* the Atlas family."

"Then stop saying 'the Atlas family'," Pan hissed.

"We are just a happy family on holiday," Mum said.

"In the most dangerous country in the world," I added.

Dad muttered "stick together", and "be ready for anything," and Mum stroked her amulet. I tried to change the subject to get them to relax.

"You read up on this tomb we're looking for, right, Pan? Quezakillall?"

"Quetzalcoatl," Pan said.

"Yeah, him. Give me your top five facts."

"History isn't about 'top five facts' lists, Jake."

"Then give me your top three."

Pan tried to look annoyed, but she couldn't resist. Mum edged closer too, but pretended not to listen.

"Quetzalcoatl was one of the Aztecs' main deities," Pan began.

Clever people always said *deities* instead of *gods*.

"He created the Aztec civilization," Pad continued. "He taught them how to build cities, and write, and grow crops."

"Busy guy," I muttered. "What else?"

"There was a pyramid temple dedicated to him in the Aztec capital, where human sacrifices were made."

The queue shuffled forward, but I didn't move.

"*What* sacrifices?"

"Human," Pan repeated, matter-of-factly. "The Aztecs sacrificed humans to keep their gods happy."

"But ... how?"

"Different methods," Dad said. "But mainly ritual cardiectomy."

"You know I don't know what that means!" I said.

"They cut out their victims' hearts while they were still living."

I thought I was going to be sick. "*Still living*? But why?"

"For the blood," Dad replied. "If you're alive, you bleed more. The Aztecs wanted them to bleed a lot. They wanted waterfalls of the stuff, gushing down the sides of—"

"John!" Mum snapped. "Too much information."

"The Aztecs believed the blood fed their gods," Pan explained. "If they didn't, there would be an earthquake. The universe would collapse."

"These Aztecs sound like a horror movie."

"No, Jake." Mum said. "Don't make the mistake of thinking of ancient cultures as primitive. They were sophisticated people with profound religious beliefs. The Aztecs built extraordinary monuments and created beautiful artworks."

"It was the Spanish that were savages," Pan said. "Coming here and killing them all."

"That's not true either, Pandora. It is not our place to judge people in history."

"It's our place to steal their treasure," I added.

All this human sacrifice stuff was gross, but it was a good distraction. By the time we reached the security desk, we didn't look so worried about our fake passports.

The lady behind the desk took the passports and eyed us curiously.

"You are on holiday?" she asked.

"Yes, ma'am!" Dad said.

"Not many families come to Honduras on holiday."

"Yes, ma'am!" Dad said.

The lady looked at Dad like he was an idiot and stamped our passports.

We went straight to the car rental stall in the airport basement, where it was cooler, thank God. Pan and I slumped against a pillar as Mum and Dad sorted

96

a car. I'd rarely seen my sister look so tired: she was like a zombie, with red eyes and a pasty white face. It wasn't just exhaustion from the flight; she had looked unwell ever since we'd left the Snake Lady's house. I wondered if she was haunted by the same memory of Sami writhing in that bed, and the same gut-wrenching guilt. I wanted to tell her it wasn't her fault; it was mine. Like Sami, she had tried to hold me back. But, and I'm ashamed to say this, it made me feel a little bit better to think Pan felt guilty too – as if the burden and blame wasn't just on me.

The rental car was a big disappointment. I was expecting a jeep or jungle buggy.

"A people carrier?" I said.

"It's safe," Mum replied.

"We're going to hunt for a lost tomb," Pan said, "in the most dangerous place in the world. We're a bit beyond 'safe' aren't we?"

Mum touched her amulet. "No, we are not. We'll be on a road all the way to Trujillo, on the edge of the Mosquito Coast. That's where we're supposed to meet the Snake Lady's contact."

The car wasn't exciting, but it *was* comfortable, I had to admit. Pan and I had a double seat each to stretch out across, as Mum and Dad took turns driving. I wanted to peer out of the windows and take it all in, but I just couldn't keep my eyes open. I remember glimpses of traffic, honking horns, road works and drills. Mum and Dad arguing, maps unfolding and maps screwed up. At one point I looked up and saw a black motorbike riding close behind us.

I woke when we stopped for petrol, and ran to use the toilet at the side of the station. It was a hole in the ground, brimming with poo and buzzing with flies, but I was too tired to be grossed out. I shuffled back towards the car to get more sleep.

I stopped.

The motorbike was there again.

Even half-asleep I was sure it was the same one. There was no driver, just the bike parked on the grass verge. Had it stopped at the station? Or was it following us?

The truth is I was too tired to care. So what if the Snake Lady was having us followed? We were here to find the emerald tablet. We were doing exactly what she wanted, and whoever was following us could tell her that.

I wish now that I'd mentioned that bike to Mum and Dad. Maybe they would have checked it out, or at least been more alert to possible dangers. Maybe we'd have discovered what was really going on – right under our noses – before it was way too late...

11

I woke with sweat stinging my eyes and someone drilling at my skull. I glanced around, disorientated. Pan was curled up in the van's rear seats, and Dad was asleep too, snoring so loudly that I first thought the noise was causing the pain in my head.

I slid open the side door and stumbled outside, rubbing sleep from my eyes. It wasn't sunny. In fact, I couldn't even *see* the sun through the thick grey clouds. So how could it be so hot? It was an uncomfortable, sticky sort of heat, and the damp-laundry air tasted mouldy on my tongue.

Mum stood at the front of the car, staring down a hill. She looked back at me and tossed me a bottle of water.

"Drink it all," she said. "Dehydration is the number one killer in the jungle."

"Jungle?" I muttered.

I shuffled to join her, and in an instant I was wide awake.

Jungle.

I gazed at a small, ramshackle town sandwiched between green and blue. To one side was crystal-clear sea. To the other were hills that rose into mountains that were entirely covered in trees. It really *looked* like a jungle, even though I'd never seen one before – a thick tangle of drooping vines, spiky palms and broccoli-top trees. A thin layer of mist shrouded some of the hillsides, but I could see monkeys swinging between branches, exotic brightly coloured birds, and gigantic snakes twisting around towering trunks.

OK, I couldn't actually see them, but they were there, I was sure.

"Where are we?" I asked.

"Trujillo," Mum told me. "End of the road."

The town really *was* the end of the road. The jungle spilled down the hills and into the sandy streets, green fingers reaching between rows of box-like houses with corrugated iron roofs. Later I saw on a map that it's spelled *Trujillo* but Mum said it with an X – *Truxillo* – which sounded even cooler.

"Where we meeting the Snake Lady's contact?" I asked.

"Where *are* we meeting the Snake Lady's contact," Mum corrected. "In the café on the beach."

Neither of us looked towards the beach; our eyes

remained on the jungle. The small area of the forest I could see looked so dense, as if there was no way in. Could we really find a lost tomb in there? Alpha Squad had searched for six weeks and vanished. And they were supposed to be the best.

"Do you really think we can do it?"

I needed reassurance. I wanted Mum to bring out a map and study it and then tell me everything was fine. But she didn't look at a map. She looked at me, and I knew what she was thinking – could *I* really do it?

She sighed. "I don't know, Jake. But we'll try."

I'd never seen Mum so tense. I decided not to tell her about the motorcycle I'd thought was following us here. One hint of danger and I feared she'd bundle us all back in the van and speed back to the airport. And, anyway, I couldn't see the bike now. Maybe it was nothing.

We waited for Dad and Pan to wake up, and walked down to the town together. Trujillo was an amazing place, all scruffy and sandy, with sagging power lines overhead and rubbish scattered around narrow streets. The buildings looked the same – breezeblock huts with corrugated roofs. They were laid out in neat rows, like a maze, so we had to wind between them to get to the beach. Locals sat outside their homes, selling stuff. An old woman had spread DVDs on the pavement, and an even older man sold watermelons from the back of a pick-up truck. I have no idea who they expected to buy them; we were the only tourists, as far as I could see.

"Stay alert," Mum warned. "Jake, stay calm."

"Why me?"

"Check out that beach!" Pan cried.

We rushed from the tarmac and onto sand that was so white it looked more like snow. Hammocks hung between palm trees, and mangy dogs slept in their shade. The sea was so clear it could have been glass. I wanted to dive in to escape the sticky heat, but remembered we were on a mission, not a holiday. I'd swim once Sami was safe.

The café where we were meeting the contact was a shed with a grass roof. A neon sign said PEDRO'S PLACE, except half the letters had broken. A dented Coca-Cola fridge hummed loudly, and an extremely old man watched us from the bar. He wore a turtleneck jumper despite the mad heat, and was drinking a fruit shake with several straws and a paper umbrella sticking out from the top.

"Are you the contact?" Dad asked.

The old man nodded, slurping his shake.

"We're the Atlas family."

The old man nodded and slurped again.

"I don't think he's the contact," Pan muttered.

The man reached a shaky hand under the bar. In a flash, Mum moved in front of me and Pan to protect us from whatever weapon she expected him to bring out. But instead he handed us menus.

"Have whatever you want," Dad said. "The Snake Lady is paying."

"No fizzy drinks," Mum added.

Dad ordered, speaking in fluent Spanish. I never knew he *could* speak Spanish, but I'd got used to discovering new things about my parents' lives, so I didn't mention it.

Mum ordered some fish thing, Dad asked for a whole crab, Pan wanted a vegetarian omelette, and I ordered a triple cheeseburger. In the end the old man brought us all cheese sandwiches, which was a big disappointment, but Mum said we should just be quiet and eat.

"Are we sure we're in the right place?" I asked.

"Yes."

"Maybe there's another beach café?"

"This is the right place, Jake."

I didn't know then how they could be so certain, so it felt like they were just ignoring me again, and I went into a bit of a sulk, picking lettuce from my sandwich.

"So when do you think the contact will be here?" Pan said.

"From my experience, contacts are never late," Dad replied.

I looked up. "You mean, we're being watched?"

"Just behave normally," Mum said.

"Should we fight?" Pan suggested.

"No, Pandora. Just be normal."

"That is normal, though. If this person knows about us, he'll know how much we fight. He might get suspicious if we don't."

"Pandora's right, Jane," Dad agreed. "Perhaps we should argue."

"About what?"

"Make something up. Let's debate whether the Aztecs were a predominantly agrarian or warring society."

"That's not a debate, John," Mum said. "That issue is settled."

"That's not fair either," I complained. "You three know about that. Let's fight about the best Indiana Jones film."

"We are not fighting about anything," Mum snapped.

"But we *are* now," Pan replied.

"Good job, guys," I said.

We returned to silence, which was fine too. When we weren't fighting, we were usually not talking.

Under the table, my knee began to twitch. We were just sitting here doing nothing while Sami suffered. I pictured him again, lying in that bed, twisted and pained...

The old man came to collect our plates, still grinning away. Then, as he turned, I spotted something strange. Grease stains, on the back of his jeans. Stains like those you might get from riding a motorbike. The man's hands weren't shaking anymore, either.

And why *would* someone wear a turtleneck top in this heat? Something weird was going on.

"Anyone for dessert?" Dad asked. "I quite fancy a—"

We never got to find out what Dad fancied because right then I jumped up onto the table and leaped at the old man.

I crashed into his back, causing the plates to fly from his hands, and pinned him to the sand with my knees.

"Jake!" Mum screamed.

"You were right, Mum," I announced. "We *were* being watched, but closer than you thought. This *is* our contact! He's not really an old man. He's wearing a mask!"

I reached under the guy's turtleneck, feeling for the edge of the mask. Then I started to panic. There was no mask.

"I, um... So, this was just an idea..."

Mum was about to yell again, when another voice bellowed from across the beach. In all the excitement, we'd not noticed a pick-up truck arrive. The guy that sprinted from it was dressed like a cowboy, in a Stetson hat and long leather boots.

"What are you doing to my grandpa?" he shouted.

He charged up to me, fists clenched. I think he would have punched me, but Mum caught his hand and flipped him to the sand. She pinned him there beside his granddad.

"Who are you?" she demanded.

"I'm Pedro. I'm your contact. Why are you *still* kneeling on my grandpa?"

I slid off the old man and helped him to his feet. He took it all pretty well, grinning and nodding like it was all part of the job.

Mum lifted Pedro up and Dad gave him back his hat.

"You're late," she said.

"I was getting medicine for my grandpa. I didn't think you would *attack him*."

"Wouldn't have had to if you were here on time," Pan insisted.

"You didn't *have* to, anyway," Pedro replied.

"Can we get on with this?" Mum said. "You're supposed to supply us for our mission."

The man – Pedro – helped his granddad to a seat and gave him a fresh fruit shake. He kept glancing at my parents, as if he was troubled by their presence. When he came back over to us, I thought he might yell again – but his face broke out in a wide smile, showing off teeth that were as freakishly white as the sand.

"So, you are really Jane and John Atlas? It's ... amazing."

"Amazing?" Mum asked.

"You're legends! I've worked with maybe a hundred hunters in the last ten years, and they all told stories about you two. Is it true that you found Blackbeard's treasure?"

"I wouldn't believe stories," Mum said.

"But is it true?" he asked.

"We're not interested in pirates. We're here to find—"

"But it's true?" I asked.

"That's not our current mission or—"

"Is it true?" Pan asked.

"Yes, it's true!" Mum said.

Pedro snatched off his hat and slapped it on his thigh. "I knew it!"

He broke out laughing, and went for a high five – which I totally went in for. I liked this guy already, although my parents didn't look so impressed.

"Alpha Squad," Dad said. "You were their contact too?"

That wiped the smile off Pedro's face. "I supplied them with equipment and flew them into the jungle. They were meant to contact me to arrange a pick up, but I never heard from them again."

"What do you think happened?"

"Take a guess. Bandits, traps, snakes, exhaustion. Some people just get lost out there. Those guys, they were the best I've ever seen. Yet still..." He scooped up some sand and blew it from his palm. "They vanished."

Mum and Dad exchanged another look. It was hard to read – and I'd spent months trying to decipher their "looks" – but Mum seemed worried. Not stressed or angry, but scared.

"You have supplies for us?" Pan asked.

We followed Pedro to the drinks fridge behind the bar. When he turned back to us, he was clearly trying to fight a smile.

"You want to know a secret?" he asked.

"The fridge isn't a fridge," Mum said. "It's the entrance to a secret chamber where you store equipment for treasure hunters."

"We've seen the sort of thing before," Dad said.

So *that* was how they knew this was the right place.

Pedro muttered something in Spanish, then opened the fridge and grasped a Coke bottle. The whole fridge slid to the side, revealing the chamber beyond.

"Standard," I said, as if I'd seen it before too.

We followed him into a room with metal walls, like the inside of a shipping container. It reminded me of Kit and Sami's headquarters in Cairo: cabinets with mounted gadgets, weapons in racks and a holosphere table screen. There must have been some sort of cooling system, because it really did feel as if we'd walked into a fridge.

"So what do you need?" Pedro asked.

Mum and Dad took over, barking at Pedro as they gathered things we needed for the expedition. Actually, they were a bit rude. Pedro was helping us, after all.

"Grappling gun and a bungee cord," Dad said.

"Climbing clips and ropes," Mum added.

"Water purifiers and food rations."

"What about GPS trackers?"

Pedro rushed over like an over-eager car salesman and raised a device that looked like a smartphone. "Quadliteration satellite tracker," he boasted. "Far more accurate than standard GPS. It could guide you to a single ant in the jungle."

Mum snatched it. "We're not looking for an ant. Will it guide us to Alpha Squad's tracking signal?"

"Yes, of course."

"Then we'll take it."

"A drone would be useful for seeing over the jungle," Dad said.

"Alpha Squad took the only drone," Pedro replied, apologetically. "Perhaps you will find it at their camp."

I rummaged among outfits hanging on a rail – khaki shirts and trousers. They felt incredibly light, like the desert suits Sami had kitted us out with in Egypt.

"Are these special jungle suits?" I asked.

Pedro was over in a flash. "Not just any old special jungle suits," he explained. "They have polymer crystals in the lining to keep you cool, and BioSteel fabric with graphene thread for extra protection. A crocodile could bite you and you'd survive."

"Not if it bit your head," Dad muttered. "I've seen a croc's jaws split a man's skull like a watermelon."

"John!" Mum snapped. She took one of the suits from its rail, felt the cloth. "You invented these?" she asked.

"Me?" Pedro said. "No. I just hand them out. These were invented by your friend, Dr Sami."

We all turned.

"What?" Pan asked.

Pedro took off his cowboy hat and held it to his chest, like a mourner at a funeral. "I ... I think your employers stole the technology from him. I think they stole a lot from him."

"They're not our employers," Pan said. "We're here to save Sami."

"I hope you can," Pedro replied.

"You have smart-goggles?" Mum asked, changing the subject.

"Of course," Pedro said.

"And utility belts?"

Pedro brought a utility belt out from one of the cabinets. It looked a lot like those Sami had made for us – ultra-light titanium, with slots for gadgets.

"It has the standard tools," he explained. "Smart-goggles, flare gun, ultrasonic explosive devices and a laser cutter for rock. But it's custom built for the jungle. See this button on the clip? If you need protection, press it three times. The belt will fire ultrasonic waves in every direction. A *lot* of ultrasonic waves."

"What does that mean?" I asked.

"It creates a force field," Dad said.

"Strong enough to protect the wearer from almost anything," Mum added. She sounded impressed, a rare compliment.

"But it only works once," Pedro noted, "and only for a second. It will short-circuit every other gadget on the belt, including your smart-goggles, and most likely leave you unconscious too. So don't just use it against mosquitoes. Pretty cool, huh?"

It was *very* cool, and Pedro was being great, but none of us replied. I don't think any of us were thinking about Pedro's kit at that moment. We thought about Sami. It was *his* job to supply us with technology for our missions. We were a team, and that included him. It felt like a betrayal to be wearing the People of the Snake's utility belts.

"All right," Mum said, trying to stay focused. "We'll need two belts."

An alarm went off inside me. I shot a look at Pan, to see if she'd noticed too.

"Me and Jake get utility belts too, right?" she said.

Mum and Dad looked at each other and had another of their silent eye battles. Usually they did that when Mum wanted Dad to shut up about something. This time, I sensed they were arguing over which of them should speak.

"We *are* coming with you, right?" I asked.

"I'm sorry," Mum said, finally. "You and Pandora are staying here with Pedro. Just for a week, while we hunt for the tomb and the tablet."

"What?" Pan seethed. "No!"

"It is not up for discussion, Pandora. It's too dangerous."

"We've been in danger before, remember?"

"Not like this. Not here."

"So we're just meant to sit around on a beach?"

"You'll love it here," Pedro said. "It's paradise. We can play volleyball, or go snorkelling. Although there are tiger sharks."

"No snorkelling," Mum said.

They carried on arguing, but I stopped listening. I knew Mum and Dad wouldn't change their minds. They didn't trust me, didn't think I was up to it. And how could I claim they were wrong? It was my fault that Sami was dying. But I wasn't going to play volleyball when I could be out there trying to save him.

My eyes landed on a stun gun in a weapons rack. Should I...?

No! I couldn't knock Mum and Dad out *again*.

Could I?

I felt that volcano inside me again, lava boiling in my belly. I needed to calm down, to breathe fresh air. If I could think properly, maybe there was a way to convince Mum and Dad they needed us on the mission.

I walked back to the beach and stared at the forest-covered hills beyond Trujillo, breathing in the humid, sticky air. Maybe this was as close as I would ever get to a jungle. Nearby, the black motorbike was here again. I saw its rider now too – black leather, black helmet, with a satchel slung over his shoulder. He sat on a low wall by the edge of the beach, watching us.

"You should trust your Mum and Dad."

I turned. Pedro held his hat to his chest again, looking sheepish.

"They should trust *us*," I replied.

"But this mission isn't about you, is it? They will save your friend. And anyway, we will have fun here. They say there is treasure buried in a Spanish fort along the coast. Perhaps you and your sister can still cause a little bit of trouble."

I smiled, appreciating his efforts to cheer me up. "I doubt it, Pedro. Between you and biker boy watching us, how much trouble can we cause?"

"Biker boy?"

"The guy that's been following us. One of the Snake Lady's spies."

Pedro stared at me, confused. "She has no spies. *I* am the contact here. *Who* did you see?"

I didn't answer; I was already running. This whole time I'd thought the biker was one of the Snake Lady's goons, keeping an eye on us. That had seemed harmless enough. But he wasn't with the People of the Snake. So *who was watching us*, and why?

The biker saw me coming and ran back to his bike. I heard my parents call out, but the shouts were drowned by engine noise as the rider spun the bike around and accelerated away in a cloud of dust.

I still had a chance of catching up. To reach the main road the biker would have to wind his way through the town's maze of narrow streets, but

I wouldn't. If Trujillo was a maze, I could run through its hedges.

I sprinted from the sand and onto the road. I was in that zone again, somehow just *knowing* the right thing to do. I darted through the back door of one of the houses, raced through a living room yelling apologies at an old woman watching TV, and burst out the front door. I turned, ran along the street, and darted through another back door. Another woman saw me and whacked me with a broom, but I kept running – stumbling through her kitchen and staggering out of her front door. I pelted across the road, and charged through another house, and then another.

I stumbled out onto a street and leaned against the pick-up truck selling watermelons, struggling to catch my breath. I heard cries of outrage from people in the houses, calls from Mum and Dad running after me, and the sound of the bike roaring closer.

It was coming at me, full speed down the street. I'd got ahead of it, but I hadn't planned what to do next. I let instincts take over again, ran to the back of the pick-up truck and yanked out the holding pin. An avalanche of melons tumbled onto the street, spilling across the bike's path.

The biker saw and sped up, determined to ride through. But there were too many melons. He hit one and skidded. The bike toppled over and slid on its side along the street. The biker tumbled off, rolled several times and smashed into the side of a house.

I *really* hoped he was a bad guy.

"Hey!" I gasped.

The biker staggered up and stumbled away, clutching his side. I tried to go after him but I was too breathless from the chase. I stopped near the crashed bike, where the rider had dropped his satchel.

Mum and Dad burst from one of the houses by the van, red-faced from the effort of catching up.

"Jake!" Mum wailed. "What in blue blazes?"

She saw the bike crashed against the house, the biker running away, the spilled and squashed watermelons. I think she realized what happened because she changed her line of attack.

"You let him get away?" she said.

I fiddled with the satchel, trying to undo its clasp. When it finally came open, several sheets of paper spilled across the pavement.

No, not paper. They were photographs. I picked one up – and then another and another – confused at first by what I saw. The photos had been taken from a distance, but the details were crisp and clear.

They were photographs of my family.

12

My parents stared at those photos for almost an hour, sitting at the bar at Pedro's cafe. Mum kept stroking her necklace amulet, and Dad drank a coffee, adding more sugar between each slurp. Mum didn't usually let him take sugar, but she obviously felt he needed it.

Pan and I sat with Pedro, playing cards at a table on the beach. Pedro had his cowboy hat over his eyes and spent ages studying his cards between hands.

"No cheats in this casino," he said.

"It's not a casino, Pedro," Pan replied.

"And we're playing snap," I added.

"Don't trust anyone, kids," he said. "That's the first rule."

"The first rule of snap?" I asked.

I liked Pedro, but I got the feeling he spent too much time alone with his granddad.

He looked over his shoulder, watching Mum and

Dad. They were arguing now. Their voices rose, but they were too far away to make out the words.

"Tell me more about your parents," Pedro asked.

Pan played a card – no snap. "You probably know more than us."

"You don't like each other much?"

I looked to Pan, wondering if she would agree, and glad that she didn't. Instead, she shrugged.

I played a card – no snap. "We used to hate each other," I said. "Before we found out about their past. Now they just don't trust us. Me, mainly."

"Do you expect them to?"

"What do you mean?"

Pedro turned again, but this time he looked beyond the café, to the hills and the mist-covered mountains. "It looks pretty, doesn't it? Do not be fooled. The Mosquito Coast is no test, no training simulator. It is one of the most dangerous places in the world. You are twelve."

"Twelve and a half," Pan said.

"Even so. Your parents are experienced treasure hunters. Do you know about their discovery of the lost city of Ubar?"

Pan and I sat up. We didn't, but were eager to hear.

"Tell us," I said.

Pedro was about to play another hand, but hesitated. "That is for them to say. But trust me when I tell you that your parents are very experienced at this. Perhaps it is more that *you* should trust *them*?"

117

"You told us not to trust anyone," Pan said.

Pedro finally played his card and grinned. "Snap."

Mum and Dad had begun to walk over to us, but stopped halfway across the beach to have another argument. Whatever they'd decided, Mum was still unsure about it.

As they approached, the sun was right behind them, so they stood over us in silhouette. Mum dropped the biker's photos down on the table beside the cards. She'd snatched them from me seconds after I found them, so I'd not been able to have a proper look. Not that I needed to; I remembered the scenes well enough – my family in the passport queue at the airport, waiting for our hire car; me and Mum at the top of the hill, looking down over Trujillo. The biker had taken the photos with a long lens as he followed us here to the edge of the jungle.

Pedro swore they had nothing to do with him, or the People of the Snake. So who had taken them, and why?

"We can't leave you here," Mum announced. "Not after this. You will be safer with us."

I glanced at Pan, but neither of us smiled even though we were now going on the mission. Pedro was right: we were about to enter one of the most dangerous places on Earth. It wasn't a moment to celebrate.

"We should leave soon," Pedro said. "There's a storm coming."

I looked around the sky and saw it was blue in every direction.

"I don't see a storm," I said.

"Kid," Pedro said. "There's always a storm coming."

We all stared at him. "But is there an actual storm coming?" Dad asked. "Or did you just say that because it sounded good?"

Pedro shrugged. "The other one."

"Which one?"

"The 'sounded good' one."

"Can we just go?" Mum said.

13

My face pressed harder against a rucksack as the plane jolted and shook, struggling to climb higher over the trees. The aircraft was tiny and totally rubbish, with just two seats in the back, so the four of us were squashed together among rucksacks and kit bags. The outsides of the plane were dented – damaged, I guessed, in the same crash that had smashed off the door. Pedro had hung a curtain where the door had been, as if that somehow solved his safety concerns.

I kept waiting for him to flick a switch, converting the aircraft into a high-tech military machine. But the plane really was what it looked like: a rust bucket. A rush of wind slapped the whole thing sideways, causing the engine to belch black smoke through the curtain and into the cabin.

Finally we settled into a smoother flight, and were able to talk without shouting.

"Jake, your boot's on my back," Pan complained.

"Well, someone's bum is in my face," I replied.

"That's a kit bag."

I shoved the bag to the side, and wiped condensation from a window to see the jungle. Pedro had spoken of a clearing for us to land in, but from up here it didn't look like there was a big enough gap in the trees for even a bird to land, let alone a plane. The green carpet stretched as far as I could see, broken only by a river that twisted in crazy loops like it was drunk and lost in the jungle. The brown thread weaved between two jagged peaks that rose from the canopy, gigantic shards of rock with waterfalls plunging down their sheer sides. Each mountain seemed to have its own weather system. Dark clouds swirled around their summits, stabbed with streaks of lightning, as if there were sorcerers on the mountains, casting spells.

"The Storm Peaks!" Pedro yelled from the pilot seat. "Those are mentioned in the Aztec codex."

"That's where the first marker to the tomb is supposed to be?" I asked. "The Place of the Jaguar?"

"Somewhere close to those mountains," Pedro confirmed.

"It's also where Alpha Squad went missing," Pan added.

I gazed at the Storm Peaks, watching the lightning streak around their tops. Alpha Squad had gone missing there, but someone had reactivated their tracking signal. Who, and why?

I shifted awkwardly, adjusting my jungle suit and utility belt, trying to find a more comfortable position. But the cramped seats weren't the problem. I was tense *inside*. This whole hunt was a mystery, and we couldn't afford to fail. Sami was relying on us.

"Do you think we'll find Alpha Squad alive?" I asked.

"That's not our mission," Mum replied. "We're here to find the tomb and the emerald tablet. Nothing else."

"So were Alpha Squad," Pedro noted.

Wriggling among the kit bags, I managed to slide my smart-goggles from my belt and slot them over my eyes.

"Zoom," I instructed.

The lenses turned into super-strength binoculars, so powerful it felt as if I'd been thrust from the plane. I swore at myself for being silly, and looked again through the plane window. Then I swore again, much louder.

"Down there!" I cried.

Mum and Dad forced bags aside, recognizing the panic in my voice.

"What is it, Jake?"

I looked again, praying I was mistaken. "On the ground. I ... I think I saw someone with a weapon."

"What sort of weapon?" Dad called. "We're two thousand feet up. No one could hit us with a gun from that range."

"Not a gun. It looked like a—"

"A *what*?" Pan yelled.

"A bazooka," I said.

Mum grabbed my arm. "Jake, are you certain?"

Even with my smart-goggles, I'd not been able to pick out much detail, but I'd definitely seen someone down there with something over their shoulder that *looked* like the bazookas I'd seen in films.

"Was it an M68 model," Mum demanded, "or an RL83?"

"What? How am I meant to know that?"

"By studying the switch contact on the secondary trigger!"

"Are you serious?" I screamed.

"Something just fired!" Pedro yelled.

A streak of smoke shot from the tree canopy. It was coming straight at us!

"Deploy aircraft shields!" Dad roared.

"We don't have any aircraft shields!" Pedro shouted.

"Brace yourself! Get hold of something!"

Dad grabbed me, and Mum grasped Pan. They pinned us against the kit bags to shield us with their bodies. I heard Pan scream as the missile hit.

It struck the tail of the plane, sending us into a spin. All four of us slammed against one wall and then the other. Black smoke gushed from the back of the aircraft and into the cabin, and suddenly the world was a spinning blur, like we were on a waltzer ride.

Pedro grappled with the controls. "We're going down!"

At first my mind was pure panic, whirling as fast as the plane. But then it happened: that clarity I get when I'm in danger. I grabbed kit bags and hurled them through the curtain that flapped at the plane door, hoping we'd find them among the trees if we survived. Now that I could see the cabin, I spotted a panel in the side and yanked it open. Two small bags tumbled from inside.

"Parachutes!" I called.

Mum tried to strap Pan into one, but there was no time. The door curtain flew up and I glimpsed the jungle rush closer.

I grabbed a parachute and shoved it between Mum and Pan. I didn't give them time to protest, I just pushed them both through the door.

Now there was one parachute left for three of us.

Pedro was still in the cockpit, trying to regain control of the plane. "Go!" he ordered. "Now!"

Dad pulled me towards the exit, but I shook him off and scrambled closer to Pedro. I'd drag him with us if I had to. I heard a cry and turned just in time to see Dad fly backwards out of the door. The plane's spin had thrown him out! He had the parachute!

"For God's sake, get after him," Pedro insisted.

I staggered back to the exit, coughing from the smoke and hyperventilating from fear. At least I couldn't see how high we were – the plane was spinning too fast. I gripped the door frame, willing myself to jump, but my fingers tightened their grip as the terror of the moment struck me with full force. *What was I doing?*

"Go, Jake!"

"I don't like heights, Pedro!"

"Do you like crashing in a plane? Jake, now!"

In the end the plane decided for me, its spin thrusting me from the exit in the same way that it had got rid of my dad. I shot sideways and flew through flames where the tail was on fire. Then, for a few seconds I just fell and screamed.

Get control of yourself!

Instincts took over again, and my mind broke my situation down into its key elements: I was falling fast, I would not survive the landing because I didn't have a parachute, but Dad did. So where was he?

I saw one parachute open. Mum and Pan clung on to each other as they floated down to the treetops.

Dad would have got himself into the best position to help me. I wouldn't be able to catch him up by falling, but if I was above him when he opened his parachute, I'd drop right past. Maybe we could grab hold of each other.

I looked down, and there he was! He'd managed to turn over, so he was freefalling facing upwards, screaming at me. I tried to yell back, but the words were lost to the wind.

He pulled his cord, and the parachute burst from

his pack. I attempted to steer myself away, but there was no time. The parachute slapped into me, sending Dad into a spin. I just managed to snatch hold of his ankle, so I hung from his leg. The crumpled parachute caught enough air to slow us down, but we were still falling fast...

"Jake!" Dad screamed. "How's your first parachute jump going?"

"Not the best, Dad."

"We're going to hit the trees. Try to grab hold of a branch, anything to slow your fall. Do not let go of me."

"Dad—"

"You can do this, Jake!"

My feet hit the top of a tree. From high above, the canopy had looked soft and welcoming, like a bed of moss. But the moment I hit it I knew this was going to hurt. Branches slapped and scratched me as I fell. My head struck another branch, and then I was plummeting to the forest floor. My cry was cut short as I jolted to a stop, hanging thirty feet above the ground. I looked up, surprised to see that I was still clinging onto Dad's ankle. Above him, the parachute had caught in the lowest branch of the tree.

"Are you all right?" he asked.

"Yeah, Dad, great..."

"Keep hold of my boot. I'll lift you with me as I climb the ropes."

Thick vines, tantalizingly close, hung down to

a stream that gurgled through a bed of leaves and fallen branches. Some sort of animal sat by the water, looking up at me. My eyes were watery, but I swear it was a big cat. The creature vanished into the forest as Mum and Pan charged from the other direction.

"Jake! John! Hang on!"

"We *are* hanging on!" Dad roared.

"Don't let go!" Pan added.

"That's rubbish advice!" I yelled.

"And don't look down."

"Stop saying stupid things!"

"Fine," Pan snapped. "Then I won't help you."

"How *can* you help me, unless you've got a ladder in your utility belt?"

"I'm not catching you when you fall."

"Pandora," Dad barked. "You *will* catch Jake when he falls."

"Stop saying *when* I fall. I might not fall."

"Don't be ridiculous, Jake," Mum replied. "Of course you're going to fall."

"Dad's going to climb up the parachute. Aren't you, Dad?"

"To be honest, Jake, I was just saying that. You'll fall before I reach the branches. But your jungle suit will take some of the blow, and your mother is going to catch you. You too, Pandora."

"Not until Jake apologizes," Pan replied.

My grip slipped on Dad's boot. They were right:

I couldn't hang here much longer. "Dad, if you swing me I think I can grab those vines."

"You're not Tarzan!" Pan shouted.

Dad refreshed his grip on the parachute ropes. He swung his legs – just a little at first, and then harder, to gain momentum. I swung with him, dangling from his leg with one arm as I reached for the vines with the other. I missed, and cursed.

"Watch your language, Jake," Mum called.

"Mum," I grunted, "I'm trying to save my life!"

"Even so."

Dad swung me harder. My grip slipped further down his boot. I couldn't hold on...

"This time, Jake," he urged. "Grab it."

I let go, hoping to flip from Dad to the vine like a trapeze artist. Only, my weight tore the vine from the tree. Clinging on, I swung over Mum and Pan, smashed into another tree and then splashed face forward into the stream.

Mum dragged me onto the bank. I lay on my back, looking up at my family through a haze of pain and ... well, just pain.

"That went well," I groaned.

Pan laughed. "Welcome to the jungle, brother."

14

"We are now in the most hostile environment on the planet. Step only where I step. Stay alert for everything. Do not wander off for any reason. If I say stop, stop. If I say run, run. Do you understand?"

"What if you don't say *Simon says*?"

Mum stared at Pan. "Even then, Pandora."

I'd expected her to snap at my sister. I'd *wanted* her to, so things felt more normal. But Mum's voice was calm, her eyes narrow. The last time I'd seen her so focused was in Egypt. That meant we were in big trouble.

We'd only just set foot in the jungle, and already things were going badly. Someone had shot us from the sky – who, and why? Had Pedro survived? And where was all our kit? I'd hurled the bags from the plane, so it had to be here somewhere. I'd thrown our food supplies, water purifiers and tents out too. This would have been hard enough *with* that stuff. Now all we had were our utility belts, smart-goggles and Pedro's jungle suits.

Dad put a hand on my shoulder. "Just stay alert. Losing concentration is the number one killer in the jungle."

I nodded, adding it to the list of number one killers in the jungle, while wondering which one would actually kill us. At least we had the tracker to guide us to Alpha Squad's signal. Dad slid the device from his belt and typed a code into its screen. It still worked: two flashing dots showed on a green background.

"The red dot is us," he said. "Blue is Alpha Squad. Or whatever is left of their corpses, which I doubt will be much after the wild boars have—"

"John," Mum said.

"Sorry."

"Let's get moving," Mum urged. "We have a long walk."

Walk. I was used to walking. I did it all the time – one foot in front of the other. No problems. But there wasn't much walking in a jungle. The best I could manage was a trudge, over the sodden, muddy ground. With each step, my boots sank deeper into a carpet of leaves and rotten wood. Everything was wet, even the air. The mist that floated around us was so warm it felt more like steam, as if we were trekking through a giant sauna.

Pedro had given us machete knives for hacking at

all the plants, but I'd chucked those out of the plane too, so we cleared a path as best as we could with our hands. We yanked back giant ferns and huge waxy palm leaves, and pushed away hanging seedpods and long thorny shoots that were like evil bamboo. Sometimes we crawled under tangles of vines, other times we scrambled over fallen trunks.

Pedro had warned us that it was simple to get lost here, and I quickly understood why. I could easily imagine myself walking off alone and not finding the way back. Light came down in weird ways, never just as *light*. Sometimes it fell in thin spears stabbing through gaps in the trees, at others in stripes that shone through spiky palm fronds like sunlight shining through blinds. Just occasionally, where the trees cleared, light fell in great big spotlights, like a tractor beam in an alien abduction. But most of the time there was simply *no* sunlight; the jungle canopy blocked it all, and we walked in almost constant shadow.

To make things worse, the ground always looked the same, and gazing up all we saw were branches and vines broken by dark flashes where animals scrabbled among the trees.

"What was that?" Pan asked.

"A howler monkey," Dad replied. "Don't touch that plant!"

Pan snapped her hand back from the ferny branch. "Why not?"

"It's poisonous."

131

"A *plant* is poisonous?"

"*Strychnos toxifera.* Very poisonous."

"Which bit of it?"

"Every bit."

My sister became convinced that everything in the jungle was out to get her, especially the things that moved. For a place that seemed so unpleasant, it was incredible just how many creatures had made it their home. There was so much noise, it was like a constant alarm going off. There were chirps and bleeps and blurts from insects, screeches and howls from high in the trees, and menacing growls that were usually far off, but occasionally worryingly close.

"Is that beetle poisonous?" Pan asked.

"No," Dad replied.

"What about those ants?"

"No."

"That frog?"

"Only if you lick it."

"Why would I lick it?"

"Just don't."

"What about that snake?"

Dad stopped and nudged his glasses up his nose. "What snake?"

"The one that just slid under that bush. It was black with a yellow diamond pattern."

Dad stared at Pan for a moment, and I swear his face turned a little green. "We should walk faster," he said.

"Please tell me she didn't say *yellow diamond pattern?*" Mum called.

"Just walk faster!" Dad yelled.

Things buzzed and flapped and crawled and wriggled and swung all around me – swarms of weird green flies, beetles as big as mice but with horns like a rhino, giant red ants carrying leaves five times their size. I spotted a monkey with a baby clinging to its chest and another on its back, and a butterfly the size of a dinner plate, with bright patterned wings.

Slug-like brown leeches stood up on the ends of leaves like over-excited students calling to their teacher, *"Me! Me! Pick me!"* You should have heard Pan scream when she discovered one on her wrist! She tried to slap it off, but Mum barked at her to stay still. You can't just slap leeches off. They dig in harder. You've gotta *burn* them off.

"Pedro gave us a gadget for leeches," I remembered.

"Get it!" Pan cried.

"I chucked it out the plane."

Pan swore at me and reached to her utility belt. "I'll use my sonic force field."

"Pandora!" Mum snapped. "That is for emergencies."

"This is an emergency!"

"It is *one leech*. Stay still. I'll use my laser cutter."

Mum had to get the shot just right so that the beam sizzled the leech rather than Pan's arm. There was a lot of shouting about that, but she got it bang

133

on every time. I lost track of how many leeches managed to latch onto us, but Mum was pretty handy with her laser cutter. Each of them sizzled and fell away, leaving a smear of blood where it had been sucking.

The leeches were gross, but they weren't the real problem. This place was home to all sorts of dangerous creatures – poisonous spiders, venomous snakes, big cats – but there was a reason it was called the *Mosquito Coast*.

I swear every single mosquito on the planet was in that jungle. At times the air was thick with them, the noise a constant buzz. They were huge, too, with dangling legs – the size of the daddy-longlegs I was used to back home. I'd thrown our repellent from the plane, so all we could do was swat and curse, pull our shirts up over our chins and slap our legs and arms.

I'll be honest, the jungle was pretty awful at first. It seemed like just locating Alpha Squad's tracker signal was going to use up all of our energy. How could we manage that *and* find a lost tomb?

Only Dad seemed to like the place. He kept pointing at bugs or butterflies, and telling us their Latin names, as if we were on a school trip.

"Have you been in a jungle before, Dad?" I asked.

"A few of them," he replied.

"Where?"

Dad checked the tracker device and changed our direction to stay on course. "Last time was Malaysia, wasn't it, Jane?"

Mum yanked back a tangle of vines. "Don't bring that up again."

"Why not?" I asked.

"Your father tried to befriend a tribe," Mum said. "He hoped they might give us the location of a temple if he accepted their offer of hallucinogenic drugs."

"What happened?" Pan said.

"I..." Dad hesitated, choosing his words. "Well, you have to understand that archaeology is as much about interacting with indigenous peoples as it is—"

"Your father spent two days up a tree thinking he was a monkey," Mum said.

Pan and I laughed, and even Mum joined in. I was about to tease Dad about it, but he stopped and raised a hand.

"Nobody move," he hissed.

Mum was at his side in an instant. "What is it?"

"Alpha Squad's signal," Dad replied. "We're close."

He turned a full circle, eyes fixed on the tracker device. The flashing dots were now right on top of each other.

"Mum, Dad, Pan," I said. "Move north, east and south. Ten paces in each direction. I'll take the west."

They all looked at me, surprised. I don't actually know where the command came from; it just blurted out.

"Ten paces," Dad agreed. "No one moves out of sight."

We split up and moved in separate directions.

I didn't actually know which way was west, so I waited for the others to set off and went the only way left.

I moved slowly, scanning the ground and looking up to the trees. I turned over a fallen branch, kicked a rock. Ahead, all I saw was solid jungle, so thick it looked almost impenetrable.

Unless... Was it *too* impenetrable?

I took another step, reaching for the wall of leaves and vines. My hand trembled, half expecting something to leap out and bite my fingers. Edging even closer, I slid my hand deeper into the foliage and touched something that was *not* foliage. It felt like ... a net.

I gripped it and pulled.

It came away in one go – a camouflage sheet disguised as jungle. Hidden in a clearing behind it was Alpha Squad's camp. Hammocks hung between trees, and an awning shelter protected high-tech military kit. There was a holosphere screen, and kit bags similar to those Pedro had given us, with food supplies and jungle suits. A large, spider-like machine sat on a camp table. I recognized it from Sami's tech training – it was a megadrone, a super-strong drone that could lift treasure from tombs. That was cool, but right then I was way more interested in the thing that sat beside the drone.

A Mars Bar!

I was about to rush to it, when Dad grasped my shoulder.

"Don't move," he hissed. "Put your smart-goggles on. Infrared."

I'd rarely seen him look so serious, so knew this wasn't the sort of advice I should question. I did as he said, and yelped. My goggles' infrared view revealed dozens of lasers zigzagging around the clearing. They were alarms, the sort of security you see in bank vaults in movies.

"Stay here," Dad instructed.

He rolled his shoulders and stretched his hamstrings, limbering up to weave his way through the crisscrossing beams to the middle of the camp.

"John?" Mum said. "Really?"

Dad looked at her, and then at the beams. "Actually," he muttered. "Maybe someone else should do this..."

"I'll do it," I volunteered.

"No," Mum replied.

That was all she said, no reason. She didn't warm up either, just set off into the laser beams, jumping one, ducking under another, rolling and moving again. She reached the holosphere screen and activated it. Several files whooshed up, and a few seconds later the lasers cut out.

I'd like to tell you that I went into high alert, searching for clues as to what happened to Alpha Squad. In fact, Pan and I both just collapsed into hammocks, scoffing half of the Mars Bar each and agreeing it was the nicest thing either of us had ever eaten. I couldn't stop myself; the chance to rest was too tempting. Everything ached from the hike – my legs, my back. My head throbbed, and there can't have been a drop of sweat left in my body.

It was all I could do to watch as Mum swiped through the files that projected from the holosphere. There were maps of the jungle, satellite photos and images of the Aztec codices that the Snake Lady had bought and destroyed.

"Is there anything to tell us what happened to Alpha Squad?" I called.

Mum shook her head. "They sent a status report from this camp on the evening they vanished. They'd searched almost every area of the jungle close to the Storm Peaks for the first marker to the tomb, the Place of the Jaguar, but found nothing."

"So what happened to them? This camp doesn't look like it's been attacked. And who turned their tracker signal back on?"

"Maybe just an animal," Mum suggested.

Dad had been silent this whole time, tinkering with Alpha Squad's tracker beacon. He seemed lost in thought, and from the look on his face, they were not good thoughts. He looked at Mum and nudged his glasses back up his nose.

"It wasn't an animal," he said.

"Are you sure?" she asked. "Howler monkeys are known for their intelligence."

"Are they intelligent enough to memorize a

four-digit code and key it into the beacon's touchpad?"

Even I knew the answer to that. "So someone came back here two weeks after Alpha Squad vanished," I said, "and set off the signal. But why?"

"Yeah," Pan agreed. "Whoever did it must have known another team would come looking for Alpha Squad."

Still Mum and Dad stared at each other across the camp. Dad nodded, and Mum closed her eyes and groaned, and I knew then what they were thinking. I sat up in the hammock, wondering if Pan had realized too. She had.

"Whoever set off the tracker *wanted* us to come," she said.

"The signal was bait," I added.

Mum rose from the holosphere and rummaged in one of Alpha Squad's kit bags. She brought out a machete and stared at her reflection in its blade.

"We've been lured into a trap," she said.

15

None of us slept much that night. Somehow it was even more humid than in the day, and my clothes were damp and smelly from the trek. We pulled mosquito nets over our hammocks so that we hung in protective cocoons, but I still heard the things buzzing at my ears. Each time I swatted, my hammock swung and I tumbled with a curse to the jungle floor.

And then there were the other noises. The jungle had been loud during the day, but at night it *really* came alive. Dad had set up Alpha Squad's laser alarms around our camp so nothing big could get in without us knowing. But there were things close by. Thousands of things. I heard snarls and growls, hoots and howls, all around us in stereo. I heard rustling in the trees and shuffling among leaves. I heard twigs snap yards from our camp. Pan cried out in fright several times, and I wondered if she was sleeping with her smart-goggles set to night vision. I was.

Mum and Dad stayed up in shifts, keeping watch. I offered to take a shift, but Mum told me off for not sleeping.

Somehow I *did* fall asleep. I was too exhausted not to. When I woke, sunlight trickled through branches, stinging my eyes. My head throbbed, and my back ached from the position I'd curled myself into in the hammock. My mouth was so dry it felt like I was chewing sand.

"Water," I gasped.

Dad handed me one of Alpha Squad's flasks. The water was purified with iodine, so it tasted like metal, but I downed every drop.

"Get some more rest," Dad said. "Exhaustion is the number one killer in the jungle."

I wanted to, but I was too uncomfortable, fidgety. I tried to climb out of my hammock, but messed it up again and thumped to the ground with my loudest curse of the trip so far.

Breakfast was one of Alpha Squad's vacuum-packed rations of dried food. Some were supposed to be porridge, others beef stew, but none of the foil packs said which was which, and they all just tasted of cardboard. I didn't mind – it was food and we were hungry.

We didn't wash, but Mum insisted we brush our teeth. I think she liked having something she could control. We kept our jungle suits on – they were our best protection in this place – but Mum made us change our socks for fresh ones from Alpha Squad's packs, insisting that foot rot was the number one killer in the jungle.

They were trying to act calm, as if everything was going to plan, but they were both on edge. Mum kept stroking her amulet and saying weirdly optimistic things like "Looks like it will be a lovely sunny day," or "Perhaps we'll spot a toucan today." They hoped we'd forgotten that someone had lured us here. Was it the same person that shot down our plane? Were they out there now, watching us? It didn't really matter. We had to find the tomb of Quetzalcoatl and recover its emerald tablet.

Up until that morning the jungle had been mostly hard work. But things definitely improved as we ate our cardboard sludge breakfast and made plans. Mum said Pan could help, but I was surprised she let me get involved too. Perhaps she thought it would keep my mind off the whole "we've-been-led-into-a-trap" thing.

We sat around the holosphere studying maps and projections of the Aztec codices, as well as Alpha Squad's notes, which left Mum seriously unimpressed.

"What sort of treasure hunters were these people?" she asked. "They were just randomly searching rivers near the Storm Peaks."

"Is that not good?" I asked.

Mum looked at me, surprised. "Did you not study the codices?"

"I... Which bits?"

"Jake doesn't read *Nahuatl*, Mum," Pan said. "Neither do I."

Mum didn't look convinced that that was a good enough excuse. "In the documents, the Aztecs describe two rivers close to the Storm Peaks as the location of the Place of the Jaguar."

"You mean, where the second marker is hidden?" I asked. "So which river should we look along?"

"Exactly," Dad said. "The marker can't be in two places. What Alpha Squad don't seem to have known is that the Aztec script is incredibly literal. Two rivers means two rivers."

"You mean... What do you mean?"

"A *junction* of two rivers."

Dad enlarged an area of the map on the holo-sphere, zooming in on one of the coffee-coloured rivers where it weaved between the two Storm Peaks, and then joined another, much wider river.

"There are two major rivers in this part of the jungle," he explained, "and they meet right here."

The projections gleamed off his glasses as he zoomed in even closer to where the two brown squiggles came together to form a single, larger brown squiggle.

"This is where we need to look," he said.

I was trying to act cool, but I had goose bumps all

up my arms. Alpha Squad had spent six weeks searching for the Place of the Jaguar. My parents might have found it by looking at a map for two minutes.

"Is that close?" Pan asked.

Dad studied the map again. "I'd say an eight-hour trek. If we set off first thing tomorrow, we should reach it by—"

He flinched back as another hologram shot up from the screen – a small flashing dot that expanded into a larger file. A face appeared on a live video feed. I recognized the smug smile instantly; it made me want to punch something.

Even on the fuzzy video, the Snake Lady's black eyes seemed to glint.

"There you all are!" she said. "Wonderful. How is the jungle? Jake, you haven't been causing trouble, have you?"

I swore at her. She stuck out her lip, pretending to be sad.

"How beastly," she said. "Now tell me, what is your mission report?"

Dad held her gaze, refusing to look intimidated. "We're here to find the emerald tablet. We don't have to report to you until we have."

Her smile vanished, but her eyes flashed even brighter. "Oh, don't you? *Don't you,* John? I say you *do*. You work for me, and my employees provide me with regular status updates."

"We don't work for you," Pan spat. "How do we

even know that Sami is still alive?"

The Snake Lady turned the camera, and there was Sami in the hospital bed, hooked up to life support machines.

I heard Mum gasp as she saw her old friend, and Dad's hands tightened into bloodless balls at his sides. They had come here to save Sami, but until then, I guessed, they hadn't realized how much danger he was really in. Our friend's condition seemed to have got worse. He looked even paler than when I'd last seen him, except for his veins, which were as dark as if they were flowing with ink.

A drumbeat grew faster inside me, a mix of anger and guilt. Mum must have noticed how close I was to lashing out. She gripped my arm, urging me to calm down.

"Your teeth," Mum said.

The Snake Lady turned the camera back to herself. "Excuse me?"

"If Sami dies," Mum added, "I will find you and break every one of your perfect teeth."

Mum meant it, no question, but the Snake Lady's mouth curled into another smile. She ran her tongue along her front teeth, and whispered into the camera as if she was telling us a secret.

"They are all fake anyway." She clapped her hands. "Now, your status report?"

"Someone followed us from the airport," Dad replied. "Our plane was shot down and Pedro is dead."

That wiped the smile off her face! It was the first time I'd ever seen the Snake Lady look thrown.

"I... Can you repeat that?" she said.

"You heard," Pan replied. "Did you have us shot down?"

"No," she said. "Why would we?"

I believed her. The People of the Snake *wanted* us to find the tablet. They had no reason to sabotage our mission. And anyway, her face told us that she had known nothing of our troubles so far. The glint in her eyes had been replaced by confusion.

"Listen to me," the Snake Lady said. Her voice had lost its fake sugary tone. She sounded deadly serious. "You need to be very careful. There are—"

"Thanks for the advice," Mum interrupted. "Status report over."

She flicked away the hologram, cutting off the video feed.

"Sami..." Pan muttered. "He looked bad."

Dad took off his glasses and rubbed his eyes. Mum glanced at me, and then turned away, gazing into the trees as she stroked her amulet She'd only given me a quick look, but it felt like a long, hard stare. Was she thinking what I was? That it was all my fault?

"Three days left," Mum said, finally. "Leaving us one day to get the tablet back home. It's an eight-hour march to the Place of the Jaguar. We need to get moving now."

"What was *that*?" Pan cried. "Over there, something moved!"

Dad rushed to where Pan was pointing. He slid on his smart-goggles and scanned the jungle beyond the camp.

"What did you see, Pandora?" he called.

"I thought... Something moved between the trees."

Dad looked to Mum, who frowned. From the look on her face she believed Pan had seen something. Or *someone*.

She grabbed one of Alpha Squad's rucksacks and began filling it with supplies for our trek. "Boots on," she barked. "We leave in five minutes."

16

I don't know how far we trekked. Mum had said the march to the Place of the Jaguar would take eight hours, but eight hours in the jungle felt like eighty anywhere else. All I know is that it was a long, long day.

It wasn't just the physical effort of trudging through mud or clambering over fallen trees. The jungle exhausted your mind, too. There were so many things growing all around us. Each tree was its own mini jungle, its trunk covered in mosses and ferns. It was claustrophobic, like we were imprisoned by nature. I couldn't wait to reach the river, where I could see the sky and spread my arms without fear of being bitten by some insect or other.

Pan was never an outdoors person at the best of times, but you should have seen her that day. She'd shoved headphones in her ears and had the music turned up so loud that when she swore at a bug – which happened a lot – it came out as a shout. Every now and then I noticed her hand move to her utility belt, and wondered if she might use her sonic force field to blast away the mosquitoes.

Even with nets over our heads, the mosquitoes were a constant misery. But every now and then, for reasons I never worked out, they all vanished and I actually saw the jungle, not just swarms of insects through a net. In those moments I realized how beautiful the place truly was.

I got so used to seeing green and brown, but, really, the jungle was full of colour. Even the greens were different: bright ferns, deep rich palms, yellow-tinted vines. We saw white-faced monkeys watching from the trees, purple butterflies, delicate pink orchids, minuscule blue frogs squatting on leaves, and bright red flowers that reminded me of the Snake Lady's painted lips. I stamped on one of those, and Mum told me off.

For about an hour of that trek my opinion of the jungle changed. It wasn't just beautiful, it was *stunning*.

And then it rained.

It's a rainforest, so I shouldn't have been surprised. But it wasn't just that it rained, it was how *hard* it rained. It didn't start spitting. There was no warning rumble of thunder. It just began to pour. Rain gushed between the trees, sprayed off leaves and ran in streams down trunks. And it was so loud, like a constant drum roll, so we had to use the microphones in our smart-goggles to talk to each other.

"It's just a shower," Dad insisted.

It was a *power shower*. Our clothes were soaked in seconds, clinging to our skin. Pedro had boasted about how light our jungle suits were, but once mine got wet it felt as heavy as a bear skin.

We walked hunched up, squelching over ground that changed from mud to mush to swamp. Streams trickled past our boots. We kept slipping over, cursing and sliding. At one point Pan sank right up to her shoulders in a mud pit. I was laughing too hard to help, and then laughed even harder when Mum and Dad finally got her out and discovered she was covered in leeches. There were dozens of them on her neck and arms. She even had one on her eye!

"That's so gross!" I cried, now in hysterics. "It's on your eyeball!"

"Jake!" Mum snapped. "Pandora, just relax. The leech is only on your *eyelid*."

"GET IT OFF ME GET IT OFF ME GET IT OFF ME!"

Pan was screaming now, and flapping around in panic. It took ages to get the little bloodsucker off. I'm not even sure how Mum managed it; I was laughing so hard my sides ached and I had to sit down.

"That's the funniest thing I've ever seen," I gasped.

"Jake," Dad hissed. "Don't move. You've got one on your lip."

"What? GET IT OFF ME GET IT OFF ME GET IT OFF ME!"

It poured for hours. There was nowhere to shelter,

and no time to stop, anyway. At times I couldn't see the rest of my family through the downpour, as if the storm had swallowed them up. With no one to talk to, it was hard to stop my mind from wandering and thinking about Sami.

Actually, it felt good to think about him. Jungle trekking was easily the hardest thing I've ever done, so it helped to remind myself why we were here and how important it was that we carried on, no matter how tough it got. Wondering if it might help the others too, I called out to Mum and Dad.

"You've never told us how you met Sami," I said.

"It's... It's a long story," Mum replied.

"Well, we have a long time."

We trudged in silence for another few minutes. I think Dad was waiting for Mum to answer. She was always so cagey about their treasure-hunting past. I guessed she didn't want me and Pan getting ideas. But I think Dad understood why I was asking.

"We first met him in Baghdad in 1983," he said, finally.

Mum moved faster to catch up. "Nonsense. It was in Cairo, in 1981. We were searching for the tomb of an Egyptian princess. Other hunters were after it too, so we needed to find it first to save its treasures for a museum."

"Was he working for one of those other teams?" Pan asked.

Mum laughed. "Sami? No. At that point he'd never

been on a treasure hunt in his life. We visited him in his laboratory at Cairo University. We'd heard he was the best when it came to new technologies, and needed his help in finding the tomb. We wanted him to build us a robot to explore spaces in caves that we couldn't reach. It was just one job, one invention."

Dad snorted. "Do you remember the noise he made when we told him what we did? I've never seen anyone so excited. He spent the next two hours showing us all sorts of ways he could help."

"Not just the robot," Mum added, "but other inventions too. Early versions of utility belts, and grappling lines that he'd designed for the military. He'd grown sick of selling all his gadgets to armies. The idea of using them for treasure hunting thrilled him."

"We were pretty excited too, Jane. We knew straightaway that the technology would give us an edge over other hunters. I remember giggling, all three of us. It was like we'd found a final piece of a jigsaw. We just immediately slotted together."

"And the fact that he saved our lives a few minutes later," Mum muttered.

"What?" I asked. "How?"

"Almost accidentally," Mum explained. "He was showing us a thermal image camera he'd developed, and its display revealed the heat signature of a hunter on the laboratory roof. The hunter had followed us there and was just about to attack. I think he planned to catch us and torture us for information to the princess's tomb. He was Swiss, I think."

"No," Dad corrected. "It was Adrian Kosikowski. An American."

"No, dear, Kosikowski attacked us in Ethiopia. He fell into a crocodile pit, remember?"

"Pretty sure the crocodile pit was in Zambia, darling."

"There have been several crocodile pits, dear. Anyway, there was a fight with *whoever it was*. Sami knocked one of them on the head with a dead fish – although why he had a dead fish in his laboratory I never did find out."

"So you won?" I asked. "The fight?"

"Yes, of course," Mum said. "After that, Sami just became part of our team. I can't count the number of times he or his gadgets have saved our lives. We never went on a mission without him until…"

Mum's voice trailed off, but we all knew what she had stopped herself from saying.

Until now.

It was still raining hard, but I didn't care. So what if this was tough? It was a treasure hunt; it was *meant* to be tough. I wasn't going to complain about the jungle anymore – I just wanted to focus on the mission. I was more determined than ever to put things right. Find the Place of the Jaguar, find the markers, find the tomb and get the emerald tablet.

Save our friend.

17

We kept walking and the rain kept falling. We fell into puddles and we climbed out. We slipped on rocks and we got back up. The ground grew so wet and we fell over so often that at times it felt more like walking over ice than mud.

"Stay close together," Dad called. "We must be near."

We had been hiking for almost eight hours, searching for a place where two rivers met in the jungle. I had begun to worry that we'd gone the wrong way, that there was nothing here other than rain and mud.

Still we kept going, following Dad across a hillside, where rainwater ran in thick streams down the steep mud slope. Pan slipped again, and only just managed to cling on to a tree trunk to stop herself sliding down into the darkness with the rain. I tried to help her up, but she slapped my hand away in a strop and screamed in frustration at the sky.

"Stop shrieking, Pandora," Mum said.

"I'm covered in mud, Mum."

"I know, but that shrieking is too much."

"That's not me anymore! It's Jake."

I turned, wiping mud and wet hair from my eyes. *Something* was shrieking, but it wasn't me either. Dad rubbed mist from his glasses and looked around the slope. The sound was getting louder, like a police siren coming closer.

"Everyone stop," Dad ordered.

We already had. We turned and squinted up the hill through the trees and rain. It was coming from up there.

"Monkeys?" Mum suggested.

"No," Dad muttered. *"Payassu pecari."*

"What?" Pan asked.

"Wild boars."

It sounded like a *lot* of wild boars. We couldn't see them but they were definitely getting closer. Their high-pitched screams rang around the slope as if they were charging from everywhere at once.

"Don't panic," Mum called. "They're not especially dangerous."

"Especially?" I asked.

"I see them!" Pan cried.

A dozen squat pigs covered in wiry brown hair charged down the hill. They were coming straight for us, squealing in fright.

"Don't panic," Mum said, although there was definitely panic in her voice. "If they think you're a threat they might gore you. Stand still and let them pass."

"Gore us?" Pan yelled.

Now I saw two short but sharp-looking tusks jutting from each boar's snout. The pigs didn't look like they were about to attack us, though. In fact, they looked and sounded as if they were *under* attack, like *they* were fleeing. Something bad was happening here, and it wasn't the mad pigs.

"We should move," I said.

"No," Mum insisted. "Stay where you are. They're just running."

"But, Mum, what are they running *from*?"

We remained still, staring up the hill beyond the boars. Something was coming after them. It didn't look like a creature, more like a wave – a *dark* wave, flooding the jungle as it swept down the slope.

"Mudslide!" Dad bellowed. "Everybody run!"

Dad grabbed my arm and pulled me with him down the hill. Pan and Mum ran ahead as the slope grew even steeper. The boars charged past us, shrieking. One of them took out my legs, knocking me over onto my back. The next thing I knew I was sliding, but much faster than I'd been able to run. I glanced back and saw that the wave of mud had grown into a wall. It was almost on us.

"Slide!" I shouted. "Get down and slide!"

I twisted slightly so that I slid at Pan, and

deliberately knocked her over like a skittle. She fell onto me and I clung on as we slid together, face to face. Her eyes were covered in mud, but I could see that her eyes were also wild with terror.

"Put your breathing tube in!" I screamed.

She didn't understand, or didn't hear above the shrieks of the pigs and the roar of the mudslide. I reached to my utility belt, slid the thin metal tube from its slot and shoved it at Pan's face. She bit on the mouthpiece. Then I took as deep a breath as I could manage, and the wave hit.

It swallowed us and carried us down the hill. The force tore Pan from my grip, flipped me over and sent me into a spin. The mudslide spat me to its surface for a gasp of air and a glimpse of a tree that I was heading straight for. I remembered the sonic force field in my belt. Maybe it could have saved me from the impact, but I was too late to use it.

I hit the tree hard enough to snap my spine, but Pedro's graphene-plated jungle suit took most of the blow. I was stuck pressed against it as the great mud wave battered me and bent my back. My mouth filled with mud. My nose filled with mud. I was out of breath, drowning in mud.

Then, finally, it passed. I peeled my eyes open, spitting out mud and sucking in air. I was half-buried, but alive.

"Jake!"

I pulled myself from the mud. My side throbbed

where it had hit the tree. "Pandora!"

It was Mum's voice. Dad was shouting too, screaming our names. I grunted, trying to let them know I was alive. Then I realized: Mum and Dad couldn't see Pan. She was buried!

I dragged myself up to scramble over the mud, fighting the pain in my ribs. The slide had carried us to the bottom of a gorge, and the edge of a fast-flowing river. Some of the mud had spilled into the river, while the rest of it had spread out along the bank, raising the ground level. Was Pan buried under it, or had she been taken by the river?

I was running now, calling to my parents.

"Jake!" Mum cried. "Thank God!"

"Where's Pan?"

"Spread out!" Dad roared. "Dig!"

The mud had spread fifty metres in both directions along the river bank. We'd never find her in time.

"Thermal!" I yelled.

Mum and Dad heard, and shoved their smart-goggles on. I did the same, ordering them to show me any geothermal heat signatures beneath the mud. I turned, scanning the ground, praying...

There!

I rushed to where my goggles showed a bright orange blob under the surface, and dug frantically, calling to my sister. How long had she been buried? Was I already too late?

"Come on!" I screamed, digging even harder.

Beneath me, something moved. "Pan! Hold on, I'm here!"

I reached deeper and grabbed hold of...

Oh, no. Oh, God...

One of the wild boars squealed at me as I pulled it by its leg from the mud.

"Over here!" Dad hollered.

The boar ran off. Mum and I ran to help Dad, and we lifted my sister out of her mud tomb. She looked shaken but OK, and was still sucking on the breathing tube. She barely had time to take it from her mouth before Mum grabbed her in a suffocating hug.

"I'm alive!" she gasped.

Dad burst out laughing with relief.

"And look where we are," he said.

Wiping more mud from my eyes, I gazed along the river to a point where it was joined by a smaller tributary. There, the muddy water churned an even darker brown at the point where a smaller tributary joined it, as if the bigger river was trying to stop the little one from getting in.

This was the place where two rivers met. This was where we hoped to find the second marker to the tomb.

So what now?

18

The Place of the Jaguar.

What did that even mean? My parents were experts in ancient cultures and treasure hunting, but even they had no idea. We'd hoped it might make more sense once we found the junction of the two rivers, where the Aztecs said the marker would be. But now we were here, soaked to the skin and caked in mud, and we still didn't have a clue. I'd secretly hoped to find a temple with a stone jaguar's head on it and Aztec writing saying "marker in here". But things were never that easy, were they?

We sat on the bank, letting warm rain wash the mud from our hair and faces. From here we could see along the chocolate-coloured river, towards the Storm Peaks. Lightning flashed around their summits, and a waterfall plunged down the sheer side of the higher of the two mountains.

"The Place of the Jaguar," Pan mumbled.

"Place of the Jaguar," I muttered.

"Just repeating that isn't going to help," Mum said.

We'd trekked for eight hours to get here, been soaked by rain, sucked on by leeches, trampled by boars and had almost drowned in a mudslide. We desperately needed rest, but there was no time. Sami needed us to keep going.

We had to find that marker.

I breathed in deeply and closed my eyes, letting my mind settle.

"We'll split up," I said. "Let's each take a twenty-metre stretch of the bank either side of the river junction. Set your goggles to *ultrasonic view*, to search for openings underground. Dad, we need ideas for how to cross the water in case we don't find anything on this side. Mum, we need to know how deep the river is and if there's any risk of attack by crocodiles or piranhas, or whatever, in case we need to go for a swim."

Mum stared at me, startled by the commands. I could tell that she was thinking through everything I'd said, looking for holes in the plan. In the end there was only one thing she chose to question.

"Swim?" she asked.

"The Aztecs said we'd find the Place of the Jaguar at the spot where the two rivers met," I said. "And Dad said that they were always very literal in what they wrote. What if they meant *literally* at that spot?"

"You mean *in the river*?" Pan said. "Underwater?"

I shrugged. It was just a thought.

Dad looked at Mum, and I thought I saw him smile. Mum just nodded.

"All right," she said. "That's our plan for now. We communicate through our goggles. But no one moves out of sight."

"Remember," Dad added, "the Aztecs left the three markers to guide their own people to the tomb of Quetzalcoatl. They *wanted* the markers to be found. So they would have put them in places that were permanent."

"So, made of stone?" Pan said.

"Perhaps," Dad agreed.

We split up, each taking a different strip of the riverbank to search. I still had no idea what to search *for*, so I just used my goggles' echolocation soundscape to scan for cavities under the bedrock. The mud was thick from the landslide, so at times I got down and dug randomly, hoping to find something under there. Mostly I saw ants.

"Anyone see anything?" Dad called.

"Mud," Pan replied. "Lots of mud."

I stared up at the Storm Peaks, strobe-lit by the storms above them, and wondered if anyone had ever climbed that high. From where I stood, the two mountains seemed to overlap slightly. Their edges made patterns, like shapes in the clouds. I stepped to one side and saw a face in the rocks that looked a bit like Mum being angry. I moved further along the riverbank and the face brightened into a smile, which didn't look like Mum at all.

A jolt went through me as if one of the lightning strikes had zapped my chest.

"The Place of the Jaguar..." I muttered.

Was it possible?

My heart picked up speed as I trudged along the riverbank through the mud. My eyes stayed locked on the Storm Peaks.

"Jake?" Mum said. "Don't go too far."

I heard but didn't listen. I kept moving, stopping every few paces to consider the shapes made by the overlapping cliffs. I wiped the lenses of my goggles and looked again.

"Guys?" I yelled.

I saw another face, but this time it was not that of a person.

It was a cat's face.

A *jaguar's* face.

It wasn't just my imagination. Caves formed almond eyes; cracks and ledges came together to create the shape of a wide nose and curved mouth.

"Guys?" I said again.

The face wasn't perfect. The ears weren't quite right. I got down lower – first to my hands and knees, and then lying flat on the mud – and gazed up at the Storm Peaks.

"Bingo!" I cried.

The jaguar's face glared at me from the mountains. I could see it perfectly from this spot and only this spot. *This* was the place where the Aztecs had wanted me to stand. Was this spot the Place of the Jaguar?

Pan, Mum and Dad raced closer, baffled and breathless.

"Are you ill?" Mum asked.

"Jake," Dad said. "Answer me honestly. Have you licked any frogs?"

I stared at the cat's face in the mountains, my cheek pressed against the warm, wet mud. "I see the jaguar," I said. "It's there, in the—"

I didn't get to finish my sentence, because right then something bit my face and my world exploded in bright-coloured pain.

19

I woke lying on canvas and staring up at the sky. One side of my jaw felt numb and swollen, as if I'd just had dental surgery. The other ached like the dentist had drilled there too, but without anaesthetic. A thick line of drool slid from my lips and down my chin. I tried to speak, but the words came out as a groan.

My family was close by, frantically digging mud from the spot where I'd previously been.

"What happened?"

That's what I tried to say, anyway, but my jaw was so swollen it came out as "Wrrrrr hagggnnnnnnn?"

Somehow Pan understood. "You've skived off all the work, that's what's happened."

"You were bitten by a bullet ant," Mum explained. "You're lucky you passed out. Their sting is not pleasant."

Not pleasant was an understatement. It had felt

as if someone had hammered a tent peg into my jaw.

"What are you doing?" I mumbled.

"Digging!" Pan said. "The jaguar face, remember?"

I closed my eyes, trying to stop my head from spinning. The jaguar face... Yes, I'd found the Place of the Jaguar, the second marker to the tomb of Quetzalcoatl! Not that anyone seemed to remember; they were all just annoyed that I wasn't helping.

I tried to sit up but my vision swirled and my arms crumpled, and I sank back to the canvas. My body wouldn't do what my brain wanted. I felt like I'd been drained of half my blood.

"We've hit the rock bed," Mum announced.

"Keep digging," Dad said. "Clear everything away."

"There's something here," Pan replied. "A groove in the rock. It's not natural – too straight."

"There's another here," Mum gasped. "They're edges of something."

"Spread out," Dad ordered. "Find where they meet."

All I could do was watch as they scrabbled excitedly in the mud, exploring the grooves in the rock bed. From what I could see, the edges marked a rectangle about the size of our kitchen table.

"Looks like a doorway," Pan said.

"It *is* a doorway," Dad replied.

"Mmmm rgggh brrrrr," I added.

"Look," Mum breathed. "There's a carving."

She poured water from her canteen across the

rock and wiped away more mud to study it. Her eyes were full of wonder.

"John!" she cried. "It's the symbol of the jaguar."

Dad got in closer to see, and they grinned and hugged. It was weird to see them looking so happy. Pan glanced at me and I wondered if she was thinking the same thing; right then Mum and Dad were their old selves from before we were born, when they were treasure hunters without the worry of protecting children.

"We need to get this open," Dad said. "Look for thin rocks – anything we can use to lever it up."

Argh! I wanted to help!

I gritted my teeth and rose higher on my elbows. Some of my strength had returned, but not enough to help lift that door. I could only watch as my sister rushed around the riverbank gathering rocks, and Mum used her laser cutter to slice them into thinner slabs. Dad hacked branches from a tree and lashed the rock slabs to the ends to make shovels.

By then I could move my legs enough to crawl closer. The swelling in my jaw had eased and I called to them to wait for me, but they didn't listen as they forced their shovel tips into the door frame.

"Good," Dad said. "Now heave!"

"Heave!" I repeated, trying to be involved.

They *were* heaving – even Pan, who is not a born "heaver". Her arms trembled, but excitement seemed to give her the strength to force the shovel deeper into the groove.

"It's rising!" Mum grunted.

"Hold your breath," Dad ordered.

The stone slab rose an inch. There was a loud hiss – as if they'd opened the seal on a snake pit – and a cloud of brown air rushed up from around the frame. Pan spluttered and staggered back, but Mum and Dad held on to their shovels, lifting the slab higher. Dad's face turned red and his glasses fell off. Veins bulged in Mum's neck. The slab rose another few inches, and I glimpsed darkness beneath it. But the shovels weren't strong enough to lift it any higher. Their wooden handles bent back, about to snap.

"It's going to fall," Mum groaned.

It was open! Just half a metre, but enough for someone to get inside...

This was the sort of thing Mum kept warning me about: acting on impulse without thinking about the consequences. If the marker was down there, we had to get it *now*. I could do it, I was certain.

I reached a shaky hand to my utility belt and pulled the clasp that unravelled the bungee cord wound around the inside.

"Jake?" Mum said. "What are you doing? Jake?"

By the time she saw me I was just a few feet from the entrance.

"Jake!" Dad barked. "Get back. The slab is going to fall!"

I moved faster over the mud, wriggling like a worm. My mind had been blunted by the ant sting, but suddenly it was pin-sharp, totally focused on what I knew I had to do. My eyes raked the ground, searching for a place to fix the bungee clasp, but all I saw was mud.

"Jake! I'll take it!"

Pan rushed closer, knowing what I was about to do. I thought she might try to stop me, but instead she grabbed the end of the bungee cord from my hand to help.

"Go!" she screamed.

The bungee unwound further from my belt as I slid face forward through the gap and into the darkness below.

20

"Torch."

I hung on the bungee line, slowly revolving so the light from my smart-goggles swept in circles around rock walls. I was dangling in a pit about the size of a well shaft, carved five hundred years ago by Aztecs fleeing Spanish invaders. Above, the stone slab had sealed the entrance, trapping the top of my bungee cord so I didn't fall.

I looked down, shining the light deeper underground. The Aztecs hadn't needed to tunnel too far into the bedrock, which opened into a natural cave about ten feet below my legs. Below that it looked like a long drop into darkness. Was the marker down there? Was anything *else* down there? At least my vertigo didn't seem to be a problem. It's hard to be scared of the height when all you can see below you is darkness.

"Jake? Can you hear me?"

Dad's voice came through my goggles.

"I'm OK," I grunted.

"You're grounded!" Mum snapped.

"What? What for?"

"Going through a secret door without permission."

I laughed, but the idea of being grounded at home was suddenly quite appealing.

"What do you see?" Pan asked.

"A cave," I replied.

"We're working on getting this door open again," Mum said. She sounded breathless, like she was running. I guessed she was scouring the riverbank for stronger stones to lever open the slab.

"You wait right there," she insisted.

"I'm going down."

"Did you not hear what I said?"

"I can't hear you. It's all crackly."

I was lying, but there wasn't time to hang around. I pressed a button on my utility belt, and the bungee began to unreel, lowering me deeper into the darkness. Torchlight corkscrewed down the pit walls.

"Go slow, Jake," Dad said. "Remember, the Aztecs didn't want the Spanish to find the marker. There could be traps."

"Like killer spikes," Pan added. "With poison."

"We've got your back, son," Dad said.

No, they didn't. They were on the other side of a massive stone slab. But it was reassuring to hear their voices as I descended beyond the pit and into the cave.

"Night vision."

My lenses showed the underground world – a domed cavity beneath the jungle. Stalagmites snarled up around the cave floor. Nothing looked man-made – no carvings or shrines in the walls.

I touched down in the centre of the cave, slid the flare gun from my utility belt and fired it at the ground. The firework flare fizzled on the rock bed, casting a blood-red glow around the cave walls. That was my landing site. If my family managed to get the slab open again, they'd lower some sort of line to lift me back up. I hoped...

I unclipped the belt and left it hanging on the line, then shook my head to clear the last of the fog from the ant sting. I needed to focus to stand any chance of finding the marker. Only, where should I look?

Think, Jake!

OK, I thought, so far the Aztecs had simply described what to look for: a jaguar. So why would that change now?

I moved towards a row of stalactites that hung on one side of the cave kissing the tips of stalagmites jutting from the ground. Together they looked like teeth ... or fangs. Behind them, a crack in the rock led deeper into the cave system – a low, narrow passage.

"I've found a tunnel," I said.

"Can you get through?" Dad replied.

I crouched down and used night vision to peer into the tunnel.

Then I swore. A lot.

"Jake!" Mum hissed.

"What do you see?" Pan asked. I could hear the delight in her voice; she knew I'd discovered something bad.

I looked back across the cave to the spluttering flare, and was tempted to say that I saw nothing, that the cave was empty. I almost wished that were true; then I wouldn't have to face what I'd seen in that tunnel.

"What is it, Jake?" Dad asked. "What's in the tunnel?"

"Spider webs," I replied.

"OK," Mum said. "A few spider webs won't—"

"Not a *few*. The tunnel is *full* of webs."

Seriously, I'd never seen so many. I wouldn't be able to wriggle around them. There wasn't even a *them* to wriggle around, just one huge web filling the space. I ordered my goggles to shine their torch into the tunnel, but the light barely penetrated the spider silk by a few metres before it was snuffed out by the sheer thickness of the mesh.

I heard Pan laughing. Mum and Dad began a conversation about the native spiders of the Mosquito Coast. I zoned out, staring into the tunnel. Could I really go in there?

"Jake, listen," Mum said. "Those webs were most likely made by tarantulas."

"*That* is supposed to make me feel better?"

"Tarantulas are not deadly," Dad explained.

"They bite, though," Pan added.

"Shut up, Pan! So the best case scenario is that I'm crawling into a tarantula tunnel?"

"Yes."

"Great. Thanks for that."

"Get a wriggle on, then," Pan said.

I breathed in deeply, trying to settle my nerves.

I can do this. I can do this.

No, I can't. I definitely can't do this.

I *had* to do this. I was Sami's only chance. I remembered how he had risked his own safety to help us in Egypt, turned himself into a fugitive, even, and then again to help us track down the Snake Lady. I *had* to do this for him.

I closed my eyes and slid a hand into the webs. They were even thicker than I'd thought, resisting my fingers, so I had to push harder. My hand didn't break through; the tunnel was just *all web*. I kept pushing until my whole arm was inside the mesh.

"Are you shaking?" Pan asked. "It might make the giant spiders come out."

"Shut up, Pan..."

"Bet that's the last time you just jump through a secret door, eh?"

"Shut up!"

I got down low and slid into the tunnel. The crack in the rock was shaped like an upside-down *V*, so there was space to slide through if I wriggled on my elbows with my arms tucked at my sides. That meant I couldn't use my hands to tear a passage through the webs. So I had to do it with my face.

Mum and Dad must have given me a free pass on swearing, because they didn't tell me off as my curses grew louder and I burrowed face-first through the webs. My goggles were quickly covered with web, dimming the torchlight. The mask of spider silk grew thicker on my face. Each time I swore I got a mouthful of the sticky stuff.

"Just relax," Mum said.

"That's easy for you to say! You've never been in a tarantula tunnel."

"Jake, we were treasure hunters for twenty years before you were born. We've been in dozens."

Dad chipped in. "Not an actual tunnel, Jane."

"No," Mum agreed, "but tarantula pits and tarantula traps."

"Oh, yes," Dad said, "and do you remember the Tarantula Queen of Cochabamba?"

"Fine!" I interrupted. "So what do I do?"

"Wet yourself," Pan replied. "Urine scares off tarantulas."

"Really?"

"No, Jake, your sister is teasing you."

"Mum! He would have done it!"

I was actually quite close to wetting myself, but from fear. At least I could now see an end, where the tunnel opened to another chamber.

"I think I'm almost there," I gasped.

Then I felt it.

A pat on my back.

Something landing.

"There's one on me," I hissed.

"Jake, do not panic." Mum tried to sound calm. "One tarantula isn't—"

Another pat.

"There's two," I whispered.

Another pat. Another. Another. I don't know how many I felt land on me – maybe a hundred – as I lay in their webs. Tiny legs tapped across my back. I couldn't see them, but I knew they were tarantulas; no other spiders could be that big. And they were spreading out.

"Stay still, Jake. They will crawl away."

Dozens of them tiptoed onto my head. They crawled down onto my face, over my smart-goggles...

I couldn't stay still any longer. I shot up, bashing my back against the tunnel roof to get the creatures off. I crawled faster, flicking away tarantulas as I slid from the tunnel. As soon as I was out I jumped up, brushing and slapping my limbs, convinced I was still covered in the creatures.

"Everything OK?" Dad asked.

"You big baby," Pan said.

"Where are you now, Jake?" Mum demanded.

Still struggling to calm my breathing, I wiped webs

from my goggles and took in my new surroundings in the trembling torchlight.

"A smaller cave," I said. "There's another tunnel on the other side. It could be a way out."

I crouched to see into the passage, which was larger than the one I'd just crawled through. "More webs, but they're broken up."

Dad began to speak. "What do you mean—"

"There's something else here," I said, interrupting.

A stone slab, about the size of a school desk, stood against the wall. Actually, I realized as I moved closer, it *was* the wall. The rock had been carved back all around it to form an altar.

"Jake," Mum said. "Just tell us what you see."

But what *did* I see? I edged closer to the altar, directing the torchlight at a strange shape carved above it on the cave wall. It was some sort of symbol. It may have been an Aztec glyph once, but five hundred years of rainwater dribbling through the cave had worn it into a blur. From what I could make out, the symbol had been large and elaborate before it was eroded, and must have taken time to carve. Was *this* the second marker to the tomb of Quetzalcoatl?

"Do you see the marker, Jake?"

"I... Maybe," I replied. "There's a carving on the wall."

"Take a photo, we can study it."

I blinked three times and my smart-goggles flashed. I prayed Mum and Dad could make more sense of the photo.

"Jake." Dad's voice sounded urgent. "The other tunnel... Did you say the webs were broken?"

"Eh? Oh, yeah."

"But you didn't go in there?"

"Me? No, I... "

A cold hand grabbed my guts and squeezed as I realized what Dad meant. If I hadn't been in that tunnel, then what *had*?

"Get out of there, Jake," Mum barked.

I wanted to, but suddenly my legs felt like they were made of lead.

"I just heard something," I whispered.

The sound was coming from the other tunnel. Soft footsteps.

"Was that a growl?" Pan asked.

She'd heard it through my goggles. She wasn't laughing anymore. "Jake? Did something just growl?"

"Jake!" Mum roared. "Move!"

This time I didn't think twice about the webs or the tarantulas. I scrambled back into the tunnel and wriggled frantically on my elbows. Another growl echoed around the cave behind me. Whatever creature was back there, it knew its home had been invaded.

"It's coming after me!" I cried.

"It could be harmless..."

"Nothing harmless growls, Pan!"

"Move faster, Jake!"

I was moving as fast as I could. There was web on

my lenses, web on my face, web filling my mouth. One of my elbows slipped and my chin hit the tunnel floor. I glanced over my shoulder, my torch beam revealing dozens of tarantulas scuttling towards the light. They were fleeing, but not from me.

"I see it," I gasped.

"See *what*?"

I wasn't sure. My goggles were clouded with spider webs. Something big, in silhouette, crouched to look into the tunnel. Amber eyes gleamed in the torchlight, and another snarl echoed through the passage.

I slid from the tunnel, scrambled up and ran for the flare as it spluttered and died. As I charged closer, another light beamed onto the ground beside the flare. It wasn't my torch. It was daylight! Mum and Dad had opened the pit!

A rope fell through the sunlight.

"Jake! Grab on!"

They began to raise the line before I even reached it, so I had to jump and grab hold. I clung on as they pulled me up. My goggles slipped and the torch beam cut out.

Below, a shape rushed across the darkness and sprang up at me on the rope. I screamed and kicked out at whatever creature was leaping. Claws flashed. Eyes gleamed. The animal dropped back to the cave, which resounded again with its furious growls.

I didn't see it, but it saw me. Maybe I was being

crazy, but I could swear those snarls were a warning. The creature would find me.

It would see me again.

21

I think the rain had stopped by the time we reached Alpha Squad's camp, but it was hard to tell. So much rainwater dripped from branches and sprayed off leaves that it still seemed to be pouring. I guessed it was late in the afternoon, but it was tricky to know *that* either. So little daylight found its way through the jungle canopy that it *always* seemed like dusk.

I felt like shattered glass. My jaw was swollen from the bullet ant sting, my side throbbed from the mudslide, and I was scratched and bruised from crawling in the cave. My feet were raw and blistered from the trek, and I can't tell you how badly I itched. Every single part of me was bitten. I had a bite on my lip, my eyelid, inside my ear, even. What sort of creature bites you *inside your ear*?

The moment we reached camp, I clambered into my hammock and pulled the net over the top. I know that sounds bad. If that symbol I'd photographed in the cave *was* the second marker, then we needed to act fast. Sami's life depended on it. But I *had* to rest, just for a bit.

After half an hour, Mum brought me a bowl of warm, grey mush – another of Alpha Squad's jungle rations. That food was depressing when you were tired and hurt and desperate for some sort of comfort. Dad's "food training" back home hadn't included freeze-dried cardboard-tasting gruel. Right then I would have done anything for a milkshake and a cheeseburger. I stared at Alpha Squad's drone, wondering if we could programme it to fly out of the jungle and bring back some proper food.

Mum rubbed some cream on my jaw where I'd been stung. She looked at me and stroked my hair in a way that she hardly ever does. With her other hand she slid her necklace out from under her shirt and clutched her amulet.

"Are you sure you're not hurt?" she asked.

I nodded.

"You're lucky to be alive," Mum said.

"I'm OK, Mum, thanks."

"No. You are lucky."

Hang on. She was telling me off!

Pan leaned from her hammock. "Jake may have found the marker in that cave, Mum."

"Jake hurled himself into a pit with no idea what was down there," Mum replied. "He could have fallen into a trap."

"He didn't fall. He used his bungee. And there was no trap."

"You don't consider a wild jaguar a trap?"

"We don't know it was a jaguar."

"Well, it wasn't a racoon! If Jake had properly observed his surroundings, as we have trained you, he might have noticed the animal's spores."

"Spores?" I asked.

"Its poo," Pan explained. "How was he supposed to see that? And if he hadn't gone further, then we'd not have found that carving. If that is the marker, then we need it to save Sami."

"I have known Sami for a lot longer than you, young lady," Mum snapped. "He would not want to be saved if it meant either of you were harmed."

"That's not your choice to make, Mum."

"It's exactly my choice. I am your mother!"

"Everyone be quiet!"

Dad hissed at us from across the camp, and we all shut up. He was crouching to examine one of the alarm sensors he'd hidden among the trees. He had his serious face on, jaw clenched and chin dimpled.

"What is it, John?" Mum asked.

"This alarm has been tripped."

"Maybe it was one of us?" Pan suggested.

"No, we entered the camp from the east. I was careful to deactivate only that alarm."

Bones clicked in Dad's knees as he rose and

183

rushed back to the canvas shelter. His eyes roved over the holosphere screen, the table, the drone...

"Someone's been here," he said. "Someone has looked through our notes."

Mum joined him, her hand now clasped around her amulet. "Could it have been an animal?"

"Maybe," Dad muttered.

Neither of them sounded like they believed that. *Someone* had been here. Someone was watching us. More than ever I feared there was something going on here that we didn't understand. I only knew one thing for sure: we had to find the tomb, and fast.

"This is the photo Jake took in the cave. As you can see, it's heavily calcified. I've filtered it through an advanced geo-reconstruction programme to enhance the eroded features."

We sat in the shelter, using Alpha Squad's holosphere to examine the photo of the marker. The blurred symbol was projected up beside other images of Aztec glyphs.

"It reconstructed the symbol like this." Dad swiped my photo away and it was replaced by another showing the symbol much more clearly. It was as if the Aztecs had carved it only yesterday, and it wasn't just *one* symbol.

"The marker is *two* signs?" Pan said. "Do you recognize either?"

Dad shook his head. "The reconstruction

programme just guessed. Neither is exactly what the Aztecs carved."

"Can we cross-reference with known *Nahuatl* glyphs?" Mum asked.

More files projected from the table screen, cartoonish signs from the ancient Aztec script. I remembered now – Nahuatl was the Aztec language.

Pan, Mum and Dad began to compare each of the files to the marker's weathered carvings. They discarded some of the signs and enlarged others, talking over one another most of the time.

"This sign could be a conflated logogram," Pan suggested.

"You're overcomplicating it," Mum said. "They're just phonetic glyphs."

"I disagree," Dad replied. "They're calendrical signs, nothing more."

I sank back into my hammock, grateful for the chance to rest while their big brains were on the job. I think I fell asleep for a bit. When I looked again the three of them stood together looking exhausted and elated at the same time. Only two Aztec glyphs remained, hovering beside the two symbols of the marker.

Dad touched one and slid it through the air, so it sat on top of a marker sign. It was a good fit – not exact, but close.

"This symbol means *fire*," he said.

Mum slid the other sign over its match on the marker.

185

"And this is *wind*."

I leaned out of the hammock and called, "So that's the second marker? *Wind* and *fire*. How does that lead us to the tomb?"

That set them off, and they began to argue over the meaning of the symbols. I lay back again and thought about the first marker. In the end it had turned out to mean something that was there to see, once we looked in the right place. That marker – jaguar – simply showed us what to look for; so why shouldn't these, too?

Surely "wind" didn't mean just mean *wind*. That could be anywhere. "Fire" wasn't much help either. Mum had said the Aztecs wanted the markers to last, so the word had to mean a type of fire that would stay alight for a long time. The sun burned for ever, so maybe the marker meant a sunny place where it was windy. That seemed too vague, though, and I knew my parents and sister would say the same.

A windy place, where fire burns for ever...

I shot up. "Are there any volcanoes in this jungle?"

"No," Mum said.

My head was spinning. That was a lot of big thinking for me, and it hadn't achieved much. I slumped back down and pulled off my hiking boots. My socks were soaked again, but I didn't want to take them off and see the blisters. There wasn't much point in changing them, anyway; the new ones would get soaked in seconds, and the old ones would never dry in this constant damp. I heard thunder in the distance, rumbling louder. It was going to chuck it down again soon.

"Thunder..." I muttered.

Was it possible?

I stared up into the trees as rainwater splashed off branches and showered the camp. Then I slid from the hammock and pulled my boots back on. No one noticed as I grabbed one of the lower branches of a tree at the edge of the camp and started climbing.

I was so excited about what I might have found that I didn't even notice the height. I must have been twenty feet up before my parents spotted me and shouted for me to come down. I stopped where I could see through the canopy, towards the jagged silhouettes of the Storm Peaks. Dark clouds gathered over the high tops of the mountains, whisked by fierce winds. Thunder roared. Lightning flashed.

A storm.

Wind.

Lightning.

Fire.

"Guys!" I yelled. "Did we pack climbing boots?"

22

"What can you see?"

"Rain," Mum replied.

Her eyes seemed to glow behind her smart-goggles, as she watched live video from the summit of one of the Storm Peaks. Craning my neck, I could just see a red light blinking dimly though the rain, at the top of a rock wall so steep it made me dizzy to look up. Another streak of lightning zapped the clouds, catching Alpha Squad's drone in stark silhouette. The machine looked like a bat searching for the entrance to its cave.

These mountains were called the Storm Peaks for a reason. Through the fierce winds, driving rain and flashes of lightning, all the drone was able to send us were rain-blurred images of rain-soaked rocks.

Dad yanked me back under an overhang at the

base of the cliff. He'd insisted we shelter from the rain, although I don't know why; we'd left camp eight hours ago and were already soaked to the skin. We'd followed the river towards the mountains, leaving it where it snaked around the edge of this peak to a waterfall on the other side, and then we'd trudged through swamps and over moss-covered boulders to the base of this cliff face.

Wind. Fire.

"Increase altitude ten feet," Mum ordered. *"Adjust camera angle thirty degrees."*

Whatever the machine showed, Mum saw the same thing in her lenses. "More rain," she muttered. "There's a small plateau at the top with a lake, but I don't see much else other than rocks and trees."

"Should we check the other side of the mountain?" I asked.

"We can't," Mum explained. "The waterfall there is too powerful for the Aztecs to have climbed the cliff face, let alone hidden the marker anywhere up—"

Her hands shot to her goggles, gripping the frames. "Wait."

"What is it?" Pan called.

Mum brushed the question away with an irritated wave, barking more commands at the drone. She tore the goggles off and gave the machine a final order. *"Return to operator."*

"Jane?" Dad asked. "What did you see?"

"I'm not certain. It's dark up there among the

189

clouds, but I think I saw some sort of structure close to the lake."

"Maybe a natural rock formation," Pan suggested.

"I think I know the difference," Mum snapped. She rubbed her eyes. "I'm sorry. I don't know what I saw, but there could be something up there."

The drone buzzed and whirred, rotors spinning in its "wings" as the bat-shaped machine flew lower. It landed with a splat on the jungle floor, and the lights around the wings cut out.

"What now?" Pan asked.

Mum and Dad did one of their silent exchanges, nods and shrugs and eye gestures – a secret language that Pan was beginning to understand.

"We're going to *climb* up there?" Pan said.

"No," Mum corrected. "Your father and I are."

They'd already begun to prepare, adding things from Alpha Squad's kit to their utility belts: climbing clips, ropes, a rubber mallet. I could tell from the way Mum replied to Pan that there was no chance she'd let us go with them – and this time I was OK with that. Just *looking* up the cliff face made my stomach curdle. It was *really* high.

"How long will you be?" I asked.

Dad stood back, looking up. "Up and down? I'd say four to five hours."

"Three max," Mum said. "You two will be safe here. Stay hydrated. Stay alert. If someone *is* following us they could be watching."

"What if we see anyone?" Pan asked.

"There's a flare in the bag. Get somewhere safe and fire it. We'll return as quickly as we can. Whoever it is, do not go near them."

Mum glared at me. "Do you understand, Jake? No fighting. Nothing crazy."

I nodded.

"Do you understand, though?" Mum asked.

"I just said I did."

"You nodded. I want to hear you say it."

"No fighting."

"Say you promise."

"I promise! No fighting and nothing crazy. Who am I supposed to fight, anyway?"

"You usually find someone."

I couldn't reply because they were already off, scrambling up a rise of boulders to the base of the cliff face. I watched them begin their climb, thinking how unfair Mum was never to trust me, to be convinced that I was always on the verge of doing something crazy or dangerous, or getting in a fight. That seems silly, looking back, because I was about to do something *very* crazy and *very* dangerous and get in a *really* big fight.

But still.

23

It had only been a few months since I learned that my
parents were professional treasure hunters. Every
time I discovered a skill they'd kept secret I added
it to the new profiles I was building for them in my
mind. The old versions of Mum and Dad, those stuffy
college professors, faded further from view, and my
real parents came sharper into focus.

They could rock climb.

I mean, they could *really* rock climb. The longer
we watched, the funnier it seemed that Pan and I had
wanted to go with them up the Storm Peak. By the
time we'd have sussed out how to get a grip on the
rock wall, they would have been fifty metres up.

We watched for over two hours, sheltered under
low-hanging palm leaves, with the kit bags and Alpha
Squad's drone. From there we could see almost the
whole way up the cliff, as well as along the river

that curled around the mountain, and back into the jungle behind us. Hopefully we'd spot anyone that might be sneaking after us.

Not that we were looking. Our eyes were fixed on Mum and Dad, and our smart-goggles were set to *zoom*. Mum led the climb, moving like a lizard in little bursts up the sheer face, using just the tips of her fingers and the points of her toes to cling onto the surface. She moved without dislodging a single rock, finding hand-grips and foot holds in the tiniest fissures.

Dad was the opposite, all brute force and grabs. If there were no obvious grips he created one by smashing the wall with his climbing hammer, causing chips of rock to cascade down the cliff. If Mum was dancing up the Storm Peak, Dad was fighting his way to the top.

"Not bad," Pan said.

That was a big compliment, coming from her.

"They could be a while longer," she added. "We should get some rest."

Rest. God, we needed it. We'd been up since four in the morning, and then trekked for eight hours to reach the Storm Peaks. My bones felt like they were cast from cement. But I'd not be able to sleep. Ever since our parents had set off up the Storm Peak, I'd had that tingle in my belly, that sense that something wasn't right...

"Do you really think we're being followed?" I said, thinking aloud.

193

"Well, *someone* was at our camp," Pan replied.

"But why? And where are they now?"

The more I thought about it, the less sense it made. Whoever broke into our camp hadn't stolen anything, so why had they been there?

Someone was spying on us. Maybe it was the same people behind the disappearance of Alpha Squad. If so, they were not people to mess with. As we'd hiked here, Dad had guessed it might be a cult trying to protect the tomb of Quetzalcoatl, while Mum suggested it could be another group of hunters. Either way, they would be watching us now.

"Unless..." I muttered.

I slid my smart-goggles back on and looked again up the Storm Peak's cliff face. I could still just see Mum and Dad climbing at crazy speed up the rock wall. My eyes continued up, following the path they were taking to the summit, studying overhangs, ledges...

The tingle in my belly grew into a gnawing pain.

"What is it, Jake?" Pan asked.

"What if someone wasn't just *watching* us? What if they were *listening* too? We didn't search our camp for bugs, and we weren't exactly being quiet about where we were going."

"So whoever was watching might know where the marker is too?"

Pan shoved her goggles back on as she reached the same conclusion that I had. What if someone

194

wasn't *following* us? What if they were *ahead* of us?

"Oh my God, Jake, there *is* someone else there."

I'd spotted them as well: two climbers higher up the cliff than Mum and Dad, and moving even faster. It was hard to pick out details, but it didn't look like they had ropes. They had almost reached the trees that sprouted from the highest parts of the rock wall. At that speed they would reach the summit in about fifteen minutes. Whoever they were, they were going to get the marker first.

"We should fire the signal flare," Pan said.

"No," I replied. "Mum and Dad will come back down, and we'll definitely lose the marker."

But we couldn't just sit here and watch, either. We had to do *something*. I turned, looking around, thinking. A plan came to me but... No, that was *too* crazy. Wasn't it?

"Maybe we can make a catapult and fire rocks at them?" Pan suggested.

"A catapult? Out of what?"

"I don't know! *You're* meant to be the one with the plans!"

I *had* a plan. I just couldn't bring myself to say it out loud...

"We have to get ahead of them," I said.

"How? Mum and Dad are too far behind."

"Not Mum and Dad, Pan. *Us*."

Her eyes followed mine, and I think she understood because she laughed, and then laughed harder when she realized that I was serious.

I was staring at the drone.

"No, Jake! It's not a helicopter."

"I think it would take the weight of one of us, at least," I said. "Remember in Egypt? A drone like this one lifted us all up?"

"Not *exactly* like this one! This isn't a crazy plan, Jake, it's way beyond that."

"Pan, this is the only plan we have. If we do nothing, whoever is up there will get the marker."

Pan gazed up the Storm Peak's sheer cliff, and then back to the drone. "I really don't know about this, Jake."

"It will hold one of us, I'm almost certain."

"*Almost* certain?"

"No, I'm just certain. Almost. One of us rides on it, the other guides it from the ground using Mum's smart-goggles."

"Why do you keep saying 'one of us'?" Pan asked. "*You're* riding it."

"What? Why me?"

"It's your plan!"

"Exactly. So you should do the riding."

Pan stared at me as if I'd just started talking the ancient Aztec language. "Jake? I don't do action things like this."

"Stop saying that, Pan! You're in the middle of a jungle, hunting for a lost tomb. That's pretty *actiony*."

"But I can't think as fast as you do. Not with

something like this. You have to do this, you know that. Besides, usually I wouldn't be able to *stop* you – you'd already be on it, ready to go. Why the sudden... Oh. Oh, I see."

She followed my eyes again up the sheer face of the Storm Peak to the dark clouds that swirled around the summit.

"It's high," she said.

"Yeah. It's high."

"And you don't like heights."

"I know, Pan..."

"You *really* don't like heights."

"I know, Pan!"

She was tormenting me for fun, but I could see the worry in her eyes, too. My life was going to be in her hands.

She crouched by the drone, typed a code into a screen on its side, and slid on her smart-goggles. *"Power, drone,"* she said, copying Mum's instructions. *"Rise one metre."*

Lights came on around the machine, and rotors whirred on its wings. It rose from the ground and hovered beside us.

"Hop on, then," Pan said.

Imagine trying to balance on top of a floating dustbin lid. I could *get* on, but it took me several attempts to *stay* there, lying face down on top of the machine, with my legs dangling down either side and my arms wrapped under its base.

"You sure about this?" Pan asked.

I wasn't at all, but I nodded.

"OK, here we go," Pan said. *"Rise twenty metres."*

I clung on tighter as the machine obeyed, and Pan steered the drone over a rise of boulders, to the Storm Peak's cliff face. Each tilt and jolt caused me to cry out in fright, and so I clung tighter to the shuddering machine. We weren't even that high yet, but already vertigo had begun to kick in, and the ground and safety seemed a mile away.

Pan's voice yelled in my goggles. "Hold on!"

"I *am* holding on!"

I couldn't hold on any tighter as the drone carried me up, about ten metres out from the rocks. The higher I rose the stronger the winds grew, and the harder the machine shuddered. It was like being on a fairground bronco ride, only if I fell I was dead. Ferns and scrubby bushes sprouted from rocks, and small trees jutted from crevices like gangly arms. I fought an urge to grab one and cling on. It seemed safer there than on this shaking death machine. I felt physically sick with fear. I might actually have thrown up had I not heard someone yelling my name.

It wasn't Pan. The voices were closer, screaming.

Mum and Dad clung to the cliff face, watching me rise past them on the shaky drone. They looked as if they'd just woken from a nightmare. Was that really their son flying into a storm on a tin can?

"Jake!" Mum screamed. "You promised!"

I tried to explain, but a roar of thunder drowned my shouts. The rain was pelting down now, and wind battered me from all sides.

"Jake?" Pan called, still talking to me through my goggles. "Can you see the other climbers?"

I looked up, struggling to see anything through the storm. The higher I rose into the clouds, the darker it became. A streak of lightning lit the top of the mountain, but I didn't spot anyone on the rock face. Had the mystery climbers already reached the top?

I forced myself to stay still as the drone carried me closer to the top of the cliff. From the ground the mountain had looked needle-sharp, but now I saw that the summit was a rocky plateau. Trees surrounded a round crater lake, like a basin, with a swirling whirlpool of rainwater. But Mum had thought she'd seen something else up here...

"I'm close, Pan!" I screamed. "Land me on the top!"

"I'm trying!"

She shouted orders, but the drone didn't respond. Instead it flew further up, carrying me even higher over the mountain.

"Too far!" I screamed again.

"I'm losing control, Jake!"

Rain lashed at my face, and my goggles clouded. As I tore them off they slipped from my hand and fell and, stupidly, I looked down. My stomach somersaulted and I actually threw up. I'd never been that scared, but I couldn't let fear take control.

Without my goggles I couldn't talk to Pan anymore. I was alone, clinging onto a tiny machine thirty metres above a mountain. Suddenly the flimsy drone felt like my best friend in the world, the only thing between me and the storm. I tried to think what Mum would say to me now.

Jake, you're grounded!

No, not that.

Concentrate, Jake! Clear your mind and think!

I breathed in and held the breath. And right then it was as if the storm clouds suddenly parted and were replaced by brilliant blue sky. I knew exactly what to do.

I slid an arm slowly from under the drone and pulled the grappling gun from my utility belt. In one quick move I sat up and fired it at the mountain top. At the same time there was a flash so bright it blinded me for a second. I sank back to the drone, crying out in fright. Black smoke rose from the machine and was whisked away by the wind. There were spots in my eyes, white flashes. Had the grappling gun back-fired? No, the shot had worked. A wire trailed from the device and down to the trees on the plateau. Had someone else fired at me?

Another flash of lightning lit the sky. Sparks flew up from the drone and it spluttered and swayed even more violently.

Then I realized: No one was shooting at me! The drone had been struck by lightning! I'd ridden a tin can into a lightning storm! One more zap and I was sure it would conk out. I had to get off this thing.

"Pan!" I screamed, praying she might still hear. "Get me down!"

She'd lost control of the drone. It was up to me now. I sat up a fraction and tugged the grappling line. Somewhere on the summit, its hook snagged a rock or branch. That was something, at least. I slid the device under the drone and used a climbing clip from my belt to connect it to its own wire, so the line was fixed to the machine. I unclipped my utility belt and slung it over the wire.

Another flash of lightning, this time even closer.

Get off this thing!

Except... Really?

Now, you idiot!

I gripped the ends of my utility belt and jumped.

I started sliding immediately, clinging onto the belt as it scraped down the grappling wire. I rushed closer to the mountain top, screaming the whole way. Just as I reached the treetops, I let go. I crashed into the branches, crashed *through* the branches, and landed facedown in something soft.

I lay, groaning and gasping, wondering how I'd survived. From what I could make out, I'd landed in a bed of sticks and grasses and...

"Eggs?" I mumbled.

Something stabbed the back of my neck. I cried out, fearing I was under attack from whoever had climbed here ahead of my parents.

Another stab, harder. Feathers hit my face, and something squawked. It wasn't a person – it was a bird! It was too dark to tell what *type* of bird, only that it was huge, and with talons as long as kitchen knives. I'd landed in its nest and it wasn't happy.

I thrashed my arms but I was too dazed to fight. The bird's claws pinned me to its nest, and now its razor beak jabbed at my face. I managed to shift so the attack missed my eyeball and sliced my cheek.

"Get off me!" I screamed.

The bird was about to take another stab at my eyes, when something crashed against the rocks a few metres from the nest. The drone had finally died and dropped from the sky. The bird squawked in fright and released its grip. I wriggled away from its nest.

I rose, wiping rain and blood from my eyes, and blinking away lightning spots. It was as dark as midnight inside the storm, and I'd dropped my smart-goggles, so I had no night vision. At least my utility belt had landed close. I strapped it back on, glancing around the plateau. I didn't see any torch-light. Had I got here first? And where was the marker?

Another streak of lightning offered a glimpse of the mountain top. Rainwater washed in streams into the small lake at the centre of the plateau, whisked by the wind into a whirlpool. Around the lake, trees creaked and swayed in the storm. It felt as if I was on the deck of a ship that was about to be wrecked.

There was something else there, though, on the other side of the lake. It looked like a rise of natural rock or ... a building!

I ran for it, slipping over and staggering up. More lightning revealed a small temple, with stone steps leading to an entrance carved with patterns and symbols. Two stone creatures jutted from its corners, grinning snakeheads with glaring eyes and plumed feather collars. It was the feathered serpent, Quetzalcoatl!

I scrambled up the steps and through the entrance into a dark chamber. I stood, breathing hard, waiting for another flash of lightning. When it came I saw that the chamber was empty other than a stone altar. Standing on the altar was a clay plaque carved with an Aztec symbol.

"The marker!"

It wasn't heavy, but my arms were so tired I could barely even lift it from the altar. Instead I stood still as another flash of lightning – and then another – illuminated the mountain top. I stared at the marker, trying to carve its symbol into my mind.

Another roar of thunder, this one so loud it caused the temple walls to tremble.

And then a voice.

"Jake Atlas! We know you're in there."

Torchlight beamed through the entrance, catching me in terrified silhouette. The voice called again.

"Come out with the marker and we might let you live."

I turned, staring around the temple walls. There was no other way out.

I was trapped.

24

"Jake Atlas. Come out with the marker, or we will come in and take it from you."

You know what? I didn't actually care who was outside the temple. I should have. These people had spied on us, shot us from the sky, killed Pedro, even. Who were they? How did they know my name?

But I just didn't care.

I stood in the torchlight, soaked and shivering, and staring at the symbol carved onto the clay plaque on the altar. I'd risked my life to get to that marker. If those people saw it, all of that was pointless. They'd beat us to the tomb of Quetzalcoatl and the emerald tablet. I thought about Sami again, lying in agony in that bed. If he died he'd never know how much I'd let him down. But *I* would. I couldn't let that be his deathbed. I had to find a way out of this *with* the marker.

A different person spoke, a woman with a voice as rough as sandpaper.

"Jake Atlas, this is your last warning."

"There's no marker in here!" I yelled.

"Don't lie to us," the man growled. "You're out of your depth now, son. You don't have to get hurt, but don't think for one moment that we'd care if you did."

"You killed Alpha Squad, didn't you?" I called.

Like I said, I didn't care, but I needed to buy time to think.

"Who we are isn't important," the man said. "What's inside that temple is all that matters. Bring it out now, son."

"There's no marker in here," I repeated.

"This is getting tiresome," the woman warned.

"I promise you," I replied. "There *was* a marker."

I rushed to the altar and picked up the plaque, my arms trembling from its weight. Then I hurled it as hard as I could against the temple wall. Clay smashed against stone, and the marker shattered. I sank to the ground, found the fragments with the carving, and crushed them against the temple floor.

"But now there's only *bits* of the marker," I added.

Torchlights bobbed and brightened. Boots thumped over stone.

"Don't come any closer!" I cried. "I saw the marker and I'm the only one that did. It only exists in my head now, so if you want to know what was on it, you'd better back off."

The boots stopped. I heard whispered arguments.

"Let's do a deal, son!" the man shouted. "You tell us what you saw and we'll let you go. Then it's just you against us to reach the tomb. An old-fashioned race."

"Why would I believe that?" I replied. "You killed Alpha Squad."

"Not quite, son. We *are* Alpha Squad."

That was a surprise, and there was something in the man's voice that said he wasn't lying. Now that I'd destroyed the marker, I wanted to know more.

"I'm coming out," I said.

"No sudden moves," the woman warned.

I wasn't capable of sudden moves. I'd got here on desperation and adrenaline, but now I mostly felt pain. My legs were bruised and stiff, and my left ankle wasn't working too well. Cuts on my arms stung like someone had rubbed vinegar in the wounds, and one of my fingernails had split down the middle. It sounds silly, but it *really* stung.

I gritted my teeth and hobbled out into the torchlight.

A flash of lightning lit up the plateau, giving me a proper glimpse of the two figures that stood by the whirlpool lake. The woman looked like a mad pirate, with wild ginger hair undercut at the sides, and a patch over one eye. The man had a shaved head, bushy beard and a neck as thick as one of the tree trunks beyond the lake. They wore jungle suits and were armed with weapons that I recognized: crab-claw shaped guns with silver barrels poking from the middle. They were stun guns, but if they were the same weapons that the Snake Lady's mercenaries had used in Egypt, they also fired bullets.

"If you *are* Alpha Squad," I said, "then we're on the same side. We're working for the People of the Snake."

"It's more complicated than that," the man grunted.

The woman raised her weapon. "What did the marker show?"

"Stop pointing that gun at me," I replied.

"I'll stop when you tell us."

"How can I think when you're aiming a gun at me?"

The man glared at her, and they did that thing Mum and Dad do, arguing with their eyes. I got the feeling they were a couple.

The woman sighed and lowered her stun gun. I'm not sure she needed it anyway: she looked about ready to strangle me with her gloved hands.

"Tell us!" she demanded.

"All right, all right! I'm thinking..."

"Tell us now!"

"Stop yelling at me, then! It's intimidating. See, now I've forgotten."

She raised the weapon again. "You'd better remember fast."

"All right!" I said. "I remember. The marker was

208

a circle with two semi circles on the top. There were eyes in the circle, and a mouth..."

The woman's eyes narrowed, as she tried to picture the symbol. "I don't recognize that," she said.

"I do," the man replied. "Is he describing Mickey Mouse?"

I grinned and tried not to look scared. "Maybe the tomb is in Disneyland?"

The man smiled too. Two of his teeth were gold, and several more were missing. "I get it," he snarled. "You're trying to be brave. Well, I'm impressed. Now tell us what you saw."

"You're wrong," I said. "That wasn't what I was trying to do."

"Yeah? What were you doing, then?"

"Buying time."

There's something I haven't told you. As I stepped from the temple, I saw two other people in that lightning flash.

Mum and Dad.

The man turned and Dad socked him in the face! It was a great punch, sending the guy flying to the ground and knocking the smart-goggles from his face. At the same time Mum jumped at the woman and they tumbled to the edge of the lake. She grabbed the stun gun and hurled it so it caught the Alpha Squad guy hard on the nose as he tried to stand.

Recovering, the Alpha Squad guy pulled a knife from his belt and charged at Dad. I'd seen Dad fight against the Snake Lady's mercenaries, but this time his opponent was a trained hunter. All I saw were glimpses in lightning flashes: the knife being kicked from his hand, punches, blocks, a spinning kick...

I'd seen Mum in action before, too, and thought no one could touch her. She was in trouble here, though. She dodged a punch, but the Alpha Squad woman caught her with a flying kick and some nifty ninja moves. Mum looked dazed. Blood gushed from her forehead. Dad wasn't doing well now either; he must have taken a big hit because he was down on his knees, swaying as if he might fall into the whirl-pool. The Alpha Squad man stumbled around the side of the lake, looking for his knife.

I had to help, but I'd never thrown a proper punch in my life. I breathed in, clearing my head. My mind went into that zone again, thinking clearly, making plans. In that moment I knew four things:

1. Alpha Squad wore small backpacks.
2. They hadn't brought the bags to carry the marker. They wore smart-goggles, so they'd have planned to photograph it and then destroy it so no one else saw what it showed.
3. They knew Mum and Dad were climbing the cliff below them, so would have planned a way off the mountain that avoided a confrontation.
4. So they had parachutes in their rucksacks.

Suddenly I was running. It was as if someone had hacked into my mind and downloaded a mad plan that I had no way of stopping. I charged around the edge of the lake, splashing through rainwater streams. I was going to hit the guy and grab hold, so we went over the cliff edge together. He'd have to pull his parachute, or we'd both die.

I ran faster, my eyes fixed on the Alpha Squad guy's back. I heard something thudding. Was it thunder or my heart?

A light beamed at my face, so bright it was like a physical thing, causing me to stop and stagger back. It was all around me somehow, coming from *above*. The thudding grew louder and I realized that it was coming from the sky, too.

A small helicopter descended over the plateau, aiming a searchlight at me. Shielding my eyes, I was just able to make out the pilot in the glass cockpit.

Pedro!

He'd survived and come to help! I grinned and whooped, waving my arms. I started to yell something – I can't remember what – but I never got to finish. The words caught in my throat.

As the helicopter came lower I saw that Pan was in it too. I signalled to her, but she glared back at me, frantically shaking her head. Her mouth was covered with duct tape. It looked like her hands were tied behind her back.

She hadn't been rescued.

She'd been *caught*.

Pedro was with Alpha Squad.

The moment Mum saw Pan she dropped her fighting stance and raised her arms in surrender. Dad did the same, down on his knees, cut and bruised from the fight.

The Alpha Squad man picked up his knife. His gold teeth glinted in the helicopter's searchlight as he smiled at me through the driving rain.

"Good try, son. But it's over now."

25

"Well, isn't this something?"

Pedro unfolded a camping chair and set it gently on the temple floor. He sat on it back to front and leaned on the back rest. I think he thought he looked cool, like a cowboy.

He nudged his Stetson up to see us better in the gloom. "This is what I call an old-fashioned Mexican showdown," he said.

"It's not a Mexican showdown," Mum replied. "A Mexican showdown is a situation that neither party can win."

"It's also not Mexico," I muttered.

"And it's a racist term, you nob head," Pan added.

Pedro glanced at the two members of Alpha Squad, who both shrugged.

"Well, whatever," he said. "It's a tricky situation."

I sat with my family on the rain-soaked temple

floor. Our hands were bound behind our backs with cable ties, and Alpha Squad had taken our goggles and utility belts. The two hunters stood guard, clutching their crab-claw stun guns.

To be honest I was glad for the rest. Every single part of my body hurt. It felt as if a rugby team had stamped all over me. Mum and Dad were in a bad way too. Dad's glasses were cracked, and he had so many cuts on his face it looked like he'd lost a fight with a lawn mower. Mum had a gouge on her leg so deep her trousers were soaked with blood. She looked pained, but I didn't think that was because of the cut. Alpha Squad had got the better of her; that was what hurt.

The Alpha Squad man grinned, blood glistening in his beard from where Dad had got in one or two punches of his own. "You must be wondering about us," he said.

Dad looked up at him through cracked lenses. "Your name is Kyle Flutes," he replied. "You were discharged from the SAS for assaulting an officer. You spent two years in prison for armed robbery after firing a bazooka at a bank vault door. It didn't work. The explosion did, however, blind your wife in her left eye."

Mum took over, glaring at the lady with the eye patch. "And you are Veronika Flutes. You were a gymnast for the Dutch Olympic team until you fractured your ankle. You began to drink, and met Kyle at a group for recovering alcoholics. After your spell in prison for bank robbery you were approached by the People of the Snake. Your combined skills for acrobatics and survival make you well suited to the physical demands of treasure hunting. However, what you make up for in brawn you lack in brains. The fact that you used a bazooka on a vault door suggests you are both imbeciles."

Mum twisted her neck, getting rid of an ache with a sharp *click*. "So there is no need for introductions."

Go, Mum and Dad! I would have gone in for high fives if my hands weren't cable tied. I wasn't surprised they knew so much. They'd spent hours preparing to come out of retirement as hunters. Sami must have helped them swot up on their potential rivals.

"Wait," I said. "Your name is Flutes?"

"So?" the man grunted.

"It's just... It's not a very tough name."

"It's just my name."

"I know. I just thought it would be Steel, or Hardfist, or something. Flutes... It's not even a very cool musical instrument."

Kyle looked confused by all this, but Veronika was boiling. Her face turned as red as her hair, and wormy veins bulged at her temples. I was trying to wind them up, to keep their attention on me. I'd noticed Dad glancing around the temple and suspected he was looking for a way to escape.

"I bet you wish you'd met someone called Trumpet," I said. "Or maybe—"

"Shut up!" Veronika snapped, aiming her stun gun at me. "Shut your mouth, you little brat."

Pedro clapped his hands. "This is great," he said. "I knew you'd all get on."

"Get on?" Pan asked.

"Of course," Pedro replied. "This is a business meeting. We are all after the same thing."

"We're here to save our friend," Pan said.

"But to do so, you must find the tomb of Quetzalcoatl. That is our goal also. So why not join forces? Alpha Squad and the Atlas Family. How could we fail? Whatever treasure we discover will be divided equally."

"You're betraying the People of the Snake?" Mum asked. "That's dangerous, Pedro. Did they not pay you enough?"

"No, you misunderstand," said Pedro. "My share of the treasure is not for *me*. It belongs to this country, to Honduras. For years I have supplied hunters with equipment. Rich white people who want to take home treasure. But it is not yours to take. The people of Honduras are among the poorest in the world. That wealth will feed families, build hospitals and schools. It is our right to profit from it."

"Hang on," I said. "You want the treasure for *charity*? Doesn't that make you the good guy?"

"Good guy, bad guy. We are all on the same side. What do you say?"

"Deal," Mum said.

Pan and I turned to her, surprised that she'd agreed so easily.

"Pedro, you are welcome to the treasure," Mum said. "We only need one thing from the tomb."

Kyle laughed, a surprisingly high-pitched noise for such a big man. "The emerald tablet is ours," he growled.

"This is tricky," Pedro said. "My original deal was with Alpha Squad. I get the treasure for my nation, and they get the tablet."

"Then you'll have to renegotiate," Mum insisted.

"You're not in a position to negotiate anything," Veronika spat.

"Actually we're in a fine position," Mum replied. "It's obvious what's happened. You searched for the first marker but couldn't find it. So you contacted Pedro and told him you needed someone else out here, another team who actually had some brains. You made Alpha Squad 'vanish' and waited for us to arrive. Then you, Pedro, saw a chance. You knew the People of the Snake would come after you if you double-crossed them, but not if they thought you'd died in a plane crash. Instead you watched us, hoping we'd lead you to the tomb."

"And you were impressive," Pedro agreed. "Everything they said about you is true."

"And now you're going to take us to the tomb," Kyle added. "If Pedro wants to give you half of his treasure, that's his business. But the emerald tablet is ours."

"Why do you want it so much anyway?" I asked.

Kyle looked at Veronika, as if seeking permission to answer.

His wife shrugged. "Tell them."

"The group you called the People of the Snake," Kyle said. "What do you really know of their operations?"

"We know enough," Pan said.

"Ha! You know nothing at all."

"They're trying to destroy particular tombs," Pan replied, "to hide some secret history of the world. The people buried in the tombs were the survivors of an ancient civilization, far older than the Ancient Egyptians, which was wiped out. Those people were remembered as gods: Osiris in Egypt, Quetzalcoatl in Central America, and others. Their symbol was the snake eating its own tail. They were buried in crystal coffins, clutching emerald tablets marked with some sort of script. Together the emerald tablets form a map, although we don't know where to."

Kyle stared at her. Blinked. "Oh. You actually know quite a lot. Then you know how valuable that tablet is, far more than any gold or jewels. Wherever it leads, *that's* the real treasure. So the tablet is *ours*."

"But if we don't get it, our friend dies," Pan said.

Veronika Flutes jabbed her stun gun at my sister. "Right now you should be more worried about saving your own lives."

Mum sat up, snarling at the woman like a wildcat.

"If you aim that gun at my children one more time, I will shove it—"

Actually I won't tell you what she said, but it wasn't a threat. It was a promise. Veronika grinned, although she lowered her aim.

"This is a business meeting," Pedro said, "so let us negotiate. Alpha Squad, would you be prepared to reconsider your position on the emerald tablet?"

"No," Kyle replied.

"Could you share it, perhaps? Alternate weeks?"

"No," Dad said. "You need *us*, Pedro. You won't know how to use the third marker to find the tomb."

"And you don't *have* that marker," Mum added. "But we do."

They were on fire! Pedro gave me a sly wink that said what I was thinking: *your family can be pretty cool.*

For a second I thought Veronika was winking too, but in fact her eyelid was twitching with rage. She raised her stun gun and aimed it right at my face. "You will tell us what you saw on that marker or else I'm going to—"

I never found out what she would do, because right then Mum shot up. The top of her head smacked into Veronika's jaw. There was a horrible *crack*, a spurt of blood, and Veronika collapsed to the temple floor.

Mum sat back down, her hands still tied behind her back. "I warned her," she said.

Kyle roared, a proper wild animal noise. His stun

gun clattered to the ground and he pulled his knife from his utility belt. Now Dad jumped up and got in front of Pan and Mum. I braced myself, ready to dive at Kyle's legs. It was all about to kick off again, when Pedro rushed between us, waving his hat in panic.

"Whoa there, cowboys! Kyle, Jane did warn Veronika. Your wife pointed a gun at her son's face."

"A stun gun," Kyle seethed.

"At his *face*, Kyle."

Pedro crouched and inspected Veronika on the ground. She wasn't moving, but her shallow breaths suggested she was just unconscious.

"Kyle?" he said.

Kyle was at boiling point. His knuckles were white around the handle of his knife as he glared at my dad.

"Kyle!" Pedro snapped. "Help me take Veronika outside. I suggest we all take a bit of time to think."

Kyle's grip finally relaxed on his weapon. He slid it back into his belt, and helped Pedro carry his wife from the temple. As he left he snarled a final warning.

"The emerald tablet is ours. You're not leaving until we have the marker. Not alive, anyway."

26

"Stop wriggling, Jake."

"Mum, I'm trying to get free."

"Yes, and that's exactly what it looks like. Pass me that tooth."

"What tooth?"

"By your leg."

It was one of Veronika Flute's teeth, which Mum had knocked from her jaw with her head-butt. Did Mum want it as some sort of memento? With my hands still tied behind my back, I scooped the tooth up and tossed it towards her.

Mum knocked it against the stone ground, causing it to split, so one of the fragments was razor sharp. She began cutting her cable tie binds.

We sat back-to-back on the temple floor. Rain sprayed through the entrance, puddling the ground, but the storm had begun to calm. The clouds must have started to clear, because slivers of moonlight beamed through cracks in the walls. Without the thunder, we spoke in whispers, scared we'd be heard by Pedro and Alpha Squad outside.

"Jake," Dad said. "Did you really destroy the marker?"

Here they went! Our lives were at threat, but they couldn't resist a chance to tell me off.

"If I hadn't," I hissed, "Alpha Squad would have it now."

"I wasn't telling you off, Jake. You did the right thing."

"Oh. I did?"

"As long as you remember the symbol you saw."

Oh God. I'd been dreading this moment. I *had* seen the marker, but Alpha Squad were yelling at me, and I was yelling back, and dazed from the fall from the drone. I wished Pan had seen it; she had a photographic memory. I sometimes struggled to remember my own name.

I won't tell you everything that was said over the next twenty minutes, but it mostly involved Mum urging me to think, me insisting that I *was* think-ing, Pan telling me to think harder, and Dad calming everyone down and then suggesting I think again.

Mum groaned. "You smashed the marker so only *you* knew the symbol. If you can't *remember* the symbol, then it wasn't a very clever plan, was it?"

"At least Jake *got* the marker," Pan replied.

"Your father and I were in control of that situation, Pandora."

"You knew Alpha Squad were ahead of you?"

"Yes. Shortly into the climb it became obvious someone else had recently scaled the cliff face."

"Then why didn't you say?" Pan complained. "We're meant to be a team."

"No, we are not!" Mum shot back. "We are your parents. We don't have to tell you anything."

"Everyone calm down," Dad said. "Jake. The marker?"

I did my best, scrunching my eyes shut and picturing the symbol I'd seen on the plaque. Actually I was surprised at how much detail I was able to tease from my memory. Dad drew what I described into the temple floor using a fragment of the broken marker plaque, scratching out about ten different symbols until I was satisfied that one was right. In the half-light we could just make out the shape – another Aztec pictogram, this time in the shape of a wave.

"Do you recognize it?" I asked.

"It looks like the sign for water," Mum replied.

"Or flood," Pan added.

"Yes, good thinking, Pandora."

"But what does it mean?" I asked. "Water? Floods? The whole jungle is flooded every time it rains."

"The marker has to point to something permanent," Pan reminded me. "Something the Aztecs thought would last. A river?"

223

"That's too vague," Mum said. "Two major rivers flow through this jungle, and hundreds of tributaries. The marker would be more specific."

"Wait!"

I sat up sharply, as if the rain-slicked ground had been zapped with electricity. Mum's comment had jolted another memory loose in my mind. I hadn't *only* seen that flood symbol on the marker.

"There was something else," I whispered, remembering that Alpha Squad was probably trying to listen. "Above the flood symbol there was a picture of Quetzalcoatl, like the one from your books, Pan."

"That makes sense," Mum said. "It's telling us that this marker will lead us to Quetzalcoatl's tomb."

"But what does the marker mean?" I asked. "A river? The lake on this mountain?"

"None of those," Dad said.

While we'd been talking, Dad had cut his wrist ties and scrambled to the side of the chamber, just out of view of our guards outside. Using another fragment of the broken marker, he drew on the wall. It was immediately obvious what he was sketching; the summit plateau and its crater lake, and the temple in which we were being held prisoner.

"This is the Storm Peak we're now on," he whispered.

He drew the other side of the mountain, another steep cliff beyond the temple. "This is the mountain's east face," he added. "We couldn't climb this side because of the waterfall."

224

Dad looked at Mum and they had one of their "moments" – wide eyes, excited by a discovery.

"Waterfall," Pan said, realizing what Dad meant. "*That's* what the marker means. It's telling us to look for the tomb entrance under the waterfall."

"No," Dad disagreed. "I don't think so, not quite."

"Not quite?" I asked.

Mum turned to me, struggling to keep her voice low in her excitement. "Jake, you're certain the image of Quetzalcoatl was drawn *above* the flood symbol?"

"I... Yes."

On his drawing of the mountaintop, Dad scribbled swirling lines inside the crater lake. "This lake is the start of the waterfall," he said. "The basin sucks rainwater down through a tunnel in the mountain, and sprays it out here, halfway down the cliff face."

"So?" Pan said. "Why can't the tomb entrance be somewhere under the waterfall?"

"Remember that Aztec pictograms were incredibly literal," Dad explained. "Wherever possible they showed exactly what they meant."

"So?"

"So, if the image of the god was *above* the flood symbol, then I don't think the marker is telling us to look *under* the waterfall."

Dad stared at his drawing and slowly shook his head, as if he could hardly believe what he was about to say.

"It's telling us to go *over* it," he said.

27

"OK, we're coming out."

"No sudden moves," warned Kyle Flutes.

"What counts as a sudden move?" I cried.

"You'll know if I shoot you," replied Veronika.

"No one is shooting anyone," Pedro insisted. "We're all friends here."

"Shut up, Pedro!" Pan yelled. "No one is friends with anyone here."

Mum and Dad led the way, shielding me and Pan as we edged out of the temple and into the glare of Alpha Squad's torch beams.

I noticed Pan shaking and wondered if it was because of the cold wind, and the rain that had soaked our jungle suits, or just plain fear. Either way, I didn't blame her. The plan Mum and Dad had hatched to escape this situation was almost as crazy as one of mine.

They believed the final marker was telling us to jump *over* the waterfall that plunged down the side of this mountain. Dad was going to make the jump – that bit of the plan wasn't up for discussion – but he wasn't just going to leap off a cliff and hope. He needed two things: a utility belt and one of Alpha Squad's parachute packs. It was my job to get them.

I'd agree to tell Alpha Squad what I'd seen on the marker. As we all discussed it, I would deliberately be very annoying, so no one cared when I slipped away. I'd get what Dad needed, cause a distraction to get them to him, and then he would run and make the jump. Alpha Squad would think he'd either escaped or fallen to his death. They'd have no idea he was going after the tomb and the emerald tablet.

Simple, right?

We shuffled further from the temple.

"Good luck, everyone," Dad whispered.

"No sudden moves!" Kyle Flutes barked.

"Seriously, stop saying that," Pan snapped.

I shielded my eyes from the torchlight, and glanced around the plateau. The parachute packs were close by, at the side of the temple. Our utility belts, though, were in a heap by Pedro's helicopter, which he'd landed on the other side of the whirlpool lake. Could I get them without being seen?

"Everyone, stay calm!" Pedro called. "We're all friends..."

"Stop saying that too, Pedro," Pan yelled. "They're

pointing stun guns at us! I'm better friends with the leech that got my eyeball than we are with Alpha Squad."

"Agreed," Kyle Flutes snarled. "The Atlas Family ain't exactly on our Christmas card list." He raised his weapon higher. "Just come out slow and tell us what we need to know."

We shuffled further from the temple, and our plan began. Dad agreed that we'd take half of any treasure discovered in the tomb, making it more believable by trying to negotiate for three quarters. I described the marker exactly as I saw it, because Pedro had a gadget pointed at me that could tell if I was lying. Credit to Mum and Dad; they'd anticipated that.

Pedro brought up the symbol on a portable holosphere and everyone crowded around it, like they were at a campfire. Light from the projections shone off flushed faces.

Alpha Squad kept their grips on their guns.

"Looks like a wave," Kyle said.

"I believe the symbol is guiding us to a river," Mum said, lying.

"Disagree!" I blurted. "It means swimming pool. Are there any swimming pools in the jungle?"

Everyone stared at me, and then back at the holosphere.

"Or maybe it means rain?" I continued. "We need to look for any place in the jungle where it's rained in the past five hundred years."

"It's a rainforest," Kyle growled. "It rains everywhere."

"OK, smarty pants," I replied. "What about a water slide? Is there one of those around here? A water park?"

They all looked at me again.

"Can I shoot him?" Veronika asked.

"Be my guest," Mum said, with a smile.

She actually smiled! At Veronika Flutes! I knew she was faking, but that really stung. I realized then why Mum had given me this job: because no one took me seriously. I was the one with the stupid plans and silly ideas, who no one would notice slipping away...

Pan pushed me gently away from the discussion. It was her way of reminding me of the plan, and it worked.

I moved further from the group and around the edge of the crater lake. Just as Mum had predicted, Alpha Squad either didn't notice me leaving or didn't care that I had. They were just happy that I was no longer interfering with the effort to decipher the marker.

I tried to walk casually, fighting the urge to make a sudden run for the utility belts, which would draw their attention. Even so, my heart was going like I was in a flat-out sprint, fearing one of Alpha Squad would spot me at any moment and open fire with stun darts. I made it to Pedro's helicopter and leaned against it as if I was bored. I checked again that no one was watching, then crouched and grabbed one of the utility belts.

So far so good. Now for the parachute.

I set off again, the utility belt clipped around my waist beneath my sodden jungle shirt. I tried to act calm, but this time my legs betrayed me and I walked faster back to the temple.

Veronika Flutes must have finally noticed I was missing – she glanced around, and her grip tightened on her stun gun as she spotted me.

I sat on the temple steps. I was five metres from the parachutes, but Veronika was watching me. I reached under my shirt, pretending to scratch my belly as I felt the utility belt for anything I could use as a distraction. I hadn't paid attention to *which* belt I grabbed, but knew now that it was Dad's. It was equipped with a UED – an ultrasonic explosive device. Pan and I had used one of these little bombs to blow up a tomb in Egypt, although we hadn't meant to. The explosion had helped us escape a trap and save Dad but, even so, Mum had made us swear we'd never touch a UED again. Only Dad carried two on his belt, for emergencies.

Emergencies like this.

I slid the device – which was round and flat like a hockey puck – from the belt, and gripped it in my palm. I planned to set it to detonate in five minutes, then get back to the group and somehow warn my family. When the bomb went off, I'd throw Dad the belt and he could grab the parachute as he ran for the edge of the plateau.

I grinned at Veronika, who was still watching me, hand on stun gun. "You're not so good with all the brainy stuff either, eh?" I called. "Wanna join me here on the stupid step?"

Her eyes flashed with rage and her weapon rose, but she turned to rejoin the group.

As soon as she wasn't looking I tapped on the UED's glass screen and set the timer to five minutes. I looked around for somewhere to fix it, but there was only this temple. Mum's warning rang in my head.

Jake, whatever happens, do not damage this temple.

Sorry, Mum.

I fixed the UED low down on the wall using its fastening clips, and pressed the activation button on its side. A five-minute countdown began on its screen.

Four minutes.

Three minutes.

Hang on....

"Oh, God," I gasped.

I'd set it to five *seconds*!

I screamed, turned and ran, but didn't even make two steps before the bomb detonated. The force threw me forward like a rag doll. My neck snapped back and my whole body twisted. I must have blacked out because when I came to I was lying among rubble from the temple. There was smoke and dust in the air, blood on my face. People were

231

shouting, but the ringing in my ears was louder. The blast had caused part of the temple to collapse. Mum and Dad were fighting with Alpha Squad, and Pedro was screaming at them to stop.

Pan grabbed my arm and helped me stand. Something hit the rubble beside us, and chips of stone flew up. She yanked me to the ground, screaming in my ear.

"They're shooting at us!"

Alpha Squad had switched the settings on their weapons. They were firing bullets!

"Get into the temple!" Mum yelled.

Pan and I scrambled up and into the bomb-damaged temple. Mum and Dad bundled in beside us, and we hid behind a half-collapsed wall.

Mum's eyes were wild; I'd never seen her look so desperate. "Are either of you hit?" she demanded.

I didn't get a chance to reply before Mum grabbed my arms.

"What were you thinking, Jake?"

There was no time to explain, and it wouldn't have mattered anyway. I had screwed up again, and because of that they were now trying to kill us. My ears were still ringing from the blast, but I could hear Pedro hollering at Alpha Squad to stop shooting. Another bullet hit the side of the temple, causing an explosion of stone shrapnel.

I snatched a look over the ruined temple wall, and spotted Pedro lying on the ground. Blood ran from the side of his head, trickling down into the whirl-pool lake. Had Alpha Squad killed him?

Right then it felt as if the storm had raged its way into in my head. Pedro had betrayed us, but he only wanted to help his country. He wasn't a bad guy. I grabbed a chunk of stone and hurled it at our attackers. The shot caught Kyle Flutes in the chest, and he fired again.

"Stop!" Mum cried. "My children are in here!"

"You shouldn't have brought them, then," Veronika replied.

"You think I don't know that?" Mum screamed. "You can *have* the emerald tablet."

"No, you can't!" I shouted.

"We can make a deal," Dad hollered.

"Too late for that now," Veronika snarled.

She fired again at the temple. Dad shielded me and Pan, and a flying stone shard cut through his jungle suit and sliced his shoulder. He grasped the wound to stop blood flowing.

"Jane, we have to get out of here," he said.

Mum's fists clenched at her sides as she watched our attackers through a crack in the temple wall.

"I can take them," she hissed.

Dad put a hand on her shoulder. "Not these two, Jane."

Mum slapped the hand away. "I can, John!"

I groped my belt, feeling the holstered gadgets. "There's one UED left," I said. "We could use it as a distraction to reach the helicopter. Can either of you fly one?"

Dad nodded, then cursed under his breath. "Maybe we could reach it, but they'd shoot us down before we were ten feet off the mountain."

"Then we have to take the waterfall," I said. "It's our only escape route. We jump into the lake, and let it spit us out with the waterfall, like the Aztecs wanted."

Mum shook her head, refusing to listen.

"Jane," Dad said. "Jake could be right."

Another shot hit the outside of the temple. Alpha Squad were stalking closer.

Mum glared at Dad with a rage I'd never seen before, and I've seen Mum angry *a lot*. I wondered if really she was furious at *herself*, for letting us get into this situation. She gazed around the ruined temple, desperate for any escape.

"There's no other way out, Jane," Dad insisted. "You know what the marker is telling us to do. We have to trust the Aztecs."

"John..."

"Jane, we can do this."

"They're our children, John."

"That's why we have to go. If we stay here we'll die."

"How did this happen, John? We were retired. We were safe from *this*."

"You're not retired," Pan said. "You're *here* now.

234

Dad's right, we have to follow the marker."

Mum stared at her, and then Dad. She clutched her amulet – Isis, the mother and protector goddess – and whispered something that none of us heard.

"All right. But we do it together."

Mum snatched the UED from my belt before I had a chance, and set the timer for five seconds. She gripped the device, ready to press the activation button.

"Run straight for the lake," she said. "Stay calm, let the water take you. Trust the Aztecs. Remember your training."

I nodded, praying there was no *actual* training for jumping off a waterfall that I'd somehow missed. I'd never seen Pan's face so pale. I knew what she was thinking – that she couldn't do this, that she didn't do "action" things, like she kept insisting. That was crazy, and anyway, she had no choice. She *had* to do this.

I gave her shoulder three quick taps, our training signal to turn. "Race you," I said.

"What?"

"Race you to the tomb. Last one in has to call the other 'lord' for the rest of the mission."

She stared at me, but couldn't resist the challenge. Almost immediately some of the colour came back into her cheeks.

"Get ready to be humiliated, brother."

"*Everyone* get ready," Mum whispered.

"Good luck, everyone," Dad said.

Mum pressed the activation button on the UED. I glimpsed the five-second countdown begin as she hurled the bomb out over the temple wall.

"Go!" she cried.

28

I started spinning the moment I hit the water.

The blast from the UED was still loud in my ears as I sank into a world of bubbles and panic, and firelight from the explosion. At first the shock of the cold overrode all other senses. Hitting the lake felt like jumping into an icebox, and I screamed bubbles, wasting precious air. By the time I was aware of anything other than the cold, the whirlpool already had me in its grip.

I remembered Mum's instruction – *let the water take you.* But instinct caused my legs to kick, and I struggled against the swirling current. I was moving too fast to see any of my family. Had they even survived the dash from the temple? I struck the side of the lake basin and screamed more bubbles, wasting more air. The whirlpool spun me faster and sucked me deeper, down into the cold darkness.

Let the water take you.

The water *was* taking me. I was too disorientated to stop it. The whirlpool whisked me like a sock in a washing machine, so I hit the side of the lake again and then again. I was near the bottom, about to be sucked down the sinkhole.

And then I dropped.

Have you ever been on a waterslide? You know the moment when the slide spits you from its end? This felt the same, except that I was screaming and thought I was about to die, and that my family was also probably dead.

I fell maybe ten metres in darkness, and splash-landed in a shallow pool. Water gushed onto my head from the sinkhole. I thought I heard someone shout, but it was hard to tell beyond the roar of pouring water. I tried to call out but I was on the move again, rushing on my back down a surface that felt like it had been deliberately smoothed into a slide. Water splashed up my face, and I was desperate for light; the darkness was so disorientating. Then I glimpsed some, and I wished I hadn't.

Daylight.

The slide was about to spit me straight out of the side of the mountain. I was about to become part of the waterfall.

Let it take you!

No, don't, stop it from taking you!

One moment I was sliding on stone on my back, and the next there was nothing beneath me but sky.

The chute fired me from the cliff face amidst the spray of the waterfall. It must have been a hundred metre drop, but there was no time to make a plan, no time to do anything but fall, kicking my legs and flailing my arms, as if I might somehow be able to control the drop.

At the last moment I tucked my arms into my sides and locked my legs together, so I hit the plunge pool like a harpoon and shot down deep. I had to get to the surface to breathe, but it was hard to tell which way was up – the force of the waterfall hitting the pool turned everything into bubbles, flipping me like a bath toy and driving me deeper underwater. At the same time, another force pulled me down, as if I was being sucked to my death.

Let it take you.

I had no choice now, anyway. I was too weak to get to the surface. I'd drown here in the plunge pool if I kept trying. Fighting every instinct, I stopped swimming and finally let the water take me.

I shot through another sinkhole at the bottom of the pool, and slid along a pitch-black tunnel, snatching frantic breaths between waves of water that slapped my face.

Get control! Remember your training!

There was no light anywhere, not even a sliver. I reached up and my fingertips scraped against the rough tunnel ceiling as I slid down a tunnel that grew even steeper, taking me deeper underground.

It's not easy to stay calm when you're rushing down-hill in total darkness with no idea where you're going to end up, but I tried to remember that this was all part of the Aztecs' plan...

I splashed into another pool, a build-up of water at what felt like the entrance to a narrower tunnel, forced myself through and slid again. This passage was half the size of the last, so the water was now all around me, with just a slim space to breathe.

I slid for a few seconds before I hit another pool, another rock wall and another opening. The rushing water tried to force me through, but the hole was too tight. I could just fit, but there would be no space to breathe. But what choice did I have? There was no chance I'd be able to get back to the waterfall. I could either stay here or go on.

I screamed, slapped the cave wall and called for my family. I was desperate to know I wasn't alone down here in the darkness. Something hit me hard on the side of my head. I sank under the water and came up dazed.

"Jake! Jake, is that you?"

"Pan!" I cried.

We gripped each other's arms, so relieved not to be alone. I could feel her shaking as hard as I was, from cold and fear and exhaustion.

"Where are we, Jake?"

"Underground. The tunnel gets narrower here, but it's the only way through."

"Where are Mum and Dad?"

"I don't know, Pan, but we have to go on."

"We could drown in there."

"No, this is what the Aztecs meant for us. Mum told us to trust them, remember?"

"But what if there's no way out?"

"There will be. You have to come after me. You can't stay here. Are you ready?"

She wasn't, and neither was I. I was trying to sound confident, to give her the courage she needed to go through, but I knew there was a chance Mum and Dad hadn't made it, and that we might not either if we entered this tunnel. But we'd die if we stayed here, too; we didn't really have a choice.

"OK," Pan gasped. "I'm ready."

I took as deep a breath as I could, and went feet first through the opening. This tunnel was less steep than the last, but the water was fiercer, forcing me along the tight passage. I couldn't even reach up – the rock ceiling was an inch above my nose and the passage was entirely full of rushing water. I was running out of air. Pressure grew in my chest like someone was sitting on me, crushing my ribs.

Then, suddenly, I jolted to a stop. Some sort of creature grabbed me by the chest. I wriggled to pull free. As it gripped harder I realized that it wasn't a creature at all; it was a hand. I saw the blurry outline of a person in a hole in the tunnel ceiling.

Dad!

I gripped his wrist, but Pan crashed into me from behind, tearing me away. I slid further down the tunnel and hit another rock wall. The force of the water pinned me there as it rushed through an opening that was too tight for me to fit into. I was trapped – unable to go on, unable to swim back, unable to breathe.

Something slapped against my face. It felt like a sheet pressed against me by the force of water. I grasped it weakly and it pulled away. I realized I was holding a pair of trousers from a jungle suit. They were tied to a shirt, and then more trousers – my family had stripped off their clothes to make a lifeline to drag me back.

I clung on tighter as they pulled the line against the rushing water. I kicked my legs in an effort to help, fighting my way inch by inch back up the tunnel. It felt now like a whole herd of elephants was stamping on my chest. I had no breath left at all. My grip began to slip.

Dad snatched hold of my shirt and this time he didn't let go. He yanked me up through the hole and out of the tunnel. I was too weak to help; I just let myself be saved.

"Jake? Jake!"

I coughed out some water, and then leaned over and threw up what felt like half of the waterfall.

"I'm OK..." I spluttered.

I'm not sure that was true, but it seemed to reassure

Mum, who grabbed me in a quick hug before plonking me back down on the rock.

"We made it, Jake!" Pan said.

Dad wrung water from their jungle suits and they pulled them back on, preferring a wet shirt and trousers to exploring a lost tomb in their underpants. My suit was soaked too, but the water actually felt nice, cooling my skin against the heat of ... wherever we now were.

I sat up and tried to make sense of my surroundings. We were in an underground chamber, with carved walls that were covered in painted Aztec scenes. A square exit in one led to stone steps, and more darkness.

"I think we're inside the second Storm Peak," Dad said, squeezing more water from his shirt before he slid it back on. "The tunnels carried us underneath it."

Mum took the smart-goggles from my belt, and used their torch to study the paintings on the walls. "These scenes show Quetzalcoatl," she said.

She moved along the wall, muttering to herself as she read the paintings.

"What does it say, Mum?" Pan asked. "Is this the tomb?"

"These are written to *us*," she said.

"Us?"

"To whomever followed the markers to get here."

"So what does it say?"

Mum reached to the wall, running fingertips over the painted glyphs as she translated the Aztec writing. "*You are the chosen one. You have found the three markers that have led you to the tomb of the Feathered Serpent.*"

"So this *is* the tomb," Pan said.

Mum kept moving, kept reading. "*You are the great chosen one. Servant of Quetzalcoatl. Yours is the great duty, for you shall ... you shall...*"

She trailed off, still staring at the ancient writing. When she finally turned, she looked like someone had just slapped her round the face. Dazed, confused, pained.

"My God, John," she said, "what have we done?"

"What is it, Jane? What does it say?"

She didn't look at the writing again – she just stared at us as she recited the rest of the wall inscription: "*You shall now be sacrificed to feed the god with your blood, so that he may live for eternity.*"

She clutched her necklace symbol so tightly that it cut her hand. A line of blood slid down her wrist.

"This whole time we've thought the Aztecs wanted their people to find the tomb," she said, "but that wasn't it at all. The markers weren't meant to *lead* us to the tomb. They were meant to *lure* us here. The Aztecs wanted us to become sacrifices to the god. They led us here for one reason. To die."

29

I wanted to go first, but Pan went for the opening before me. Mum grabbed her arm and pulled her back, so *she* could go first. But Dad grabbed Mum's arm and pushed his way in before everyone. By the time we entered the secret tunnel I was somehow at the back, and we were all annoyed with each other.

"Night vision," Dad said.

He used the smart-goggles to lead us deeper into the darkness of the mountain. We climbed stone steps, and then shuffled along a tunnel that was so narrow I could touch the arched walls on either side. The stone was hot, as if we were walking into a pizza oven. The air was thick and stifling, and smelled of damp.

The Aztecs had led us here as victims, to be sacrificed to Quetzalcoatl. That meant there would be traps, maybe lots of traps. We kept bumping into Dad as he stopped and used the goggles to scan the walls and ceiling, ordering them to switch to *thermal*, *torch*, and then back to *night vision*. He was being sensible, but I kept thinking of Sami in that bed, relying on us here and now to save him. The deeper we moved into the mountain, the tighter my insides twisted with impatience and frustration. Did we really have to go *this* slowly?

"We need to move faster!" I called.

"Jake," Mum snapped. "Your father knows what he is doing."

I bit my lip; arguing with them wouldn't help.

Squelches from our sodden jungle suits echoed along the narrow passage, but the shirts and trousers didn't take long to dry in the intense heat of this place, so we soon walked in silence. The path rose and twisted, as if we were climbing a helter-skelter inside the mountain. It grew even steeper, turning again and again – and then it ended, and we all stood and stared in the light of Dad's torch.

We'd come out at a crack inside the mountain, ten metres wide and at least fifty high. One wall was sheer rock. The other was covered with skulls. Human skulls – thousands, packed so tight I could barely see a sliver of rock between them. Empty eyes glared down at us. Jaws hung open, as if the skulls were laughing, like an audience of skeletons at a comedy show.

"What is *this*?" I asked.

Mum stroked one of the skulls at the bottom of the wall. Her hand trembled a little, as if the brittle jaw might snap at her fingers. "It's a *tzompantli*," she said.

"A what?"

"A *skull wall*," Dad explained. "The skulls of sacrificial victims put on display for the gods. These were common on Aztec temples and tombs."

"This was *common*?" I asked. "There must be ten thousand skulls here."

Mum moved along the base of the wall, scanning the grotesque decoration. "I'd say *thirty* thousand."

"Hang on," I said. "So as well as the coffin of Quetzalcoatl, the Aztecs dragged thirty thousand skulls with them here? But why?"

"They needed them to survive," Mum replied.

"Survive?"

"Human sacrifices kept the gods happy," Dad said. "The Aztecs believed the world had been destroyed four times because the gods hadn't been fed enough human sacrifices. These skulls were a sign to those gods that they were behaving."

"So if they were put here for Quetzalcoatl to see, then his tomb must be close, right?" Pan said.

Dad turned to Mum, and light from his goggles caught her worried glance back at him. She was stroking her Isis amulet again, which was not a good sign. I remembered their lesson: the closer you got to a tomb, the more dangerous things usually became.

Dad turned and looked up, so the torch beam

shone up the crevasse wall opposite the skulls. Tiny holes pockmarked the sheer rock face, but they were too far apart to use as handholds and there were no other cracks or ridges. The cliff looked like it had been deliberately smoothed to prevent anyone from climbing. There was only one way up.

"We have to climb the skulls," I said.

"Looks like there's a ledge at the top," Pan added.

Dad grasped one of the skulls, seeing if he could pull it from the wall, and then prodded its eye sockets. "They seem sturdy. You couldn't really ask for a better climbing wall, with all these hand grips and footholds."

Mum tested the skulls too, mumbling disapprovingly, but finally sighed and nodded. "Pan and Jake, you go first," she said.

I looked at her, surprised. She trusted us to lead?

"So we can catch you if you fall," she explained.

I'm guessing you've never scaled a wall of human skulls. I don't know how the Aztecs fixed them so firmly to the cliff, but they didn't slip as they took our weight. It was as if they had been carved straight from the rock. It wasn't as good a climbing wall as we'd hoped, though. We could get our fingers into eye sockets, but our boots wouldn't fit into the jaws. We'd have to widen them.

"Can I kick the skulls?" I asked.

"No," Mum said, her voice echoing up the crevasse. "These need to be recorded. Archaeo-anthropologists can study them for insights into—"

I kicked the skulls. It was the only way to climb and I think Mum knew it because she didn't tell me off as I toe-punted one of the jaws. Bits of bone showered over Pan and my parents.

"Hey!" Pan snapped. "Stop spraying me with skull."

"Jake, warn Pandora whenever you're about to kick a skull."

"Hey, Pan? I'm about to kick a skull."

I kicked harder, covering her in bone.

"I got some in my mouth!" she wailed.

"Better keep it shut, then."

"Stop squabbling!" Mum ordered.

I reached up and dug my fingers into a skull's nose cavity. As I climbed higher I stared into its hollow eye sockets, and for the first time since we'd come to Honduras, I felt cold.

"Who were all these people?" I asked.

"Prisoners of war," Dad replied. "The Aztecs attacked other tribes to capture victims to sacrifice."

"How did they kill them?"

"Most had their hearts cut out with knives."

"You mean ... while they were still alive?"

"They weren't alive for long after, but yes. Others were killed with arrows. And there was one particularly unpleasant ceremony in which victims had their skin—"

"John," Mum interrupted. "That's enough."

A jawbone came away in my hand. I was about to

fall, but Pan pressed me back into the wall, instinctively coming to my rescue.

"Thanks," I gasped.

"What's going on up there?" Mum asked, struggling to see us higher up the wall. "You're not fooling around, are you?"

Pan looked at me, rolling her eyes. "No, Mum."

"You two wait there," Mum said. "I'll climb past to lead."

"We're fine, Mum," I said.

She was already moving to get above us. Something in me snapped. It was stupid, but I refused to let her lead. *We* were leading, and we were doing fine. She just couldn't let herself trust us. Or trust *me*.

I climbed faster, kicking footholds into brittle bone. Mum's shouts grew louder, rattling the skulls. She was gaining on me.

"Jake! Stop this instant!"

I reached and grabbed another skull by the jawbone. It slipped a fraction from the wall, and something *happened*. I didn't know what until it *had* happened. I heard a creak, and felt a rush of air. Something stung my cheek and the skull exploded, spraying shards at my face.

Mum pinned me to the wall to stop me falling. "Are you OK?" she demanded. "Jake?"

Blood slid down my cheek and into my mouth. I wiped bone from my eyes and saw an arrow stuck into what remained of the skull. It had fired from a hole in the opposite wall, missing my head by inches.

"What happened?" Dad called.

"The skull," I breathed. "It shifted from the wall when I grabbed it."

Mum leaned to inspect the skull, and then turned to see the hole in the rock face behind us. "There are bows behind that wall," she said. "They're rigged to fire when we touch certain skulls. We need to get down straightaway."

"Down? It's just as dangerous that way as it is going up."

"This isn't a discussion, Jake."

"But we're closer to the top now," Pan said.

Mum closed her eyes and breathed in, containing her frustration. I knew what she was thinking: *Never again.*

Dad noticed too. He tried to sound calm, as if everything was under control. "We'll carry on, but carefully. We look for the holes in the opposite wall, and avoid the skulls that they face."

"I'll go first," I said.

"You certainly will not," Mum replied.

I didn't have time to argue; she was already climbing – slowly, now, inspecting each skull before she touched it, and then turning to make sure there was no hole in the opposite wall. She reminded me of a sloth inching its way up a tree.

"Follow my path exactly," she insisted.

It was painfully slow, but suddenly I didn't

mind – none of us wanted an arrow in our neck. I thought of all the bows hidden in the cliff behind me, arrows loaded, drawstrings twitching...

"Watch out!" Mum warned.

One of the skulls fell past us down the wall. It hit another about ten metres below, and an arrow fired, shattering that skull.

"It was just a loose one," Mum said. "Be careful."

I looked down, watching the falling skull hit several more on its descent. Below, another arrow fired, and then another. Only ... the falling skull hadn't hit *that* many others. Arrows were firing where they shouldn't have been.

Dad saw it too. "It set those others off too. But we're safe up here."

An arrow shot into the wall a metre from Dad's arm.

Another smashed into a skull right beside Pan.

"They're all going off!" she screamed.

"Everybody climb!" I cried.

"No," Mum called. "Stay still. Don't move!"

I was already climbing, kicking footholds, racing to reach the ledge at the top. Pan was right behind me, and Mum and Dad must have followed because I heard them roaring at me to stop.

Another arrow slammed into the wall above Pan's head.

"Keep moving!" I yelled. "We're almost there."

Bone fragments showered over us, cutting my

cheeks and getting in my mouth. I spat them out, grabbed an arrow shaft and used it to pull myself onto the ledge. I reached to help Pan up, and then Mum and Dad.

We lay at the top of the skull wall, coughing and wheezing. We were covered in bits of skull, sweat and dust from the rocks, and cuts from bone shrapnel.

Mum touched her amulet, took a deep breath and held it. It was the same calming technique that she'd taught me, only it didn't work. She whirled at me, glaring. "What were you thinking, Jake? I told you to stay still."

"We might have been killed," I gasped.

"We almost *were* killed. We should have stayed where we were."

"We'd have been sitting ducks," Pan said.

"I said *stay*," Mum snapped. "That was the right plan, to wait for them all to fire."

"And you're certain that none of us would have been hit?" Pan asked.

"Of course not, but it was less risky than—"

"Well, I am certain that none of us *were* hit," Pan interrupted. "So Jake's plan worked."

"It wasn't a plan! It was dumb luck. I gave you an order."

"An order?" Pan laughed. "We're not in the army."

"Enough," Dad barked. "We made it. Maybe it was the wrong decision, maybe not, but we're alive."

"Then it was the right decision," Pan muttered.

"I said, enough," Dad repeated.

Pan and Mum both sighed, as if they each felt they would have won the argument. But Dad was right: if we hoped to reach the tomb, we had to focus on whatever dangers lay ahead, not those we'd already survived. We were all alive – but for how long?

30

It wasn't enough for Mum that we had climbed a wall of skulls, dodged dozens of arrows, and survived. She was upset about *how* we'd survived. She kept rubbing the goddess's wings on her amulet. It was amazing she'd not worn the thing away.

She was convinced that I'd panicked, but that wasn't true. I *had* taken a chance by continuing to climb the skull wall, but it would have been just as risky to stay still. I'd made a plan, and we'd all lived.

Pan was properly fuming about it. Lurking at the back, she'd gone into one of her mega-sulks. Her long fringe rustled with her constant sighs and muttering.

We walked in silence through another carved tunnel, following the shaky ribbon of light from Dad's torch. Sweat gushed down my forehead and stung my eyes. The air grew drier, parching my mouth. I pressed a hand against the rock. It wasn't just warm, it was *hot*, and it trembled against my palm. It was almost as if we were heading deeper into a living thing, an artery to the heart of the mountain.

"Remember your training," Dad said. "Be alert for anything."

But this wasn't the same as the tombs Sami had created in the simulator. Those were labyrinths, with passages leading from passages, wrong turns and dead ends. This was different. Dad kept looking for secret doors, but there was only one path, and it was the one the Aztecs wanted us to follow. To them we were here for a single purpose: to die.

"There's an opening ahead," Dad called.

The passage led to another cave. It was wide, with a high domed ceiling. A stone pier stuck out about thirty metres into a chasm, like a giant diving board. On the other side of the chasm, another small ledge jutted from the cave wall. A stone pillar rose from it with a reed basket fixed near its top. A stone ring – like a sideways basketball hoop – jutted out of the pillar above the basket.

Dad pulled the flare gun from my belt, and fired it up into the arched darkness. As the firework rose, its livid red light shimmered off the stalactites. Bats wriggled, irritated to have their sleep disturbed. We watched as the flare fell past our ledge into the space below, and then slid down the sloped side of a pit that looked like a giant stone funnel. Still sizzling, it disappeared through a hole at the bottom.

"What *is* this place?" I asked.

Dad looked at Mum, who nodded.

"It's a sports field," Dad said.

"Sport?"

"An Aztec sport called *ollamalitzli*," Mum explained. "See that stone hoop on the pillar? Two teams fought for a ball and tried to get it through the hoop."

"Like basketball?" I asked.

"Sort of," Pan agreed. "Except it was played before sacrificial ceremonies. The losing team had their hearts ripped out."

"Of course they did," I muttered. "Those Aztecs *loved* ripping out hearts."

"Remember, Jake, we are not here to judge them."

I did remember Mum's lesson, but it was hard *not* to judge. The Aztecs wanted us dead – although I couldn't see how *this* was a deadly trap.

A small wooden table sat at the side of our ledge, with a ball about the size of a tennis ball on it. I picked it up. It felt like hard rubber.

"They want us to play the game," Mum said, talking about the Aztecs as if they were alive now. "We have to throw the ball through the hoop."

"See the basket under it?" Dad added. "My guess is that if the ball goes through and lands in the basket, that will trigger a door to open ... somewhere."

"And if we miss?" Pan asked.

"The ball falls into the pit, and we're stuck here."

"But... That's it?" I said.

It wouldn't be easy – in fact, the shot seemed almost impossible from so far away – but I'd expected something far more unpleasant, like deadly snakes, or spiked walls. I noticed Mum's shoulders relax too, relieved that she wasn't putting her children's lives at risk again.

"I'll take the shot," she said.

"What?" I held the ball away. "Pan's the best shot by far."

"Jake, give me the ball."

She reached for it, but I turned away, refusing to hand it over. "It's Pan's shot, Mum."

"Jake, I am not asking. I am telling you to—"

"And I'm telling *you*. Pan's got this."

This whole time Pan was glaring at me. I think she meant for me to leave her out of this, but I couldn't. I honestly did think Pan was the best person to take the shot, and she knew she was too. But also, it was another chance to show Mum and Dad that we were good enough to be here.

I handed Pan the ball and, still glaring at me, she clenched it so tightly her knuckles were white. Mum tried to grab it from her, but Dad put a hand on her arm.

"Jake's right, Jane."

For the next ten minutes, Pan and Dad stood at the end of the stone pier, discussing the best angle for the throw. The more I considered it, the harder the shot seemed. Imagine standing at the bottom of a house and trying to chuck an apple into a tiny attic window. Then imagine having to do that when your friend's life was on the line, and maybe your family's lives too.

Mum stayed with me on the ledge, rubbing her amulet as she watched. I suspected she was fighting an urge to march up the pier and snatch the ball. But she knew Pan had to concentrate. Instead, she turned and snapped at me.

"Jake, focus!"

"Eh?"

Mum looked a bit flustered at her outburst. "I... If Pandora manages the shot," she said, stressing the word *if*, "some sort of door should open, but perhaps only for a short time. So we have to spot it fast. It must be somewhere here."

I nodded and looked along the ledge. It didn't seem like there was any door in the rock. In fact, this whole thing was weird. A ball game? Was that really all there was to this? Or were we missing something?

"OK," Dad called. "We're ready."

The only thing Pan looked ready to do was throw up. Her grip hadn't relaxed on the ball since she'd taken it from me, and the uncertainty in her eyes had given way to something more like terror. Was she thinking the same thing as me? This one throw could decide whether we found the tomb or not, whether Sami lived or died. No wonder she was clutching the ball so tight.

She was overthinking it, I realized. The times we'd seen her sharpshooting before had all been under pressure, when she'd barely been thinking, just acting on instinct. That's what she needed now, a little bit of panic.

Suddenly I charged towards her along the pier, waving my arms and yelling, like I was fleeing some sort of monster. "Pan!" I wailed. "Throw the ball! There's something coming!"

Pan and Dad both turned and looked back, more confused than scared.

"Eh?" Pan said.

"What's coming, Jake?" Dad asked.

"I don't see anything," Mum muttered from further back. "Are you seeing things? Maybe you should lie down?"

I sighed and shrugged. "No... It was just... It doesn't matter."

Pan grinned. "I don't need the help, brother," she said. "I got this."

And then she turned and took the throw.

I held my breath, as if breathing might send the shot off course. The ball flew up and across the arc of Dad's torchlight. It sailed straight through the hoop, and landed in the basket!

Pan squealed with delight and high-fived Dad. She rushed back along the pier and gave me a playful shove. "Sharp shooting, eh, Jake?"

I smiled, but Pan was actually looking at Mum.

Mum said something that sounded like "well done", but it was tricky to tell. She was already moving along the ledge, inspecting the rock wall.

"Did anyone see a door open?" she asked. "Look for splits in the rock."

Pan and Dad rushed to search, but I stayed where I was on the ledge. That tingle in my belly was growing stronger, a sense that something wasn't right. I walked to the end of the pier and stared across the gap to the pillar and hoop. The basket had tilted from the weight of the ball, just as Mum had predicted. But the Aztecs *wanted* us dead, that was the whole point of luring us into this mountain. Why would they have given us a way to survive?

Unless they wanted us to think we could survive. They *wanted* us to make that shot.

What if *that* was the trap?

A grinding sound echoed around the cavern, like scraping rocks. The stone pillar began to tremble, and then tilt forward. I stepped back, realizing what was happening. The pillar had been perfectly balanced, so that even the small weight of the ball was enough to tip it over...

The pillar fell.

I staggered back and slipped over as the top of the stone column crashed against the end of the pier. Stone shards skittered towards me and dropped into the funnel pit below.

I sat up, shaken but relieved, and flashed my

family a grin to show them I was OK. Mum and Pan had begun to rush along the pier, but stopped suddenly, staring.

"That wasn't so bad," I said.

"Jake!" Pan screamed. "Behind you!"

Dark cracks spread along the pier. It was breaking up!

I scrambled up and ran. Behind me, chunks of rock fell into the pit as more and more of the pier collapsed. The darkness was chasing me, catching up...

"Jake!"

I grabbed Mum's hand just as the ground gave way under my boots. She fell with me. Pan grasped her wrist and she fell too. Only Dad was left on the ledge, clinging on to Pan with one hand and the cave wall with the other as we swung below him in a human chain.

"Hang on!" Dad grunted.

"That's a stupid thing to say!" Pan yelled.

"Just do it!"

"Obviously we're doing it! That's why it's a stupid thing to say!"

"Just hang on!"

"Stop saying it!"

And how long could *he* hang on for? Pan screamed as Mum slipped from her grasp. At the same time, Dad let go of the wall and we all fell.

We hit the sloped side of the pit and slid among rubble from the pier. I scrabbled at the surface, trying to slow my descent, but I was sliding too fast.

I shot through the opening at the bottom of the funnel, and into a stone chute. I fell again and slid again, along another tunnel and into another cave, where the ground finally levelled out and I stopped sliding. The rest of my family tumbled in after me, and we lay in the darkness, coughing and swearing.

"Is anyone hurt?" Dad gasped.

"Me," Pan said.

"Me too," I said.

"Is anyone seriously hurt?" Mum asked.

"Still me."

"Still me too."

"Has anyone got anything other than bumps and bruises?"

It was hard to tell. I had a lot of bumps and bruises on my arms and legs, and a cut on my head. I tasted blood in my mouth, but I didn't think any of the wounds were deep.

"Where are we, anyway?" I wheezed.

"A tunnel," Pan said. "Maybe we were meant to keep sliding."

She didn't sound convinced. Mum had said that everything in this place was designed to kill us. Again I sensed that we were not seeing everything here. Was that slide really all there was to this trap?

A growl echoed around the chamber.

"Jane?" Dad asked. "Are you hurt?"

"I'm fine," Mum replied.

Another growl, deeper.

"You don't sound fine," Pan said.

"That noise wasn't me..."

Dad scrabbled in the rubble until he found his smart-goggles. He ordered them to switch to thermal. He turned, peered deeper into the cave and sat up sharply.

"Nobody move," he gasped.

"What is it?" Pan asked.

"There's a jaguar in here with us."

Pan's breaths quickened. "You mean jaguar as in the big cat?"

"What other type of jaguar could he mean?" Mum hissed.

"I don't know ... the car."

"Why would there be a Jaguar car in here?"

"I was ... I was just hoping."

"Just don't move," Dad repeated. "It is twenty metres away, watching us. Don't panic. Jaguars only attack if they are threatened."

"Threatened how?" I whispered.

"If they feel cornered, or their lair is invaded."

"You mean exactly the situation we are in now?"

"I think it's moving," Pan breathed.

"We have to stand up and get back," Dad said. "We need to show it we are not a threat. Jake, don't startle it in any way."

"Why me? You think I'm going to go and poke its nose?"

"Just stay quiet..."

I slid back, helping Pan up from the rubble. Her hand tightened on my wrist as another growl filled the tunnel.

"*This* can't be the trap," I said.

"Is a man-eating cat not enough for you?" Pan replied.

"But the Aztecs can't have planned *this*," I said. "Not five hundred years ago."

"Let's deal with one problem at a time," Mum said. "It can see us, remember? Just get as far back as possible, so it knows we're not a threat."

Snick-clank!

Warm air rushed from behind. Instinctively, I pulled Pan and Mum forward as something dropped from the tunnel ceiling and slammed into the ground. Sparks sprayed up at our faces, and in the brief light I glimpsed a grey wall behind me where there had been no wall before. It had fallen from the ceiling, separating us from Dad, and trapping us in with the jaguar.

"What was that?" Pan cried.

"Keep your voice down," Mum warned. "The cat..."

The snarling grew louder. I don't know if the creature was getting closer or angrier, or both.

We backed up against the slab. It was cold and smooth, cut from a glassy stone that didn't feel the same as the rest of the cave.

"What is this thing?" Pan demanded.

Dad spoke to us from the other side of the stone barrier, which can't have been more than an inch thick.

"This is cut from obsidian," he said. "Looks like it fell from a groove in the tunnel roof. The bottom is razor sharp."

"Obsidian, John?" Mum insisted.

"Just don't panic..."

"What's so special about obsidian?" I asked.

"Just stay by me," Mum insisted. "I don't think the jaguar's coming closer."

"But what's so special about obsidian?"

"It was a precious stone to the Aztecs," Pan said. "They used it to make special knives."

"What type of knives, Pan?"

"Knives for human sacrifices."

Snick-clank!

Another stone guillotine fell from the ceiling, this time a few feet in front of us. We pressed back against the first as the new weapon struck the ground, causing more sparks to fly. Beyond it, the jaguar hissed and spat.

"Ha!" I yelled. "You can't get us now!"

Then the obsidian wall rose. So did the one behind it, sliding back into its groove in the cave ceiling. We staggered back into Dad's arms.

"Night vision," Dad barked.

Whatever he saw in his goggles caused him to grab me and Pan and pull us further back.

"It's coming," he warned.

I reached for my belt, feeling for the laser cutter. "I'm going to laser it."

"No, Jake!" Mum warned. "You'll anger it."

"It's *already* angry, Mum."

"Just get behind me."

"You get behind *me*. I've got the weapon."

"Everyone calm down," Dad said.

"Calm down?" Pan spat. "There's a man-eating cat attacking us from one direction and giant knives in every other place. Please tell me this is one of those funny situations you've been in loads of times before and know a way out of?"

"Not exactly this, no," Dad muttered.

Snick-clank!

Another obsidian blade dropped from the ceiling, blocking the cat off again.

Snick-clank!

"Move!" Dad roared.

He shoved us forward as a blade fell from behind, landing where we'd just been gathered.

Snick-clank!

The next blade came down inches in front of us. Now that one shot back up into its ceiling groove, and so did the one behind us.

"Get back into the tunnel!" Dad called. "If we can find out how we triggered this trap we might be able to stop it."

I tried to move back, but another blade landed in the way. The Aztecs hadn't meant for anyone to leave this chamber. We were sacrifices, to be sliced apart to honour their gods.

Snick-clank!

Snick-clank!

Blades rose and fell like pistons, spraying up sparks. I dived forward to avoid another as the rest of my family moved the other way.

"Get to the back!" Mum screamed.

What if there was no way of stopping these things? We'd be trapped. Moving forward seemed even crazier. Above the clatter of the rising and falling blades, I could hear the jaguar going berserk. But it had got *into* this cave; surely it knew a way out? *That* was the way we had to go.

I looked up from the ground, trying to see the grooves from which the blades were sliding. It was too dark, and my eyes were blurred with sweat.

"Pandora! Jake!"

Another obsidian blade fell from its groove. I slid back far enough to save my life, but not my shirt. The blade caught my sleeve, pinning me to the ground. I tried to tear it free but the shirt was made of BioSteel. It was like pulling on a chain.

Snick-clank!

I slammed my body into the blade in front of me as another crashed down behind. It caught my other sleeve and pinned *that* one to the ground too, so I was stuck. If there was a blade right above me, I'd be sliced in half.

I kept screaming until both blades rose back into their places in the ceiling. I'd got lucky – now I had to *use* that luck. I stayed where I was, trying to think through my fear. There was no groove directly above me, so the distance between the two that tore my sleeves was about a metre.

"Jake!" Pan screamed.

"Get up against a blade!" I yelled.

"What?"

"Next time one comes down, press up against it," I called. "When it goes up, take one step forward and stay still. Another will come down in front of you, then do the same thing."

"Jake, I—"

"Just do it!"

I knew she'd understand, but would she trust me? And where was the jaguar? I tried to listen, but the clashing blades were too loud as they continued to rise and fall along the cave.

Another blade came down in front of me. I fought the instinct to stagger back and instead rushed forward to stand against the slab. My nose pressed against its cold stone.

The blade rose and I stepped forward and waited, summoning every scrap of courage to stand still. A few seconds later, another blade slammed down an inch in front of me. I cried out and moved forward a small step. I clenched my fists, urging myself to stay still again. I had to forget about all the other blades, and the jaguar at the end. My whole world was the blade in front of me, the blade behind and the slim gap in the middle.

The blade lifted. I stepped forward.

My fear increased with each step. How long could my luck hold? I pinned my arms against my sides to stop them from shaking. Another blade rose. I moved again, stopped again.

"How many more can there be?" I hollered.

Another blade crashed down ahead of me, causing sparks to lash up at my face, so I lurched forward in shock. I froze, realizing I'd lost track of how far I'd moved. Was it one metre? Two? How far should I go back?

I stood for a moment, a dozen obsidian blades clashing and sparking behind me, before I realized that there were none *in front* of me. I'd reached the end of the trap!

Except...

In the dark I could just see the jaguar ten metres away, crouched low and curled back against the tunnel wall. Its ears were pinned back and its mouth was open, showing me its dagger teeth, but the cat made no noise. I wish I could tell you I saw respect in its eyes, or something like that. I didn't. I saw a wild, terrified animal whose home had been invaded. I remembered my utility belt and its force field. Pedro had warned us to use it only in emergencies, and I couldn't think of a bigger one than this...

"Nice kitty," I whispered.

Very slowly I reached to my belt. My finger hovered over the button beneath the clasp.

Maybe the jaguar thought I was standing my ground, rather than just being paralyzed with fear, because it turned, scrambled up the tunnel wall and vanished through a crack in the rock.

Something touched my arm. I whirled around, so startled I almost pressed the force-field button. It was Pan! She'd trusted me and followed my plan.

"Did we reach the end?" she gasped.

I grabbed her in reply and hugged her tightly. "We did it!"

"But where's the jaguar?"

My grin grew even wider as I pointed to the crack in the cave wall. "There's a way out."

The rocks around the crack began to tremble. Several fell from the ceiling and thumped to the ground, and a creaking sound echoed around the cave. It sounded like some sort of mechanism was grinding to a stop above the ceiling.

Then, all at once, the blades retracted back into their grooves. It had felt like we'd walked miles, when in fact the cave was barely thirty metres long.

Mum called to us from the other end. "We found the trigger. But we can't keep the blades up for long."

"Hurry, then," Pan replied. "There's a way through."

"No, come this way," Dad demanded.

"We need to look for a way out," Mum added.

"What?" I said. "No, we have to go *on*. The tomb is this way."

"Forget the tomb!" Mum shouted. "Our mission now is to stay alive. That means going back."

"No!" I yelled. "Our mission is to save Sami. We need to go on, *this* way."

"You almost got killed just now," Dad replied.

"But we *didn't*. We found a way through."

"This is not a game, Jake. You got lucky."

"It wasn't luck," I insisted. "I made a plan and it worked. Sami doesn't have much time and we're wasting it now. There's a way out here."

"Jake," Dad said, "we all want to find the tomb. But sometimes you have to admit defeat. To plan again and rethink."

"But not now," I replied. "Why would we admit defeat when we just won?"

"Listen to us," Mum said. "We know what we're talking about. So far we've been lucky."

"Stop saying we've been lucky!" My voice rang around the cave walls. "It wasn't luck. If you had trusted us, you would be over here now too."

"This is not up for discussion," Mum said.

"Not up for discussion? We're meant to be a team."

"Stop saying that! We are not a team. We are your parents."

"Mum," I said. "You have to trust us."

"Really, Jake? Should I have trusted you when you got Sami poisoned?"

"That wasn't our fault!"

"No, it was *your* fault. You walked right into a trap. And you'll walk into another if you go that way. If we go back, we can find a way out."

"We didn't come here to find a way out. We came to find a *tomb*."

"Not today," Mum replied. "Come back this instant."

"Come forward!"

"Everyone just calm down," Dad said. "We can talk about this."

"The blades are going to come down again," Mum warned. "For God's sake, John, get over there and grab them."

"If you try," I warned, "I swear I'll use my sonic force field."

The cave filled again with the creaking. The walls trembled even harder, and more rocks thumped down around us. The blades were going to come down any moment now. We'd be cut off from Mum and Dad.

"Jake..." Pan hissed.

"No, Pan. We don't need them, anyway."

"Jake!" Dad roared.

He hurled his smart-goggles across the cavern. They landed beside our feet just a second before...

Snick-clank!

One of the obsidian blades fell and crashed into the cave floor. I heard Mum yelling at us, but the sounds were drowned by the clash and clang of blades rising and falling again along the tunnel.

"I can't see them," Pan yelled. "Jake, I can't see them!"

Her voice was filled with panic. I think she'd only just realized that we'd separated ourselves from our parents.

She stared at me. Her arms were shaking and even in the gloom of the cave I could see that her face was almost white. "Jake, what did we do?"

I stared at the obsidian blades, and hoped our parents were able to find another way out. The truth was, I was as scared as my sister about continuing without them. I'd insisted that they trust us, but my confidence came from knowing they were there, ready to correct our mistakes. Now we really were on our own. But what choice did we have? We *couldn't* go back. So I tried to sound as if that was fine by me.

"We did what we had to," I said. "For Sami."

"So what do we do now?"

I picked up Dad's goggles and used their torch to study the crack in the rock. I prayed the jaguar was gone, but feared that the creature might be the least of our problems once we climbed through that gap. The Aztecs wanted our blood. They weren't done with us yet.

31

"It's a dead end, Jake."

I swore, kicked the cave wall, and swore louder. We'd squeezed through the crack in the wall, convinced that we were getting even closer to finding the tomb of Quetzalcoatl. But the path seemed to lead nowhere – another narrow cavern, another rock wall.

"We could go back," Pan said.

"No," I insisted. "There's no way back."

We could still hear the obsidian blades clashing against rock in the chamber behind. Even if there was a way to get through them, I wasn't going back. That meant giving in, and giving up on Sami. It also meant admitting to Mum and Dad that they were right, that I was just a hothead whose plans they couldn't trust.

My blood was boiling from the argument. After everything we'd been through, how could our parents still not trust us? We were meant to be a team, but they just wanted to tell us what to do. If we did find the tomb, well, that would *really* show them.

"It feels strange without them," Pan muttered.

"Feels better," I replied.

That wasn't true – I was just raging. It *did* feel strange, and scary. The last time Pan and I were in a tomb we'd been searching for Mum and Dad. This time we were running away from them, and maybe into danger. But we were ready for danger; that was the point of our training. Mum was so determined to keep us safe that she refused to take any risks. She'd said that this wasn't a training simulation, but that was my point too – this was real, and if we failed, Sami was dead. We had to go on, despite the risks.

I turned, guiding the shaky torch beam around the cavern. "The jaguar isn't here," I said, "so there must be a way through."

We searched the walls, climbing up and pulling back rocks, using night vision, then thermal vision, and ultrasonic.

"There's a crack in the cave ceiling here," I said, directing the light up into the tight space. "Looks like it runs higher into the mountain."

The opening, which was less than a metre wide, was curved and sharp, like a rock-monster's grin. It looked like a natural crack rather than anything the Aztecs had carved. The torchlight startled several long bugs, like giant millipedes only with sharp pincer fangs.

"Scolopendra," Pan said.

"Are they deadly?"

"They kill bats."

"Good job we're not bats, then."

"What? We can't go up there, Jake. It's too dangerous."

"It's meant to be dangerous. We're in a lost tomb. But I think that's where we're meant to go."

My sister saw what I saw, but at the same time something totally different. "Jake, it's just a crack in the rock. We could get stuck, or slip and fall."

"Pan, the tomb is close. It has to be."

"We're just in a cave system, Jake. The only thing we'll find up there is the jaguar. We should go back."

"We're not going back."

"We have to. Come on."

She gripped my wrist and tried to pull me back the way we'd come. Instinctively, I lashed out and shoved her. She tripped; stumbled back and bashed her head against the cave wall.

The push was harder than I had intended, but she looked at me as if I'd plunged a knife into her chest. We used to fight all the time: punches, shoves, hair-pulling. A few months ago she'd have responded with a kick, or picked up a rock and launched it at me. But since we'd started training as treasure hunters, Pan and I had become friends.

"I'm sorry," I said. "Look, you go back. Tell Mum and Dad where I'm going. They listen to you, Pan."

I reached to help her up, but she slapped my hand

away. "I'm not letting you go on alone!" she insisted. "You're not thinking, Jake. That's what you're usually so good at, thinking and making plans. But you're so angry about Mum and Dad, you're not using your brain right now."

"I am, Pan. That crack is—"

"That crack is not a plan! You might die. Do you think Sami would want that? We could have died half a dozen different ways since we've been in the jungle. Sometimes you act like this isn't actually dangerous. And you wonder why Mum doesn't trust you."

I glared, as if this time she was the one who had attacked me. I'd always known that Mum trusted Pan and not me. She let her help decipher the markers, and asked her questions about the Aztecs. She saw Pan as a real treasure hunter, but not me. I knew that, but hearing my sister say it still felt like a punch to the gut.

Pan sighed and reached out her hand. I finally helped her up.

"Mum's just scared, Jake."

"Scared I'll mess up."

"No, scared that you *won't* mess up."

"What do you mean?"

"Look," Pan explained, "me being clever isn't a worry. I read books, look at pictures, learn a language. Mum can handle that. But you doing what you do best is different. You're at your best when things are at their most dangerous. If Mum trusts you, that means willingly letting you into all sorts of danger. She was pleased to see you fail in the simulator back home because it helped convince her that you weren't ready. It gave her a reason to keep you out of danger."

"I'm not here to get into danger, though. We're here to save Sami. That's worth the risk."

"To you, but not to Mum or Dad, and probably not Sami. Not to me either, Jake."

I didn't know what to say. I understood; I just didn't agree. We were closer than ever to the tomb. We couldn't give up now.

"I promise we'll be careful," I said. "Take it slow."

Pan looked back to the hole we'd crawled through, and then at the crack we were about to climb into. She closed her eyes and groaned.

"I'll help you up," she said.

Getting into the crack wasn't easy. In the end we had to gather rocks from around the cavern and stack them in a pile so we could reach and pull ourselves into the tight space. Climbing it was simpler, and actually something we'd trained for back home. We wedged ourselves in, backs pressed against one side of the crack and feet hard against the other, and started to shimmy up.

We heard a voice, distant and echoey. "Jake! Pandora!"

Pan yelled back so loud that bugs scuttled up the wall in fright, but we didn't hear a reply.

"Mum and Dad are looking for us," Pan said.

"There's an opening ahead," I grunted.

My feet almost lost their grip as I wriggled faster and reached for the ledge at the top of the crack. I was forgetting my training, taking no precautions before entering an unknown chamber. At the very least I should have thrown a few stones up there to alert any animals that I was coming. I didn't, even though Pan hissed at me to do it. I reached and pulled myself up into the chamber, flashing my torch around the darkness.

"Pan!" I gasped.

I helped her up and we stared along a passage with stone gargoyles jutting from the walls – dozens of them, sticking out in rows on either side. They were the same creatures I'd seen decorating the mountain-top temple, the grinning snake with the swirling eyes and feather collar.

"Quetzalcoatl," Pan breathed. "Jake, we *must* be close."

We rushed along the passage, following the line of snakeheads and the shaky beam of torchlight from my goggles until we reached an opening to another split in the core of the mountain. This wasn't just a crack – it was a *chasm*, a huge crevasse running as far as we could see up into the mountain and down into darkness. Three long ropes made from twisted vines stretched across it, tied at either end to wooden stakes wedged into the rocks. One of the ropes was at foot level, while the other two were at waist height and sagged slightly in the middle.

"It's a monkey bridge," Pan said.

I gripped one of the lines, surprised by how strong they remained even after five hundred years. We'd been taught about these bridges in training. They were the simplest type of crossing, with the lower rope for our feet and the upper two as handrails. Only, they usually had safety netting at the sides to stop you from falling if the bridge leaned with your weight – which happened a lot when you tried to cross these things...

The rope bridge stretched fifty metres across the chasm, to a square entrance on the other side. Even from so far away we could see that the opening was carved all around with Aztec patterns.

"That's it, Pan," I said. "That's the entrance to the tomb."

"Jake..."

I knew what she was thinking, and she was right. It would be easy to fall off this bridge, and stupid to cross it without some sort of safety line. I reached to my waist, feeling the remaining gadgets holstered on my utility belt.

"We can use the climbing clips," I suggested. "They'll fix us to the ropes in case we fall."

"Jake! Pandora!"

The cry echoed around the chasm, so loud that at first we couldn't tell where it came from.

"Up here!"

My torch spotlight swept up the chasm until it found them – Mum and Dad. They were leaning from a ledge higher up on the other side of the chasm, about thirty metres above the end of the bridge.

"We've found it," I called. "The entrance to the tomb is there, across the bridge."

"Just stay there," Mum shouted. "We'll find a way to reach you."

"It's right here, Mum!" I yelled. "We can get across."

"No, Jake, do not cross that bridge."

"Why? We'll get the emerald tablet, and then get to you. We can cut the bridge from the other side, and throw the rope so you can lift us up the wall."

"It's not safe," Dad bellowed.

"We're already well past *safe*," I replied.

"This whole mountain is one big trap, Jake," Dad said. "Every single part of it is designed to kill us. The Aztecs wouldn't just build a bridge to take you to the tomb. The bridge is a trap. *Everything* is a trap. You have to trust us on this."

"You have to trust *me*," I insisted. "The tomb is right there."

"Jake..." Pan said.

"No, Pan! They don't want us getting in because if we do that *proves* we're good enough. *We* will have found the tablet where *they* couldn't, so they'll have no excuses anymore to stop us from being treasure hunters."

"Use your head!" Pan protested. "Do you really think there won't be another trap at the end of this bridge? The Aztecs want us dead. It would be suicide to go across."

I wish I'd remembered my training, that I'd breathed in and controlled my emotions. They were right; I know that now, and had I just paused for a moment, then maybe I might have seen the sense in their warnings. But that volcano was rising in me again... I was *convinced* Mum and Dad didn't want me getting to the tomb first, simply because that would prove them wrong and that I *was* good enough.

I did know that Mum was right about one thing. The bridge was obviously a trap. But I'd seen something else when I looked over the edge of the chasm...

There was *another* opening, fifty metres below the supposed entrance to the tomb. It wasn't just a crack in the rock; it was definitely an entrance, although it wasn't decorated with sculptures like the one at the end of the bridge.

"Jake, we can't walk across this bridge," Pan said.

"We're not going to walk across it," I replied.

"Good," Pan said. "Now you're thinking straight. Maybe we can go—"

"We're going to swing across it," I added.

"What?"

"Look down there. *That's* the real entrance to the tomb. The one at the end of the bridge is a trap. But look at the distances. If we cut this rope, we can use it to swing right through the real entrance down there."

"You're joking, right?"

I shook my head. I don't think I've ever looked less like I was joking.

"Jake, you've lost it. You've finally lost it."

"We're working on a way to get down to you," Mum called. "Jake, do not cross that bridge."

"I'm not going to cross the bridge," I promised.

"He's going to swing across it!" Pan yelled.

I grasped one of the vine ropes and tugged, pulling in just enough slack to twist my wrist around the line and get a grip. The moment I cut the rope it would shoot out, yanking me with it as it swung.

"Jake!" Mum screamed. "Just stay there. We can talk about this."

I slid the laser cutter from my utility belt. It was made for slicing stone, so should cut through this rope like it was tissue paper.

"Jake!" Dad roared. "You listen to your mother."

My hand trembled as I held the cutter to the line. I looked up and smiled at my parents.

"I know you don't trust me. I know you think I'm not up to this. But you'll see that I am. I'll bring back the tablet."

"Jake, don't!"

I don't know which of them shouted the last warning; they were all yelling now, even my sister. I blocked out the sound, breathed in and held the breath, calming my nerves and controlling my fear.

Then I cut the rope.

I knew it would yank me from the ledge, but not how *hard* it would yank me, or that Pan was going to jump onto my back as I cut the line.

"No, Pan!" I wailed.

I should have known she would come; I would never have left her to go on alone either. She clung on tight as we dropped into the abyss, and then began to swing, flying across darkness towards the entrance to the tomb.

Then, suddenly, the line jerked, as if something *else* had grabbed hold. That was impossible, unless...

I looked up. "What are you doing?" I cried.

Mum and Dad had jumped from their ledge too! They had timed their leap perfectly, so they were just able to grab the rope as we swung across the chasm.

"Jake," Mum snapped. "You're grounded."

"Grounded?"

"Look out for the wall!"

The extra weight had swung us off course. Instead of swinging to the entrance, we were going to hit the rock wall ten metres to its side.

"Hold on!"

I managed to twist so we slammed sideways against the chasm wall, dislodging rocks and knocking the wind out of us. My grip slipped and I was about to fall, taking Pan with me, when Mum did the most incredible thing I have ever seen. She must have anticipated us letting go because she did too, a fraction of a second earlier. She dropped about ten feet, grasped hold of the rope again just above Pan and me, and then used her legs to pin us back into the wall.

It was amazing – the timing, the awareness – I see that now. But as I grabbed the rope again I just felt annoyed. She'd *assumed* I would mess it up. She hadn't trusted me.

"Hold on," she grunted. "The rope will swing us to the entrance."

Pan tightened her grip on my shoulders as the rope slid across the cliff to the hidden opening. Mum, Pan and I tumbled inside, but rocks dislodged as Dad climbed down, and he slipped back into the darkness. Again, Mum acted crazy-fast – dropping low and snatching hold of his hand, so Dad clung on and dangled below the entrance. Pan got down too, gripping Mum's waist so she, too, was anchored to the ledge.

I should have helped. I know that now. We were supposed to be a team, but at that moment, when they needed me, I wasn't even looking at my family. I had turned, guiding the light from my goggles deeper along the passage from the entrance. There were more carvings on the walls here, more leering snake-heads. We were *so* close. What if there was another trap, with some sort of timer – what if we only had moments left to find the coffin? Mum and Pan didn't need my help saving Dad; they had that covered.

Was that really why I left them, and ran off? Partly, maybe. I did genuinely think we needed to keep moving. But it wasn't just that. I still wanted to get there first, to show Mum that I could do it without her – that I could be trusted. No, "wanted" isn't the right word. I had become obsessed.

I heard Mum call out, but didn't look back as I stumbled from the passage into another chamber.

I stopped.

"Treasure!" I gasped.

It was everywhere I looked. Stone shelves displayed gold beakers, gold plates and small gold statues of gods. Wicker baskets overflowed with jewellery: dangly gold earrings, chunky jade bracelets, necklaces with turquoise snake pendants. Lifelike gold masks stared at me from another shelf, and there were skulls, of course. The Aztecs *loved* skulls. But these were different to any skulls I'd seen so far. They were real, with real teeth, but covered in a mosaic of polished turquoise, and with shiny black stones for eyes. Below them, Aztec weapons stood propped against the wall – spears, bows and quivers full of arrows, a shield covered in gold and turquoise...

"Jake!" Mum called. "Stay right there."

I kept moving, breathless with excitement, following my torch beam from the treasure chamber and through a square doorway. I stopped again, confused at first by what I saw, and then horrified.

Stone stairs led down into a square room sunken into the rock, but I could only see the first two steps. The rest of the floor was covered with bones. Piles of human skeletons filled the chamber, stacked right to the top of the steps. I couldn't see any skulls; just arm bones and leg bones and rib cages and spines, *thousands* of them, like a gruesome ball pool filling the sunken space.

I'd heard enough about the Aztecs to know these were the remains of the sacrificial victims whose skulls we'd already seen on display. Some of the bones were still covered with the ragged remains of clothes; ribcages of others had been forced open when the Aztec priests cut out their hearts. It was totally gross, but right then I didn't care. My torchlight had settled on something else. In the middle of the skeleton pit, rising from the dusty heaps of bones, was the top of a stone plinth with snakeheads leering from its corners.

On the plinth was a coffin.

"It's here!" I cried.

"Jake," Mum called from back along the passage. "Stay there. Don't move."

For a moment I *couldn't* move. I had seen coffins almost identical to this one, in Egypt, but I was still mesmerized by the sight. It wasn't because of everything we'd gone through to find it; it was just that it was so *beautiful*. It was made of solid crystal, its sides carved with symbols I recognized from the emerald tablet, but which even my parents hadn't been able to decipher, signs that looked like maths equations mixed with ancient pictograms. But we knew the symbol cut onto the coffin's lid well enough. It was carved on the chamber ceiling too, directly above the coffin – a snake, curled in a circle and eating its own tail. It was the symbol of the ancient people who were buried in these crystal coffins around the world, and whose civilization had been wiped out.

The coffin was ten metres away. To reach it I just had to walk over the top of the skeletons, which wasn't such a big deal, right? I reached a foot over their surface, and pressed it down. The bones creaked and snapped, compacting beneath my weight. The surface was wobbly, uneven, but it seemed strong enough to walk on.

I breathed in and took another step. A few bones slipped out from under my feet, but others crushed more tightly together. I took another shaky step, and then another, holding my arms out for balance. As I got closer to the coffin, my goggles' torchlight could just make out a blurred shape of the figure buried inside, and the green glint of an object that the person was holding.

"The emerald tablet," I breathed.

My boot broke through a ribcage, and suddenly I sank into the bones until my boots hit the floor of the pit and I was up to my neck in skeletons. I cursed and tried to shove the things aside to climb back up, but more headless skeletons fell in their place, wrapping me in gruesome hugs. I gave up trying to get back to the top and instead tried to force a passage through the bones to the plinth and the coffin.

I managed another step, but the ground sank a little. A grinding sound echoed around the chamber. All around me the bones began to tremble.

I knew immediately what I had done – the realization was like a knife to my chest, so sharp that I cried out, staggered back, tumbled into skeletons. All around me the bones rattled harder.

"No..." I gasped. "Please..."

I had stepped on a trigger stone beneath the bones. I had set off a trap.

I scrambled around the chamber floor, shoving aside bones, trying to find the trigger stone, but it was too dark and there were too many bones. Panic took hold and I thrashed at the skeletons, somehow managing to haul myself back up to the surface of the pit. I looked back and saw a stone slab begin to slide down over the entrance to the burial chamber. It was going to seal me in!

I moved instinctively – not to the exit, but to the coffin – and ran my hands around its sides. I could see the emerald tablet through the casket's thick crystal lid. It was right there! But I knew from Egypt that only the People of the Snake knew how to open these coffins. I glanced back and cried out again in a mix of anger, fear and frustration as the slab slid even lower. There was no way I'd get this coffin out of the chamber in time.

For a second I knelt on the bones, staring at the dull green object beneath the crystal. Sami's life was right there, and my family's happiness. It was so close...

Leave the coffin! Get out of here!

I turned and tried to run back to the entrance, but sank again up to my neck in the bones. I shoved them away, digging frantically.

"Jake? Jake, get out of there!" Dad warned.

I didn't need to panic. The slab was closing slowly; I still had time. I scrabbled at the bones, pulled myself back up to the top and crawled over the surface to the exit. I managed another couple of metres before I sank back under, as if the skeleton arms had dragged me down.

"Jake, get out!"

I kicked and thrashed. Only my head was above the surface now. The door slab was barely a metre from the ground... I knew I wasn't going to make it. It was hopeless. Any second now I would be trapped in here, alone.

Then, just at the last moment, I saw something else.

Mum!

She slid feet first through the tiny gap under the door slab. But the gap was too small, and closing too fast. The slab was going to crush her head! I tried to move closer, but sank even deeper into dusty bones, losing sight of Mum as the slab sealed the chamber with a hollow *thud*.

32

"Mum? Mum!"

I called louder, above the cries from my Dad and Pan on the other side of the stone slab. I'd seen Mum slide towards the burial chamber seconds before the entrance sealed. Had she made it through, or had she been crushed beneath the door?

I managed to shove aside piles of skeletons and force a path back towards the exit.

"Thermal," I gasped.

My smart-goggles' torch cut out and my view changed to the dull grey fuzz of a geothermal map. As I scrabbled around, two orange heat signatures appeared in my view, beside one another. They were Dad and Pan, yelling at us from the other side of the slab. I kept turning...

There!

"Mum!" I yelled. *"Torch!"*

The beam guided me to her, and I forced my way to where she lay. She had sunken into the bone pit, right down to the chamber floor. The bones around her were spattered crimson; blood flowed from the side of her head.

"Mum…"

I scooped her up so her head rested on my lap, and tried to push the bones away to clear space. It was hopeless; even more toppled onto us in their place. I leaned over Mum, shielding her as best I could.

Dad called out again. I'd never heard him sound so desperate.

"I'm here," I replied. "I've got Mum."

"Is she alive?" Pan screamed.

"I–I don't know. The door hit her head. She's bleeding. She's—"

"She's alive," a voice groaned.

I cried out with delight as Mum's eyes fluttered open. She was barely conscious, her breathing shallow and forced.

"Are you OK?" she asked.

She was asking *me*? I nodded.

"Then … get … that light … out of my face," she said.

I hadn't realized I was shining the goggles' torch in her eyes. I yanked them off and slid them back into my belt. My eyes began to adjust to the darkness, so I could still just see Mum on my lap.

"Stay calm!" Dad hollered. "We're going to find a way to get you out."

Mum rasped a reply. "No way out."

"What do you mean?" Pan called.

"The Aztecs meant to lock us in here," I said. "They trapped us in here, to serve the gods. They'd have made sure there's no way out."

"Well, we're going to damn well find one!" Dad shouted.

I heard them tossing aside the treasures in the room, searching for a catch or lever to open the door. Dad swore, which he almost never does, and I heard something crash to the ground; I guessed he'd yanked away another item of Quetzalcoatl's grave goods in his search.

Mum heard too.

"John?" she asked, weakly.

"Dad!" I yelled. "Mum's talking to you."

Dad rushed back to the slab. "What is it, darling?"

"If you damage one more item in that room, then I'm going to haunt you for the rest of your life."

"Dad, she said—"

"I heard," Dad said. "But you are not going to die in there. Jake, can you find the stone that triggered the seal? See if you can lift it back up."

Mum smiled at me, as I laid her head back on the ground. I turned and burrowed back through the skeletons towards the coffin plinth. I scrabbled around the ground, shoving aside bones as I looked for the trigger stone. I found it, eventually, but it was no use to us. About the size of a dinner tray, it had only sunk a few inches into the ground but there was no way to force it back up. I wondered whether the seal would open even if I *did* manage to raise the stone. The Aztecs had designed this trap to lock us in here; I doubted they would have added an escape route.

"Jake, what about your utility belt?" Pan suggested.

We pretended to be hopeful as I forced my way back through the bones and used the belt's few remaining gadgets on the door slab. But I knew none of them would work, and I suspected Pan and Dad did too. The seal was at least half a metre thick. The compact drill ran out of power thirty centimetres in, and even if it *had* got through, it would only have drilled a tiny hole through the slab. The laser stonecutter might have helped, but I'd dropped it on the rope swing.

"What about the bungee cord?" Pan asked.

"What about it?" I said.

"I don't know! Do something clever with it!"

"Dad," I called, "I still have Pedro's sonic force field."

I heard Dad's boots stomping over stone. He was still charging around, searching for any other way into this chamber.

"I hear you, Jake," he said. "It's worth a try."

"No, it's not," Mum rasped.

I took her arm and helped her climb the steps, pushing away skeletons until she sat with me on top of the bones, her back against the door slab. Blood covered the side of her face and had soaked her jungle shirt, but her eyes looked a little sharper than they had a few minutes ago.

"The force field will repel animals," she said, "but it won't smash through a two-foot stone block. It will just knock us out."

"Both of you just wait there," Dad said. "I'll get out of here and find Alpha Squad. They'll be looking for us. They can have the emerald tablet, have whatever they like, if they help us get this slab open."

"They'll kill you as soon as they see you, John."

Dad knew that too. And anyway, I doubted he'd find a way out of this mountain. No one was meant to leave this place alive. That was the Aztecs' plan.

"So what do we do, then?" Pan asked.

"Nothing," Mum said.

"Nothing?"

"Sometimes that's the best plan. Just breathe and think."

Mum shifted down a little, rested her head on my lap again and closed her eyes. I stared at her face – a mess of blood and bruises and sheer exhaustion – and then gazed across the bone pit to the crystal coffin. That casket, and what it contained, had meant everything to me, for so long. But right then I'd gladly have given it all up to get my mum out of that chamber. I'd messed up so badly. I'd been so blinded by the hope of reaching this tomb, of proving that I could reach it, that I'd forgotten even the most basic treasure-hunting lessons.

"This is my fault," I said.

"You're damn right it is," Dad barked. "What were you thinking, Jake? You just charged right in there. It was as if we'd taught you nothing."

"I just wanted to get the tablet," I said.

"We all wanted to," Pan said. "We all care about Sami, Jake. But you stopped thinking. Of course there was going to be a trap in there! It's the burial chamber. That's the trappiest bit!"

"I know..."

"Damn it, Jake," Dad said. "This is exactly why we wanted to stop. Because you weren't ready."

"I know, Dad, I'm sorry."

"Sorry is not good enough. It was just a matter of time until you—"

"Why are you trying to teach me a lesson after I've already doomed myself and Mum to die?" I shouted. "You can stop now, Dad. I get it. I'm not good enough. I'm not you or Mum or Pan. I'm reckless, and now it's going to get me killed, as well as Mum and Sami. So, yes, you were right, you were both right the whole time. I never had the brain for this, like you three. I realize that, OK?"

I scrunched my eyes to stop the tears, but they found a way out anyway and dripped onto Mum's head. I pictured Sami looking weak and desperate on that bed, imagined him reaching for help, but finding only the Snake Lady. I saw her smug smile and her black eyes. I pictured Mum, Dad and

Pan hunting for this chamber without me. Making it, getting the emerald tablet, getting out. Doing it properly.

"I should never have been part of this team," I said. "I screwed up."

"Screwed up?" Mum said, softly. She opened her eyes again and looked up at me. "That's funny, Jake."

I sniffed back tears, stared at her through watery eyes. "Funny?"

"Yes."

"I don't understand."

"It's true, Jake, you made mistakes. At the Snake Lady's house, and here in this chamber. In those moments, you forgot your training and let your emotions take control. That was always our concern about you."

"I know..."

"But what about the rest of the time? Jake, darling, it was you who caught the motorcyclist in Trujillo. It was you who saved us from the plane crash by acting the fastest. You found the Place of the Jaguar, and recovered *both* of the markers. You saved your sister's life in the mudslide by putting your breathing tube in her mouth. You chose to climb the skull wall when we were under attack from arrows, and we survived when we might not have had we stayed still. You got through the obsidian blades, and you found this burial chamber. That was all *you*, Jake. Without you on our team, we would still be scratching our heads in the jungle camp, at best, and Sami would almost certainly be dead."

"I..."

Words stuck at the back of my throat. I'd never heard Mum talk that way about me, or anyone. I was so used to her criticism that I didn't know how to reply. More tears dripped down on her.

"I just wanted to impress you," I said.

"And you have, darling, so many times. I've never known anyone to think so fast under pressure. Jake, you are a born treasure hunter, but that doesn't mean you know everything. You hurl yourself into danger, and a lot of the time you find a way out, but not always. Those few times when you lose control, those are the moments we worry about. It just takes one of those, one step on the wrong stone, and it's all over."

"I know, Mum..."

"Your father and I did this for twenty years before you were born. That experience is something you should learn from. You say we should trust you, but we can't until you trust *us*. If we tell you to stop, it's because there's a reason to stop. We're not just being annoying parents. We're looking out for you, with all the experience that we have. We needed to know you trusted *us* enough to listen."

She smiled at me. "First rule of treasuring hunting: always trust your parents."

That sounded like a pretty good first rule to me. "I wish I had," I said. "We wouldn't be stuck here now."

I gazed around the chamber, noticing for the first time the decoration on the walls – brightly painted scenes of Aztec people carrying the crystal coffin, and grisly images of victims having their hearts torn out to honour the god.

"I really don't like the Aztecs," I muttered.

"It's not your place to like them or not like them," Mum said.

"You're still defending them, after everything they've done to us?"

"No," Mum said, "I'm choosing not to judge them. You look across this room and see murder. That's not what the Aztecs saw. Killing these people was their religious duty. It served a greater purpose."

"Because they thought sacrifices would stop the world from ending," I said.

"That's right. When you look at an ancient people, look from their eyes, not yours. You might see things differently."

"Why are you giving Jake a history lesson in there?" Pan called.

"Because that history lesson might save our lives," Mum replied.

I eyed her curiously. "Mum, do you know a way out of here?"

"I have an idea. Just an idea."

She sat up and rubbed her bleary eyes to see better around the chamber. "John," she said. "I know you've been thinking it too."

"The fifth world?" Dad replied.

"The fifth world," Mum agreed.

"Oh, man, you're doing it again!"

"Doing what?"

"That thing when you have a discovery, but draw it out for the drama."

"I do that?" Mum asked.

"You *all* do," I said.

"I definitely do," Pan confessed. "It's fun. Really annoys Jake."

"Actually, we do too, Jane," Dad admitted.

"You're doing it now!" I protested. "What's this about a 'fifth world'? Wait, I remember that. The Aztecs thought there had been four worlds before this one, and each was destroyed. These sacrifices were meant to stop that happening again, right?"

"Right," Pan agreed. "If the gods weren't happy, then the fifth world would be destroyed by an earthquake."

"What destroyed the other four worlds?" I asked.

"Good again, Jake," Mum said. "That's the right question. Pandora?"

"I ... I can't remember."

"That's all right," Mum said, "it was a lot to take in. But you should know the answer because you've been thinking about it a lot since we've been on this mission. One of the worlds was destroyed by a jaguar, another by fire, the third by wind and the fourth by floods."

"Hang on," I said. "Jaguar, fire, wind, flood... Those are the markers!"

"Good, Jake," Dad said.

"How long have you known about this?" Pan asked.

"Your father and I had our suspicions after Jake found the second marker, but we were only certain once you described the last one to us."

"The Aztecs were fleeing the Spanish invaders," Dad explained. "Their markers weren't just intended to lead us here, they were also a document of history. They led us through the four old worlds, to this place – the last refuge of their own world, the fifth world. In the Aztecs' eyes, this mountain was all that was left of their empire."

"But how does that help us?" I asked.

"Maybe it doesn't," Mum said, "but once you see the world through their eyes, new possibilities appear. We need to keep thinking. What might this mean?"

"The Aztecs wanted us to become sacrificial victims," Pan said. "To keep Quetzalcoatl happy. But what if we didn't die? What if the god was unhappy?"

"Their world would be destroyed," Mum said. "By an earthquake."

"Dad," Pan said, "you said the Aztecs saw everything literally. Do you think they might have planned a way to destroy this mountain if we *didn't* die, so it seemed like an earthquake? If we can trigger that, then maybe there is a way out of here.

Maybe we can make this whole tomb collapse."

"That is how they thought," Dad agreed, "but there would have been no way for them to know if we did or didn't die in these traps."

We'd run out of ideas. The Aztecs had led us to this place, the final stand of their world, and they needed us to die to keep it from being destroyed. But they couldn't have known if we did *actually* die. So there was no way for them to tell if the god was or wasn't happy.

Unless...

I rose from our bed of bones, staring at the coffin in the centre of the chamber. Maybe there *was* a way of telling if Quetzalcoatl was unhappy.

"The Aztecs wanted to protect that coffin, right?" I asked.

"Right," Mum replied.

"Agreed," Dad said. "Disturbing it would have been a sure way to anger Quetzalcoatl and bring about the end of their world."

"But how would they know if we *had* disturbed it?" Pan asked.

"Because it was *moved*," I said.

Mum looked at me, and a small smile curled the corners of her mouth.

"Because it was moved," she repeated.

Dad's voice came back, suddenly full of hope. "Jake, can you get to the coffin?"

"I think so."

"Not without me," Mum insisted.

I helped her up, and we moved together over the top of the bone pit. This time I spread my weight out by crawling, so I didn't sink down into the skeletons. I should have done that before, but I hadn't been thinking clearly. Now, though, I was focused, ready to get this right. If I still could...

By the time we reached the coffin, all the pain and worry had vanished from Mum's eyes; they were sparkling as brightly as the casket's crystal lid. She traced the snake symbol's circular shape with a finger, and leaned over to examine the markings on the side of the casket.

I remembered that she had never seen one of these crystal coffins. In Egypt, it was Pan and I who had found one in the tomb of Osiris and seen others inside the headquarters of the People of the Snake.

"This is beautiful," Mum said. "But it isn't Aztec."

"Pan said the one in Egypt wasn't Egyptian either," I replied. "Whoever is buried in here is from some sort of lost civilization, from way before ancient times. The Snake Lady and her organization are trying to wipe out that history."

Mum looked up at the chamber ceiling, and the carving of the snake eating its own tail – the symbol of that lost civilization and of the Snake Lady's organization.

"We won't let them," she said.

I know we were in a dangerous situation, but

I couldn't stop myself from grinning. I'd wanted to hear Mum say that for so long. Being here, seeing this, it had relit a fire in her. She'd stopped being a worried mum and she'd become a treasure hunter again.

"What can you see?" Pan yelled.

"We're at the coffin," I replied. "It's on a stone plinth."

"Can you see the base?" Dad shouted.

We dug deeper, clearing away just enough bones to see the chamber floor. There was a groove around the base of the plinth where it seemed to go deeper into the ground.

"John, it's a sliding trigger," Mum called.

"A what?" I asked.

"This plinth isn't just a plinth," she explained. "It does something else."

"Like set off a trap?"

Mum nodded slowly, considering the coffin and the plinth. "If we move this coffin, it will trigger the Aztecs' final trap. It will anger Quetzalcoatl and bring about the end of the fifth world by somehow setting off an earthquake that will destroy this entire mountain."

She looked at me, and smiled. "Possibly."

"If we bring down the mountain," I replied, "the door seal could shatter. Maybe we can escape."

"Maybe?" Pan said.

"*Maybe* is better than we had before," Mum said.

"John, you and Pandora need to find a way out of this mountain right now. We'll give you an hour to get clear, and then we'll push the coffin from its—"

"No chance," Pan said, interrupting. "The only way we're going to get out of a collapsing mountain is *together*."

"John? You have to get Pandora out."

"She said no chance, Jane. If we're doing this, we're doing it together. That's how we got this far."

Not quite, I thought. We'd argued and split up, and that's why things had gone so wrong. As much as I wanted them to get to safety, I also knew they were right. We needed them, and they needed us. We were a team.

Mum pressed her palms against the coffin's thick crystal. "I'm going to count to three, and then we're going to push this coffin from its plinth and see what happens. Everybody get ready. Remember your training. If things get crazy, our direction is daylight, wherever we see it."

I placed my hands beside Mum's on the coffin, as she began the countdown.

"One ... two..."

"Wait," I said. "Are we pushing *on* three or *after* three?"

"On three," Mum replied. "It's *always* on three."

"You never taught us that."

"Well, there's your lesson. All right. One ... two... "

"Wait!" Pan yelled. "Just to be clear, we're not

307

joking? We're really going to deliberately cause this whole mountain to collapse on us?"

"Why would we be joking?" Dad asked.

"I don't know. It sounds like a joke!"

"We can do this," Dad said. "We can all do this."

"So we're going on three, or after three?" Pan said. "I didn't hear."

"Oh, for heaven's sake," Mum sighed.

Then she shoved the coffin.

33

The crystal coffin slid away far more easily than I'd expected, with a smooth movement that caused me to tumble forward into the plinth. It didn't come off completely; one end remained on the stand while the other dropped down, crushing the skeletons.

"Guys?" Pan called. "What's going on?"

Mum yanked me back from the plinth, as if she expected the whole mountain to collapse on us right there and then. We knelt together on the bones, breathing hard for fear of what might happen next, but at the same time hoping that something *did* happen.

"Stay focused," she warned. "Be ready for anything."

I tensed my hand as it rested on the surface of the plinth, trying to stop it from trembling. No, it wasn't my hand that was shaking, I realized. It was the *plinth*.

"Mum..." I hissed. "Something's definitely happening."

We slid further back over the skeleton surface as the shaking grew into shuddering. The plinth began to sink slowly into its grooves in the chamber floor.

Maybe we could use it as an elevator to take us out of here? I was about to jump on top and call to Mum to follow, but I stopped myself and looked at her instead. Was this the sort of risk-taking she had warned me about?

"Should we get on?" I asked.

"Not until we can see what's down there."

Maybe this was all there was to it; this was the Aztecs' idea of an earthquake. We watched the slab sink, scraping against skeletons as it slid deeper into the ground. I blinked, momentarily blinded as dust rose and stung my eyes.

"Are you OK?" Mum said.

"Just dust," I muttered.

"What dust?"

She was right – the plinth was sliding smoothly into the ground; it wasn't causing any dust to rise. The dust was coming from above, where a thin crack had formed in the chamber ceiling. For a long moment – too long – we stared as the crack grew wider, splitting the snake carving in two...

"Jake, move!" Mum roared.

She grabbed my arm and pulled me down a second before half of the chamber ceiling caved in. It would have squashed us flat had Mum not pulled me into the gap beneath the crystal coffin, where it rested half-on and half-off the plinth. We huddled together, sheltered from the impact, as the ceiling crashed down around us, crushing bones into powder.

"Jake! Jane!"

We crawled from under the coffin, sweeping our arms to clear the bone powder that filled the chamber like smoke – and I saw Dad and Pan. The door slab had collapsed too. We were free! They rushed to us, scrambling over rubble and shoving aside smashed up skeletons.

I grinned, wiped powdered bone from my face. "That wasn't so bad."

"Jake!" Pan snapped, "why did you have to say that?"

"Eh?"

"*That wasn't so bad.* Now it's obviously going to get worse."

"Come on, Pan, how much worse can it get than a ceiling falling on us?"

"Jake!" Mum protested. "Why did you say *that* now? Of course it can get worse."

I helped Mum up from the rubble. "I'd like to see how," I muttered.

As if in answer, the chamber walls began to shake. Suddenly, a pile of rubble and shattered skeletons dropped away and vanished, just a few metres from where we were gathered by the plinth. Now another did the same, only even closer.

"The floor is giving way!" Mum yelled. "Run! Get out of here!"

We ran, leaping the remains of the door slab, back into the treasure chamber. Behind us I saw rocks and bones drop away as more of the burial chamber floor collapsed. The crystal coffin tipped up and plunged down, like the Titanic going under.

"Keep moving," Dad shouted.

We staggered through the treasure room as rocks rained down from the ceiling, crushing the golden burial goods. Everything was shaking now – the ceiling, the ground, the walls all around us. My feet slipped and I tumbled over just as a crack opened in the ground beneath me. I landed with an arm and a leg on either side of it, staring down into an abyss that was growing wider as the crack spread. I was about to fall when Dad grabbed my arm and pulled me to safety.

He helped me up and for a second we just stared, spellbound by the sight of the crack opening even wider along the treasure room floor. It looked as if the entire mountain was splitting in two.

"Come on!" Dad barked.

I followed him back along the passage to the chasm, where things were even crazier. The Aztecs had thought this mountain was all that was left of their world; well, this really *did* look like the end of the world. Massive splinters of rock tore from the sides of the chasm, like icebergs breaking from a glacier. They tilted into the space and then fell, plummeting into darkness.

"What now?" Pan gasped.

Mum and Dad looked up, searching the walls as if they might spot a safe way out of this – but there was nowhere safe.

"Look out!" Pan warned.

We staggered back from the ledge as a chunk of rock fell from higher up the chasm. Streams of water fell with it, and shafts of light beamed from somewhere above. Looking up, we saw a circle of sunlight and swirling cloud.

"The top of the mountain has caved in!" Dad cried.

"Daylight!" Pan yelled. "Can we get up there?"

"Even if we can," Mum replied, "the whole mountain is coming down. It will take us with it. We need to get *down*."

They began to shout over each other, trying to agree a plan. I didn't listen. Instead I breathed in, trying to control my fear and think. I watched another giant rock slab tear from the side of the chasm and fall. My mind cleared and I went into that zone again, eyes moving fast, studying the destruction, my mind instinctively processing the sights and forming a plan that might save us. We had to get down, and maybe there was a way if we timed it right...

"Follow me!" I called. "Jump when I jump."

"Jump?" Pan asked. "Why are we jumping? Mum?"

Mum had been watching me as I stared around

the chasm. She had that look on her face, like she was about to tell me I'd done something wrong.

She reached and touched my shoulder. "Are you sure, Jake?

"I... Yes."

"Then everyone follow Jake."

Now she trusted me? I'm not sure Dad was so certain, but Mum gave him a glare, and he sighed.

"Let's get out of here," he said.

I turned back to the chasm, praying I wasn't about to get my whole family killed. Then, just as another slice of rock carved from the cliff, I jumped. I fell six feet and landed on top of the rock slab, windmilling my arms to stop myself stumbling off the edge. I crouched to keep my balance as the slice of rock leaned further into the chasm. I glanced back and saw the rest of my family landing behind me on the rock.

Just before the rock splinter broke from the wall, I leaped and landed on another chunk that had begun to come away from the opposite side of the chasm. I jumped again, landing on an even lower chunk, and then again and again, through sunlight spotlights and past falling rocks, using the leaning slabs as a ladder down the chasm. Smaller rocks plunged from above, smashing against the larger ones and sending shards flying.

"How much further to the bottom?" Pan screamed.

I looked down and saw spots of sunlight glinting

on water. Broken rocks sank under and vanished. We'd come down far, but there was at least a hundred metres to go.

"Almost there," I yelled.

"That's a lie!" Pan shouted.

"Jake, don't lie to your sister," Mum called.

"You're telling me off? Right now?"

"Concentrate, Jake. We need to move."

I was just about to leap to another rock below when a boulder crashed down onto the one we were on, behind the rest of my family. Instinctively I covered my head, protecting myself from flying shards. I heard a scream and looked back – Mum and Dad were there, but Pan was gone! We all cried out and dropped to our knees. My heart stopped as I looked down over edge of the slab, expecting to see my sister falling to her death...

"Pan!" I screamed.

"Down here!"

"Pandora!" Mum called. "Oh, thank God!"

Pan had managed to grab hold of a jutting rock on the underside of the shard. She was hanging by one hand. Mum and Dad began to climb down to her, but her fingers were slipping. Pan wouldn't be able to hold on long enough...

Move, Jake! Now!

I didn't think; I just acted. I yanked the clasp of the bungee cord from my utility belt, jammed it in a crack in the rock, and jumped. The cord unwound from my belt as I fell through darkness ... and then jolted to a stop. The bungee line ran out just as I grabbed hold of Pan's arm as she fell.

I swung on the line, holding onto her as she dangled below. I only had a weak grip on her wrist. The line was swaying hard, threatening to tear her from my grasp.

"Stop kicking your legs," I grunted.

"I can't! They're just doing that! Pull me up!"

"I'm trying..."

I gripped her tighter, but now the bungee jerked even harder as Mum and Dad slid down the line to join us.

I stared up at them, baffled. "What are you doing?"

"You said *follow me*," Dad replied.

"Follow me on the jumping bit, not on the saving Pan bit!"

"How were we supposed to know there were two bits?"

"Who's going to pull me back up?" Pan asked.

"Who's going to pull *any of us* back up?" I replied.

"Just get me up!"

Mum and Dad slid further down and managed to lift Pan higher. We all swung together in a strange sort of hug as the chasm walls shuddered. I doubted we'd manage to climb back up; the bungee clasp wouldn't hold all our weight for long enough, and the rock slab we'd jumped off was going to fall at any moment. We'd fall with it and it would crush us as we landed.

The slab had blocked most of the light from the collapsed mountain top, but enough got through to see it glinting off water about fifty metres below, at the bottom of the crevasse. There was something else down there too, glinting even brighter. Something crystal...

"So what now?" Pan wheezed.

"We have to cut the line," I said.

"Jake, that drop will kill us even if we land in the water."

I looked up to Mum and Dad as we swung harder on the line. "We haven't used my belt's sonic force field yet," I said. "You said it wouldn't smash through rock, but will it bounce us away from the water, so we don't hit it so hard?"

"I ... I think it might," Mum said.

"I'm not so sure," Dad replied.

"I have no idea," Pan added, "but this line isn't going to hold us much longer."

She was right; we needed to take control.

"OK," Pan said. "I'm ready. Dad, cut the line."

"What with?" he asked.

"What?"

"It's a bungee cord!"

"Jake," Mum said. "What else is left in your belt?"

"Nothing. We used it all up."

"So how do we cut the line?" Pan said.

"I'll unclip the belt so we all drop."

"We *need* the belt, Jake," Mum reminded me.

"Unless you have a spare sonic force field in your pocket."

"Bite through the line," Pan said.

"I can't bite through it," Dad replied.

"Why not?"

"Because I'm not a great white shark! It's a bungee line! It has an extremely high tensile strength. You can't bite through it."

"All right, it was just an idea."

"It was a silly idea."

"Wait," Mum said. "I've got a *great* idea..."

Maybe she did, but we never got to hear it because right then the bungee clasp tore from its crack in the rock, and we all fell.

34

In books, heroes sometimes say that time seems to slow down just as they attempt something horribly dangerous. We needed that as we fell towards the base of the collapsing mountain; but if anything, time seemed to speed up.

We dropped fifty metres though darkness, clinging to each other and screaming. Dad shouted at me to use the sonic force field, but I hadn't forgotten: my finger was on the button under the clasp of my utility belt. I glanced down, saw the crystal coffin bobbing on swirling water, and I pressed the button three times.

There was a sound like cannon fire right by my head, so loud it felt like my ears had burst. Then things got *really* weird. Instead of splashing down, water splashed *up* at my face as ultrasonic waves blasted in every direction. The sound waves bounced off the water and thrust us ten metres back up into the air. Around us, falling rocks suddenly changed direction as the sound waves fired them against the pit walls. I slammed against a rock wall too, then plummeted into the water and went under.

Dad pulled me back to the surface, where I could just see him in the light beaming through the collapsed top of the mountain. He was yelling instructions so loudly that veins bulged in his neck, but all I heard was a distant murmur. The sonic blast had messed up my ears. It looked like Pan and Mum had been affected the same way; they were banging their's and shouting to be heard in the water.

Another chunk of rock crashed down onto the crystal coffin, shattering into shards that flew in every direction. One of the falling rocks would hit us soon; we couldn't just stay here.

"Stay here!" Dad screamed.

Before any of us could protest, he dived underwater. Mum dragged me and Pan closer to her and gave us a thumbs up, as if everything was going to plan.

"What's that supposed to mean?" Pan cried.

"I was trying to be encouraging," Mum yelled back.

"Encouraging? We're stuck in a pit with boulders falling on us. How could our situation be any *less* encouraging?"

Then everything went dark.

Above us, the slab of rock that we'd fallen from tore even further from the side of the chasm, totally blocking the sunlight. Any moment now it would fall and crush us into pulp.

Dad burst to the surface. He shouted to us, mouthing the words clearly so we understood. "The water is flowing out through a tunnel. I think we can get through."

"John, Alpha Squad could be out there," Mum warned.

Dad saw the rock slab looming over the chasm. "We'll have to take that risk," he said.

He was right; we had to get out of here fast. Only, we'd gone through so much, and the emerald tablet was so close... I looked back at the crystal coffin. It was covered in dust and rubble, but hadn't actually been damaged by the collapsing mountain. It was too dark now to see the emerald tablet inside, but it must have still been there. We had to try to take it with us, didn't we?

"Dad, the coffin!"

"Leave it, Jake, we have to go."

"We can't let Sami down," Pan screamed. "We can't have gone through all this for nothing."

Dad glared at Mum, hoping she might convince us to give up the coffin and follow him underwater, but Mum shook her head.

"We have thirty seconds until that rock comes down," she decided. "That's enough time if we work together."

I don't know how much time Mum usually allows

for removing coffins from collapsing mountains, but her confidence gave me and Pan the courage we needed to swim to it rather than dive down and escape. Dad came with us. We wasted a few seconds scrabbling at the edges of the casket, looking for a way to get the lid off.

"We'll never open it," I said, remembering that only the People of the Snake knew how. "We have to get the whole coffin out."

"We can push it under," Pan insisted. "Dad, come this side with me. Mum, you push with Jake. Everyone, now!"

We all heaved, forcing the coffin underwater against its will. We dived down with it and saw daylight glimmering from the entrance to a tunnel. The end of the coffin thumped against rocks, but we managed to redirect it through the narrow opening. Now we had to push and hope.

Enough daylight filtered from the other end of the tunnel for me to see the outline of the body inside the coffin, and the emerald tablet in its hands. Maybe the others saw it too, because we all found extra strength to push the casket harder underwater. Then, suddenly, the whole tunnel jolted.

I turned in time to see darkness rushing at me. Behind us, the slab of the chasm wall had crashed into the pit, sending a surge of rubble and water shooting along the tunnel. The force of it slammed me against the coffin and then swept me along the tunnel and out into the daylight.

I burst to the surface, gasping. There was a cut on my head, and blood ran into my eyes, so the outside world appeared through a crimson haze. The tunnel had spat me out into the river that ran between the Storm Peaks, with a ringside view of the end of the world – or the Aztecs' world, at least.

More and more of the mountain collapsed and fell into the jungle, sending great plumes of dust rushing up over the trees. Other slabs splashed into the river. What remained of the Storm Peak seemed to wobble like a jelly as brightly coloured birds flapped from its ledges, and monkeys leapt from cliffs, all fleeing for their lives. The whole mountain was about to come down.

"Jake! Over here!"

Mum, Dad and Pan clung onto the crystal coffin as the river swept them away from the destruction, deeper into the jungle. I swam after them, struggling against the current to get across the river. Another chunk of rock splashed into the water close by, sending me into a spin. I sank under, swallowed water, and screamed bubbles and blood. The current was so fierce, and I was so disorientated, that I think I would have drowned had a hand not yanked me back to the surface.

"I've got you," Dad grunted. "Just hold on."

I don't know where he got the strength. Even with me clinging onto him, Dad managed to swim against the current, and carry me back to my mum and sister. They all looked as banged up as me, their faces covered in cuts and bruises, their eyes wild with fright.

"Are you all right?" Mum gasped.

I nodded vaguely and clung on to the coffin like a life raft. From somewhere I managed something like a smile. Somehow, we'd done it. We'd escaped the mountain and we'd got the coffin. If we could get it open, and get the emerald tablet back to Britain in time, we still had a chance of saving Sami. At least we were out of danger.

"Everybody, look out!" Mum screamed.

Something struck the river close to us – not a rock, but something smaller and faster, spraying up water. I turned, blurrily aware of a dark shape rushing from downstream. Another object hit the side of the crystal coffin, so loud and close that it snapped my mind back into focus, and I realized what was happening. It was Alpha Squad – they were coming after us in a motorboat!

"They're shooting at us," Pan said.

"Get under the coffin!" Dad yelled.

We dived underwater, using the coffin as a shield. A bullet pinged off the side of the casket, and another shot past us underwater in a trail of bubbles. But the river was getting shallower; we couldn't stay under the coffin much longer.

I hit the riverbed, scraped through mud and stones, and burst to the surface. Alpha Squad's boat was only fifty metres downstream, and catching up fast. Veronika Flutes stood at the front, taking pot shots at us with her crab claw gun. She looked more like a pirate than ever, with one eye patched, the other gleaming wildly and her flame-red hair lashing in the wind and spray. A crazed grin spread across her face as she raised her weapon for another shot.

"Oh, my God," Pan breathed. "Look!"

She wasn't looking at Alpha Squad. She was looking *past* Alpha Squad, where what was left of the Storm Peak was finally collapsing, like a building being demolished. An entire cliff face sheered away from the mountain and fell towards the river – a towering wall of blackness coming right for us.

"Swim!" Dad roared. "Swim for your lives!"

35

I didn't look back, and nor did any of my family. We just swam, splashing and gasping, frantic to get as far as possible from the great wall of darkness that had broken from the mountain. We were far enough away to escape being crushed, but we weren't out of danger. When that cliff crashed down it would do more than just crush what was beneath it.

"Keep moving!" Mum screamed. "Don't look back!"

Of course I looked back *then*, and I stopped swimming. I knew I had to keep going, but I just couldn't. I was transfixed by what I saw, partly out of terror, but also just plain astonishment.

The entire cliff slammed down on the river and the banks, sending up a ten-metre tidal wave of mud and water. It happened so fast that there was nothing we could do to escape it. The wave swept us up and hurled us into the jungle. I crashed against a tree and looked up just in time to see something flying towards me like a missile. The crystal coffin! I rolled away a second before it slammed into the tree so hard it snapped the trunk in half.

I lay on the jungle floor, staring. It wasn't the *whole* crystal coffin.

"It's just the lid..." I gasped.

The falling cliff had smashed the coffin open!

I scrambled up, wiping wet hair and blood from my eyes to gaze around the flooded riverbank. I saw Kyle Flutes leaning against a tree, tearing off his mud-soaked jungle shirt, struggling to gather his senses. I saw Mum and Dad helping each other up, calling out for Pan and me. I saw Pan farther along the riverbank, climbing down from a tree that the wave had thrown her into. I turned, scanning the rest of the riverbank. Was it there? Could I see it? My breath quickened and my heart picked up speed...

"There!"

The rest of the coffin lay on the edge of the bank, half in and half out of the water. The body that had been inside it lay a few metres away, face down in the flood water. Was it still holding the emerald tablet?

I ran for it, dodging between trees, slipping over, staggering up. I heard a cry, but didn't look back. I could see the body better now; a slim figure partly wrapped in cloth. One of its legs had torn free and was twisted at a horrible angle. The limb was thin and dark, like a stick of charcoal.

I heard a cry but kept running. There was absolutely no way I was stopping until I reached that mummy.

Then I stopped.

"Oh, God..."

I stood, staring, unable to believe my bad luck. Dark red ants surrounded the body, swimming frantically where their nest had been washed over by the floodwater. *Bullet ants.* I'd felt the sting of just one of those things; there was no way I could wade through a puddle of thousands. There were several other nests too, all along the riverbank...

I spotted a fallen branch and picked it up. Leaning over the puddle, I dug the end of the branch under the mummy and tried to flip the corpse over. Almost immediately, dozens of ants scrambled onto the wood and rushed towards my hands.

Behind me, Kyle Flutes limped closer along the bank. I heard another cry, like a tiger's growl, as Veronika charged from the other direction. She'd lost her gun, but the crazed look in her eyes suggested she'd rather beat me to death with her fists anyway.

I gripped the branch tighter, ignoring the army of ants rushing closer to my hands. "Come on."

The mummy finally flipped over, and I dropped the branch and staggered back. Its face was even more gross than the ancient corpse I'd seen in Egypt: it was dark and frazzled, with peeled-back lips and hollow black eyes. Its spindly hands were twisted over its cloth-wrapped chest, but the emerald tablet they'd once held was gone.

I turned and scanned further along the river – and there it was, glinting in the sunlight on the bank fifty metres downstream, beside Alpha Squad's upturned motorboat.

I started running again, but Veronika had seen it too, and she was closer. Reaching it first, she picked the emerald tablet up and raised it triumphantly.

"I got it, Kyle!" she hollered.

She saw Pan running towards her, and the grin spread even wider across her mud-splattered face. She had the tablet *and* she'd get to hurt someone. Pan must have seen the look in her eyes, but she didn't slow down. I'd never seen my sister look so determined. She'd always insisted that she didn't "do action" but now she was charging straight into a fight with a psychopath. It seemed like suicide – she couldn't beat Veronika!

"Pan!" I cried. "Don't!"

Then, just at the last moment, Pan seemed to chicken out. Instead of attacking Veronika she dived to the ground and slid under the upturned motorboat.

Veronika laughed, a proper witch's cackle. "Smart girl. You stay under there."

But her grin faltered as the boat's motor spluttered to life. Pan had turned its engine on. The outboard motor began to whirl like a lazy electric fan.

Veronika snorted. "Is that meant to be scary?"

"No!" Pan shouted. "But *this* is."

She jammed the boat's throttle, revving the motor so it started to spin in a blur. The rush of air sprayed anything close to it on the riverbank up at Veronika Flutes: mud, water – and thousands of bullet ants.

"Yeah, Pan!" I yelled.

You should have heard Veronika's cry! I swear it was even louder than the mountain collapsing. She sank to her knees, wailing and thrashing, frantic to shake the stinging creatures off her limbs. The tablet dropped from her hands and fell into the river. The current instantly swept it away.

I didn't stop to think – I just let instinct take over. I took two steps and leapt into the water. I heard another splash behind me as Kyle Flutes dived in too. He was coming after the tablet, and me.

I swam harder, keeping my eyes on the relic as it sank under and bobbed back up, again and again. Kyle was a much stronger swimmer than me, and he was catching up fast. I guessed that he planned to take me out first, and then go after the tablet alone.

The tablet shot over churning water, caught in a current that swept it towards the opposite bank. It hit the side of a tree that had toppled from the bank, and it stayed there – trapped against the trunk as the river rushed against it.

Reaching out, I just managed to grab the end of the tree, and pulled myself along it to the tablet. I screamed – a mix of delight and distress. For the first

330

time I actually *had* the tablet, but Kyle was getting closer, and he looked like he wanted to change that situation very quickly and very painfully.

I glimpsed Mum and Dad and Pan charging along the opposite bank. They were trying to keep up, but they wouldn't make it in time to stop Kyle.

I was only about ten metres from the riverbank, but doubted I'd be able to scramble up the muddy slope before Kyle grabbed me. This fallen tree was my best escape route. It rose at a steep angle up and over the bank to where it had snapped from the lower part of the trunk. If I could climb to the top, I hoped, I should be able to scramble down to the bank.

Gripping the tablet under my arm, I used my other hand to pull myself up onto the slippery trunk. The wood felt dead and rotten. It would struggle to hold Kyle too, if he came after me.

I wanted to run up the slope, but the trunk was wet and I feared I'd slip back into the water. More than ever I needed to remember my parents' lessons: *stay calm, think*. I kept moving, placing each step carefully on the trunk as I edged my way higher over the river and then over the bank. I was close to the top now, from where I could hopefully get down and flee. I looked for a good place to jump to, but spotted something else, something moving on the forest floor.

The shock of what I saw caused me to shriek and slip. I landed on the trunk and almost let go of the tablet, but managed to clutch it to my chest. My other arm hugged the trunk as I stared down at the creature pacing beneath me on the forest floor.

"Please tell me this is a joke," I gasped.

The jaguar glared up at me, its amber eyes flashing in the sunlight. It was the same jaguar – I was somehow certain – that we'd escaped in the mountain. I shrieked even louder as it leapt at me, swiping its claws, but it missed and dropped back to the bank with a snarl.

Behind me, Kyle climbed up onto the tree trunk. He'd torn off his jungle shirt; bulky muscles rippled along his arms and under his vest. He saw the jaguar directly below, and a grin spread across his stubbled cheeks as he edged closer up the trunk.

"Bad luck, kid," he growled.

"Bad luck?" I pulled myself carefully up, so I stood again on the trunk, now facing Kyle. "Bad luck is a mountain falling on you, Kyle. This is just ridiculous. A jaguar? Seriously?"

"Maybe you angered the Aztec gods, kid."

"Oh, shut up, you idiot."

Kyle's grin spread even wider as he came closer. The guy's wrists were thicker than my thighs. He'd snap my spine if he got his hands on me...

"Give me the tablet," he called.

I reached the top of the slope, where the trunk had snapped and fallen. I couldn't climb down, and there were no other trees close enough for me to jump to.

"This trunk won't hold us for long," Kyle said.

"That cat won't be happy if we come crashing down on it, and I fancy my chances against it better than yours. Hand me the tablet and I'll let you back down to the river. We'll call it even, how about that?"

"You're not having it, Kyle," I insisted.

"Listen, kid, I'm impressed. You put up a good fight. But you're not going to win this one. The smart play here is to know you're beaten. Live to fight another day, eh?"

I looked down again at the jaguar snarling and pacing below us, then back to Kyle. My mind raced. Half a dozen different plans came to me, but they all ended up with Kyle getting the tablet, and me getting dead. There was only one plan that ended differently, but it was the craziest of the lot.

I gripped the tablet to my chest.

"Don't come any closer," I warned.

"Son, just give me the tablet. This tree doesn't have long before it breaks and that jaguar's getting angry."

The tree groaned from our combined weight. Kyle was right; the rotten trunk wouldn't hold us much longer.

I looked beyond him, to my mum on the opposite bank. I'd expected her to leap into the water, to swim across to help. Instead she stood totally still, watching me. She knew what I planned; somehow I just knew that she did. Our eyes locked, and Mum nodded.

Do it.

"You know the number one killer in the jungle, Kyle?" I said.

Kyle stopped, confused. "No, kid, why don't you tell me after you give me that tablet."

"I'll tell you first."

"OK, then, what is it?"

"Not wearing a jungle suit when you fight a wild cat."

Pedro had told us that these suits would withstand a crocodile bite. I hoped they'd protect me against a jaguar's, too, because I was wearing mine, and Kyle was not wearing his.

I think Kyle realized at the last minute what I was going to do, but he was too surprised to react. He just watched, eyes bulging, as I lifted my foot ... and stamped on the trunk. That was all it took, just one hard stamp and the whole tree trunk broke in half. I heard the jaguar snarl, and my family call out, as I dropped with Kyle and the emerald tablet, down to the jungle.

The Snake Lady turned up the volume on the record player, closing her eyes as the singer's bittersweet aria filled the room. It felt somehow as if the music was inside *her* too, rushing through her veins and swelling her heart.

She closed her eyes, breathed in deeply, and held the breath. It was a calming technique she'd picked up from one of her clients, the child from the Atlas family with all the behavioural issues. Where was that boy, she wondered? Most likely dead in a ditch with the rest of his family, which was *such* a disappointment. Now she would have to arrange for another team to—

No. Do not think about work right now.

The Snake Lady breathed in again, held the breath again. Her head was such a mess at times – so many things to plan. Her therapist had urged her to clear her mind for a few minutes each day, to relax and forget about work.

She turned the volume to its maximum level. How she loved this opera. Puccini's *La Bohème*, the tragic tale of the poet and a seamstress in Paris. The seamstress's love felt so pure and perfect. Sometimes the Snake Lady dreamed of Paris and poetry, a simple life away from the burden of her work. An attic flat, a record player, a pile of books. Far from the hassle of the missing Chinese tombs, the funding issues over her organization's new headquarters in Mongolia, or the nightmare of the Honduras hunt that had her superiors in such a twist. If only they had let her run the organization as she wished, without all the form-filling. They would have *all* the emerald tablets by now, and be well on the way to solving their mysteries.

No, do not think about work.

Breathe.

She left the living room and sat with her supper at the dining-room table. As she ate, she imagined herself in that Paris flat, listening as the long-haired poet read to her—

The needle slipped and the opera stopped.

The Snake Lady sighed. She loved the record player, but it was frustratingly old-fashioned. She walked back into the living room and set the needle back on the record. The seamstress's love song continued.

This was the moment in *La Bohème* that she most loved, when the poet finally declares his feelings for the seamstress.

The music stopped again.

The Snake Lady cursed.

Relax.

Breathe.

She returned to the living room, but stopped in the doorway.

Jane Atlas was stood by the record player.

The treasure hunter was half-hidden in shadow, and half-lit by flickering firelight. She wore jeans and a shirt, the outfit of a mother at the supermarket, but there was something about her that warned the Snake Lady to remain still, to resist the urge to reach for one of the alarm buttons hidden around the room.

Jane Atlas looked like she'd had a tough time in the jungle: she had a black eye, a swollen jaw, and a dozen insect bites on her hands alone. Her face was scratched as if she'd been in a fight with an alley cat, but she also looked leaner and tougher than when the Snake Lady had seen her last, with eyes as narrow and sharp as razor blades. How had she broken in without setting off at least one of a dozen alarms? There were twelve mercenaries working beyond the walls of this room; it was their job to deal with this sort of trouble. The Snake Lady made a mental note to sack them all. But one problem at a time...

Stay calm. Control the conversation.

She forced a smile. "Jane Atlas," she said. "I take it you are not a fan of opera?"

"Where is Sami?" Jane replied.

"What, no chit-chat? At least allow me to welcome you into my home before we get onto business. Where are the rest of the family?"

"Where is Sami? If he is dead, then so are you."

She means it.

"Threats are so unpleasant," the Snake Lady said. "I made your children a deal that I shall honour. Sami's life in exchange for the emerald tablet. So, do you have it, or do you not?"

"We have it."

Thank God. That tablet is one of the most important of them all.

"May I see it?"

"You may not."

"Ah. You see, that is not how to conduct business. Dr Fazri has very little time left. So shall we stop playing games? I assume the tablet is close by?"

"Very close," Jane replied.

"With John or Pandora or Jake?"

"One of them."

"So how do you wish to proceed, Jane? You must be aware that the wall panels behind you are false. They conceal three chambers, little outposts of my organization. There are four mercenaries in each, all armed. I merely have to press one of several buttons in my immediate vicinity, and you will be captured."

This time the Snake Lady's smile wasn't forced, and her perfect teeth gleamed in the firelight. Carefully handled, this situation could work out to her advantage. With Jane Atlas captured, the remaining members of the Atlas family could surely be forced into another mission. Even without her, they would make a fine team to recover the final tablet in China, which had so far proved so frustratingly elusive. And if they died, no great loss. They would need to be disposed of at some point anyway. They knew far too much.

But, first things first. The Aztec tablet was not yet secure.

The Snake Lady edged closer to an alarm button on the side of the coffee table. "Now, where is it?" she asked.

"Give me Sami first," Jane demanded.

"You are not in a position to negotiate."

"People keep telling me that and then wishing they hadn't."

She's as tough as a pack of nails. Don't give her an inch. Let your mercenaries take her out. That's why you pay those idiots.

The Snake Lady moved her hand closer to the alarm.

"I wouldn't touch that button," Jane warned.

"Ah, you have seen it. However, you have miscalculated. You are fast, Jane, but even you could not reach me before I press that button."

"Just tell me," Jane said.

"Tell you?"

"The emerald tablets, where do they lead? Your organization must have spent millions of pounds and destroyed dozens of tombs to hide some secret. Tell me what is this all about."

The Snake Lady's black eyes gleamed like polished stones. "We have spent *billions* of pounds, and destroyed *hundreds* of tombs. Yes, to hide a secret. It is a secret that *must* be hidden, to avoid mass panic, the breakdown of society."

"But you're not destroying the tablets. You need them. Together, they form a map. Where to?"

"To a place we must find to ensure the survival of all life on Earth. You see, Jane Atlas, you regard me as a villain, yet I look upon you in the same light. By obstructing us you have no idea of the danger you cause."

"It's not up to you to hide secrets about history."

"*Is it not?* Is it not, Jane? I say *it is*, as does an international treaty of sixty-three nations that protects and funds our organization. When will your precious little family realize that we are the goodies?"

"No. You can't just wipe out history. People need to know."

"Spoken like a true historian, but also horribly naïve. You are beginning to sound like your hot-headed children, Jane. I am surprised that they are not here, actually. Jake would have charged in here

340

with some half-baked plan. Honduras must have been good for him. You finally have your children well trained."

"They're the best trained in the business."

"Indeed, they are remarkable children. I cannot wait to see them again."

The Snake Lady pressed the button.

Around the room, wooden wall panels slid up into the ceilings, revealing the three chambers hidden behind the living-room walls. The Snake Lady gasped and stepped back, as if she had been punched in the stomach.

There *were* four mercenaries inside each chamber, but all of them lay unconscious on the floor. Three other figures stood in the entrances, each breathing through a slim metal tube.

John Atlas. Pandora Atlas. Jake Atlas.

Wisps of green gas drifted from the chambers as the treasure hunters stepped into the room.

Jake Atlas yanked the tube from his mouth and grinned.

"Hello, Marjorie," he said. "We're back."

That was such a good line! I was trying to look cool, like the rest of my family, but it was hard to stop myself grinning. You should have *seen* the Snake Lady; she was *totally* freaked out to see us step from her secret chambers. She always seemed so calm and in control, but right then she looked like someone had just slapped her in the face with an electric eel. Her mouth was a twisted expression of shock and disbelief. Her black eyes moved from me to Pan to Dad and then Mum, growing wider with panic.

"It's not possible," she gasped. "Those chambers are highly secure. Without Dr Fazri you could never have broken into them."

"Hey," a voice replied. "That hurts my feelings."

She turned and saw the other members of our gang approach from the dining room. She recognized them both, but looked even more confused to see them here. Pedro snatched off his cowboy hat and greeted her with a quick bow. Beside him, leaning against the door frame for support, was Sami.

He was still very weak, but the antidote Dad had forced one of the mercenaries to hand over was already working, and he even managed a smile. After such an effort to save his life, we'd almost hugged the poor guy to death when he finally woke. I'd apologized about fifty times in the space of a minute, but he waved them all away with a shaky hand, muttering to Dad about something worse that he'd been through years ago in Guatemala, or somewhere. I'm not sure that was true, but it was so good to hear him talk. He'd not been strong enough to say much else yet, but his eyes told us how happy he was to see us all safe and together. I think he could tell that something had changed among us, too. The Atlas family he'd seen in Egypt was back.

"But... How...?" the Snake Lady breathed.

"Easy," Pedro replied.

He held up a device from his gadget supplies, a sort of super-skeleton key that we'd used to get past the mad security in this place and open the rear doors to the secret chambers. It was called a ... actually I'm not sure what it was called, I wasn't really listening; I'd been too excited – this had been my plan, and Mum and Dad had totally gone along with it! Pedro had kitted us out with gas bombs to take out the mercenaries, and new breathing tubes so the gas didn't send us to sleep as well.

The Snake Lady couldn't stop glaring at us. We all looked skinnier from our time in the jungle, tired from the long flight home, and bug-bitten, bruised and cut on every bit of skin that she could see. I had the worst injury: three deep scratches on the side of my neck, which I secretly hoped might scar because it looked *so* cool.

I noticed the Snake Lady looking at them, and tilted my head so she could get a better view in the firelight.

"Jaguar scratch," I said. "You should have seen the other guy."

"Alpha Squad," she realized. "Are they dead?"

"No," Mum replied, "but they'll be out of action for a while. Once they've licked their wounds, I suspect they'll come looking for us, as will your organization."

The Snake Lady nodded slowly, trying to gather

her composure. "Then why do this?" she asked. "Jane, you're just putting your children in even greater danger."

"My children can look after themselves, thank you very much."

"Then why? What do you want?"

"Information," Dad replied.

"But... What information?"

"*All* your information," Pan said. "We're going to use it to find the last tablet, and discover where they all lead. We're going to smash your secrets wide open and let everyone know what you're trying to hide."

If it was possible for the Snake Lady to look more horrified, she managed it then.

"No," she gasped. "No, you cannot. That information is classified... It is protected by an international treaty!"

"We're wanted criminals," I said. "That doesn't bother us."

That's not entirely true. The moment I'd fallen with Kyle Flutes down to that jaguar, everything hadn't just instantly changed. My jungle suit had protected me from most of the cat's attack, but it still had that swipe at my neck. Kyle was bitten on the leg but used his sonic force field to blast the jaguar into the river. After that, all he could do was roar threats at my family as we got away with the tablet. We'd been rescued by Pedro in his helicopter, and then got here as fast as we could.

Wherever the tablets led, that's where we were going next. All of us, together. But first we needed more clues.

"We just need you to stay still," I explained, "while we hack your holosphere and steal all your information."

Pan picked up one of the mercenary's stun guns from the floor. "Only, we don't trust that you will," she added. "So we have to make you."

"You look like you need a rest, Marjorie," Mum said.

"Don't do anything foolish!" the Snake Lady shrieked. "You want answers? I can give you answers. You can still work for me, all of you. I can give you new identities, even."

We stepped closer, surrounding her now from all sides.

"We like our *current* identities," Pan replied. She raised the stun gun. "Now, who's going to take this shot?"

"You're the best aim, Pandora," Mum said.

"Thanks, Mum, but you can take it if you like."

"Jake, would you like to?"

"Thanks, Mum!"

I took the stun gun and leaned over the Snake Lady as Pan and Mum rushed back to one of the chambers and began to download information from the People of the Snake's systems, using one of Pedro's gadgets. I heard laughter and gasps of excitement – *laughter*, from Mum! – as they scanned the hologram files.

"Guys," Pan called. "You're not going to believe where we're going next."

The Snake Lady glared at me. Her reptile eyes were no longer scared or confused. They were hard and focused and they gleamed with ferocity.

"You have no idea how much trouble you are in," she warned. "We will come after you with everything we've got. What makes you think you'll get away with this?"

I grinned and raised the stun gun.

"Haven't you heard the first rule of treasure hunting?" I asked.

I fired, and then answered by my own question.

"Don't mess with the Atlas family."

ABOUT THE AUTHOR

Rob Lloyd Jones never wanted to be a writer when he grew up – he wanted to be Indiana Jones. So he studied Egyptology and archaeology and went on trips to faraway places. But all he found were interesting stories, so he decided to write them down. *Jake Atlas and the Hunt for the Feathered God* is Rob's fourth novel, although he has written over eighty other books for children, including non-fiction and adaptations of such classics as *Beowulf*.

About writing *Jake Atlas*, he says, "It began on a rainy day in the countryside. Stuck at home, I watched an Indiana Jones movie and then a Mission: Impossible film straight after. I wondered if you could mix the two: classic treasure hunts but with crazy high-tech gadgets. I especially wanted to set the first adventure in Egypt, a place and history that I'd loved so much since studying it at university. But

I didn't really have a story, just an idea. Then, after becoming a father, I realized that many parents are invisible in stories for young people. I decided to write about a whole family on an adventure together. But not just any family – one with troubles and squabbles, special skills and deep secrets..."

Rob lives in a crumbling cottage in Sussex, where he writes and runs and moans about mud.

JAKE ATLAS
TOMB ROBBER,
TREASURE HUNTER,
TROUBLEMAKER

A couple of days ago I was a schoolboy
with terrible grades and even worse
behaviour – and a way of causing trouble
that drove people nuts.

Now I am a member of a super high-tech
treasure-hunting team searching for a lost
tomb so I can save my parents from being
turned into mummies by an evil cult.

Things have moved pretty fast…

LONDON
• • • • **1841** • • • •

A BOY COVERED IN **HAIR**, RAISED AS A MONSTER,
CONDEMNED TO LIFE IN A TRAVELLING FREAK SHOW.
A BOY WITH AN EXTRAORDINARY POWER OF **OBSERVATION**
& DETECTION.
A BOY ACCUSED OF **MURDER**; ON THE RUN;
HUNGRY FOR THE **TRUTH**.
BEHOLD THE *savage spectacle* OF

WILD BOY